Killer Competition

Tom Kranz

First Edition: 2018

ISBN 978-1-64467-148-1

Published by Thomas Kranz
Fanwood, NJ 07023

Dedication

To all the TV journalists I've worked with in Philadelphia and New York.

Thanks to my wife, Marianne, who puts up with my crap.

TK
Fanwood, NJ

Table of Contents

Chapter 1 - Night & Day

Burning embers rose into the darkness of the frigid night, danced in the sky, then settled back to earth on a cushion of acrid smoke. Its odor carried for blocks through old Fishtown, the venerable neighborhood that sat on the bank of the Delaware River forming the eastern border of Philadelphia. Depending on the breeze, Fishtown could smell like beer, refinery exhaust or burning trash. Tonight, the smell of an old building dying in winter was predominant.

Bill Klemmer, dangerously obese, unshaven and sweaty, but with exquisite auburn hair, pulled up on the roaring fire consuming an abandoned factory on Aramingo Avenue. He looked at his Casio watch--1:55 AM. He squinted through the filthy windshield of his 2005 Camry. The defroster hadn't worked in weeks, so he had to wipe the fog from inside the windshield with his hand.

The flames leapt a hundred feet or more into the night. There is nothing more beautiful, he thought, than a kickass fire in the dark. He struggled out of the driver's seat, a sharp fart escaping in the process. His parka made him sweat profusely even though the outdoor temperature was in the teens. He walked to the rear of the Camry and opened the trunk, revealing a pile of trash and small black case that held his camera, a Panasonic consumer model HD camcorder, small enough to hold in one hand. Its video quality, especially in low light environments, didn't measure up to Channel 7's standards. But they never complained since no one else seemed to get what Klemmer got on these overnight jobs. And here he was again, capturing flames at their very peak.

"Hey, who are you?" came a question from a firefighter wearing a white helmet, barreling towards Klemmer.

Klemmer reached into his shirt pocket and whipped out a homemade, laminated press card with the Channel 7 logo pasted in the center. "Channel 7 News, sir."

"Stay out of the way, we're bringing hoses through here," said the lieutenant harshly, unbothered by the arts-and-crafts nature of the credential. He then gestured to several firefighters dragging a large hose their way.

The fire had grown in size and intensity in just the few minutes since Klemmer had arrived. He overheard chatter on the lieutenant's radio, the dispatcher striking a second alarm. Klemmer couldn't have been in a better spot. There were no other photographers. He would have the best video, again, maybe the only video. This fire was a moneymaker.

Ice was forming on the firefighters' helmets. The lieutenant barked into his handheld radio, "Strike out a third alarm and have police establish a two-block perimeter around the scene." The increasing heat overpowered the frigid air and forced Klemmer to step back another 50 feet, his camera lens riveted on the scene before him. He thought of his dad and found himself smiling as the dancing flames reflected in his eyes.

Those eyes betrayed no questions about his good fortune at being in the right place at the right time.

Again.

Some hours later, the sun had risen and snow crunched under the feet of another parka-clad man as he trudged into his backyard with his parka zipped up to his chin. His hands were jammed into the pockets, so he would have no way to catch himself if he rolled an ankle on one of the miserable seed pods from his sweet gum tree. They were everywhere, golf ball sized and brown with jagged little spines all over. It happened more than once that he ended up on the ground after stepping on one of the little bastards.

He got about thirty feet across the yard to his usual spot, then turned around to face the house. Then, and only then did the dog come off her perch on the outside landing and begin sniffing around for a place to do her business. The highly anticipated morning dump occurred each day only after this ritual. The dog, named Beulah, would not be walked on a leash lest she be frightened by the whoosh of a passing car or the sight of another human walking too close. They had adopted her after she was found neglected for a long period of time in a mud pit in Georgia, rescued by a local humane society and transported by volunteers up to Pennsylvania for adoption by some kind-hearted humans who would live to regret it.

With the temperature hovering just above 15, it was imperative for her to finish quickly. The man's eyes were riveted on the dog's asshole, which always gave early warning that a jolly load was on

4

the way. Sure enough, the telltale sphincter contraction and expansion took place and elimination was achieved. She scampered back to the landing by the back door and the human began walking back to the same door.

"That's quite an outfit," came a male voice from over the fence and beyond the huge deposit of honeysuckle draped over it.

The head at the apex of the parka's zipped-up collar turned ninety degrees toward the source of the voice and the bare legs extended below the parka began walking towards the fence.

"I'm the new neighbor," said the male.

"Hi," came the voice from behind the parka's collar as its owner walked two more steps to the fence, and extended his hand. "Bordon. Nice to meet you."

"Lester," said the neighbor, a man of about 35 and indeterminate ethnicity, who extended his hand in return. There was a quick handshake.

It was at that moment that Bordon looked down at himself and remembered that he was wearing only boxers and his untied duty boots which, in concert with the black parka, made him look like a homeless man who had lost his pants.

"Aren't you cold?"

"Fucking freezing," replied Bordon who instantly regretted saying fuck. "Sorry. I've been coming out like this to get my dog to shit in the yard since we got her and I'm not used to having neighbors. I usually give it about two minutes and if she doesn't do it by then, we go back inside and then she shits in the living room. It's a vicious cycle."

"That's pretty funny. What else do you do for your dog?"

"That is a conversation we'll have one day when the wind chill isn't minus 10. What's your last name?"

"Noble, Lester Noble."

"Les Noble? Guess mom and dad didn't think that one through."

Lester squinted with fake annoyance. "And yours?"

"Remmick, Bordon Remmick."

"So, your parents named you after condensed milk?"

"We'll talk soon," nodded Remmick with a grin. "And maybe you should just call me Bud."

"Good enough. You gonna put pants on now?"

"Maybe. Maybe not."

Bud trudged into the kitchen, stamping his feet on the mat at the doorway, then shut the door behind him. Beulah had scampered to her spot on the couch next to the other occupant of the tidy two-bedroom ranch home in semi-rural Armitage, Pennsylvania.

"Oh, thought you'd be gone by now," said Remmick to his wife Maggie, who was dressed for work and already had her overcoat on.

"Just thought I'd wait and say bye," she said with a smile. It was a smile that had kept Remmick going during darker days. She stood up, met him in the center of the living room and leaned in for the daily goodbye kiss. Her sandy, slightly curly hair came down to just the top of her shoulders. Her understated make-up and smart outfit painted a picture of a confident, professional woman. After moving to Pennsylvania, Maggie Remmick landed a job at the Livingston County Department of Senior Services, and in less than a year became executive director. Her $90,000-a-year salary took some of the sting out of Bud's inability to find work. She'd come quite a ways since earning $19 an hour coordinating a meals-on-wheels program in Ardmore back during the dark time. Now, she supervised a range of senior services including a county-wide meal program that included delivery to homebound people and congregate meals served in senior centers, home care, transportation, nursing assessments and a grocery shopping service, all paid for by the taxpayers of the Commonwealth of Pennsylvania. Since taking over her Department, there were rave reviews from the various senior watchdog groups who previously hammered the County for cutting services. While she didn't get much more of a budget to work with than her predecessor, some diligent belt-tightening, changes to ordering procedures and a modest but painful staff reduction transformed the Department into an actual public service.

"Go take care of the old folks," said Remmick as Maggie walked out the front door towards her Subaru.

"Love you," she chirped as she walked down the path, climbed into the car and drove off.

Now it was just Remmick and Beulah.

"Why do you hate me?" he asked the dog. She cowered on the corner of the couch. He stood 15 feet away in his boxers, t-shirt and untied boots. He walked past the china cabinet and saw his reflection in the mirror.

"Oh."

Once the sun appeared, the temperature soared to 21 degrees. Inside the Channel 7 newsroom, an associate producer named Reginald sat at his computer, staring out at the Manayunk skyline where bits of steam rose from rooftops, then disintegrated in the staggering cold. The working class Philadelphia neighborhood had enjoyed a renaissance with trendy restaurants and vibrant street life hosting the men and women who labored for Lewis Recycling, drove buses for SEPTA, swept the streets and taught public school. Reginald wished he were there right now instead of sitting in front of his computer, agonizing over a piece of copy.

"Reg, this is gold, man," said the noon producer from halfway across the newsroom. "Works fine for the show and the website."

Weary from writing stupid words about cold weather, Reginald replied, "Glad it works. It's hard to make cold weather sound like anything but cold weather."

Sometime during the 1970's, broadcasters were awakened to the idea that covering the weather was cheap and easy, so why not cover it *a lot*? Thus, weather grew from its five-minute perch deep in the newscast to the lead story, complete with a Storm Team, a Storm Truck, Storm Radar and Storm Stupidity. The worst was putting reporters at the wheel of moving cars to give live descriptions of road conditions, a practice that continued despite a well-publicized accident in Kentucky in which one reporter's death-by-tractor-trailer was documented in sickening detail during her weather liveshot on I-64.

Around the corner from the news desk, separated by a portable wall and a tall pane of Plexiglas, sat Karen Sikorsky, senior producer, senior mentor, mother hen and acting news director. A veteran of twenty years at Channel 7, she believed she was the only actual journalist in the room. She was a graduate of Temple University whose first job was as a content writer for phillynews.com. Karen knew how to write, how to edit, how to assign and how helicopters worked, the latter thanks to her marriage to a great grandnephew of Igor Sikorsky, whose company manufactured helicopters. The marriage ended some time ago, but she was amused by the curiosity the name engendered.

She missed being at the nexus of the daily news gathering process, having been relegated to the administrative and wearying personnel tasks that went with being acting news director. She so wished an actual news director would be hired. She had worked for many news directors at Channel 7, almost too many to count. She never aspired to that position, always maneuvering instead to stay in the daily mix of gathering, editing, writing or assigning stories. However, today's newsroom was populated by kids. She called them kids anyway, young men and women just out of college, many with degrees in things like political science, health care communications, marketing, public relations. They earnestly believed those who counseled them that the news business demanded people of wide interests who could bring diversity and knowledge to the table. All well and good, reflected Karen, except they never learn how to write, how to tell stories, how to use pictures and so forth. So, at $34,000 a year on average, Channel 7 got what it paid for in a stable of eager, semi-clueless, ersatz journalists.

"Hey, got a minute?" came a voice from the other side of the Plexiglas, which Sikorsky had installed to afford some quiet to hear herself think. It was the Channel 7 general manager, Roy Strickland, a man of about 40 with thinning hair, no tie and a pale, white face.

Karen got up from her chair, revealing a zaftig and comfortable body dressed in a black suit and decorated with a smallish, red beaded necklace with matching earrings. Her dark hair had a few streaks of gray. She wore her new dark-rimmed glasses, obtained just days after her 42nd birthday and held a Phillies mug containing what was left of her coffee.

"Sure," she said with a smile. Strickland, though a general manager, was not a threat. "What's up?"

"No offense, but we need a news director," he said.

"None taken and yes, for Christ sake. I can't decipher one more timesheet. What have you been doing about it?"

"Interviewing a bunch of people. I can't pay what these candidates think they deserve. As you know, our numbers suck and suck hard. Viewership is down. Ad revenue is down. I can barely pay someone 75K and we're the sixth largest TV market. One guy actually giggled when I told him the salary, the little prick."

Karen tipped her mug to her mouth to get the last of the tepid coffee. "You need more than a news director here, Roy. You need a teacher. The kids here are lovely and stupid, clueless about writing, no natural curiosity, waiting to be told every goddamn thing to do. I'm tired of being their mother."

"Yea, I know."

She put down her mug and sat back down, setting her sights on her computer screen. "Well, keep me in the loop. I know you're trying."

"Yep," he said and walked away.

As Strickland left, the assignment editor, a young woman named Nancy, appeared at Karen's cubicle.

"We just got this video in from a freelancer," she said. "Pretty awesome. Raging fire, that building that burned overnight in Fishtown. Unbelievable flames."

"Any info yet?" asked Karen.

"Got calls in to the public information lieutenant at fire headquarters."

Karen turned to her computer, found the icon for the video server, clicked on an item labeled ARAMINGO FIRE. Indeed, quite a ripping good burner.

"Jeez, that sucker's going. Got there fast. Scanner hound, no doubt."

"That's how he makes his living," Nancy said.

"And this is who?"

"A guy who only sells to us. We have kind of a loose deal with him."

"We still have a couple hours. Let's get whatever info we can and make it the noon lead."

"OK," confirmed Nancy. "I'll let the producer know, and I'll stay on top of those bozos downtown."

Klemmer slept fitfully, battling with his ancient pillows and comforter, all of which emitted odors of unidentified organics. He finally awoke and peered at the clock on his night table--1:07 PM.

"Shit," he said under his breath. He'd missed the noon news. He liked seeing his work on TV. He hauled his heaving mass out of bed and ambled over to his bureau, scratching his crotch thoroughly. There lay a small pile of SD memory cards. On top was the

Aramingo Avenue fire from overnight. He picked it up, smiled at it, then laid it back down.

He yawned deeply while walking back to his night table. He picked up his cellphone and walked into the bathroom with it. He sat down on the toilet and instantly jumped up and howled. He had forgotten to put the seat down and sat on the cold, wet, hairy porcelain surface.

"What's all the screaming about?" asked the voice Klemmer heard through the phone he held to his ear.

"Nothing. I just fell into my toilet."

"Why are you calling me?" asked the voice. "NEVER call me, idiot. I call YOU."

"We gotta talk. I'm not getting my money."

"Since when?"

"Since every goddamn time. Every job, I gotta fight to get paid. They don't have a record of the job, or they can't find the authorization or constant bullshit about who OK'd the job, blah, blah." Klemmer had stood up, recovered from the shock of cold porcelain, and walked back to his bed. He fidgeted while sitting on the edge at a spot marked with numerous skid marks.

"Man up and deal with it, boy," said the voice at the other end. "And don't call me again."

Chapter 2 - Community Service

"...fifteen, sixteen, seventeen, eighteen..."

The counting was done out loud, as he had been taught.

"...twenty-seven, twenty-eight, twenty-nine, thirty." He stopped doing chest compressions and his partner ventilated the unresponsive man with the bag-valve-mask. Across the room, a third EMT dragged a Reeves stretcher into the room. After pausing to allow the ventilations, Bud Remmick resumed chest compressions.

His partner, a paramedic, left her position at the man's head, dropped the BVM and quickly positioned her cardiac monitor while the third EMT began cutting off the man's shirt. That took ten seconds during which the medic attached the leads and the machine started beeping.

"Take over bagging," she said succinctly to the EMT, who promptly knelt on the floor, placed his knees on either side of the patient's head and positioned the BVM over his mouth to prepare for the next set of ventilations.

"...twenty, twenty-one, twenty-two, twenty-three," counted Remmick in a near-whisper while compressing the victim's chest at a rate of about once a second.

"Stop compressions," ordered the medic. She studied the EKG readout for a few seconds. Flat line. "Resume compressions," she said. Remmick resumed and realized for the first time that his victim's eyes were half open, pupils dilated. The medic attached more leads and barked, "CLEAR." She pushed a button, the man's body jerked and the lines of the EKG spiked for that moment, then returned to a straight, horizontal line.

"Continue compressions and keep bagging."

"...twenty-eight, twenty-nine, thirty," said Remmick in a louder voice.

"OK, step back for a minute," said the medic as she traded places with the EMT at the patient's head, preparing her laryngoscope blade to begin intubating the man. Remmick looked at the EKG. It was not looking good. The medic worked with confidence, getting the breathing tube down the man's throat in less than a minute. She motioned to the EMT to attach the BVM to the top of the tube. "Keep ventilating once every 6 seconds, not too aggressive. He's already got a distended belly."

Too much air in the stomach while artificially ventilating meant vomiting was just around the corner.

Remmick kept up compressions. He felt a sharp crack under the heel of his hand, a rib breaking. The other EMT continued ventilating. The paramedic prepared a syringe for an injection, then interrupted to deliver another shock.

"CLEAR," she shouted. All activity stopped, Remmick and the EMT separated from the victim and another shock went through the man. His body jerked again, causing another spike in the EKG. Then, flat line.

The victim looked to be about 60. He was in his pajamas. The wife called 911 after he failed to get out of bed. Remmick and his partners pulled up in the ambulance about six minutes after their phones beeped, ran into the house, were directed to the bedroom, felt no pulse, saw no breathing, dragged the man down to the floor and went to work.

Another syringe was produced, another drug was injected, another shock was delivered, more chest compressions, more bagging, the Reeves stretcher was positioned for transporting the patient, all as the room remained quiet except for the sound of Remmick counting under his breath. The ritual continued for another twenty-five minutes.

"Everyone stop," announced the paramedic. She looked once more at the flat-lined EKG, then turned to Remmick and quietly asked, "Will you talk to the wife?"

Remmick had stopped after spending what seemed like an eternity on his knees and straightened himself up, grabbing the end of the bed to help him stand. As he slowly walked past the police officer to where the wife was sitting in the kitchen, his partner spoke into her phone, getting the official pronouncement from the doctor at Regal Medical Center.

It wasn't the first time Remmick had to deliver the news. It required a moment to gather himself, take a deep breath and clear everything else out of his mind. He approached the frightened woman and their eyes met.

She knew.

Driving the ambulance back to quarters with his paramedic partner in the passenger seat, Remmick felt the ache in his knees, not surprising after spending a half hour kneeling on the floor. He was rubbing his right one while keeping his eye on the highway.

"Getting old," he said.

"*Getting* old? You *are* old, mother fucker," said paramedic Tiffany Shaw with a stupid smile. "I feel bad for that poor woman."

In the back sat young EMT Chris McCall, still on probation, futzing with his smartphone.

"Yea," replied Remmick. "Hard to argue with sudden cardiac arrest."

Tiffany, younger than Remmick but not by much, was a veteran paramedic who had truly seen it all in her eighteen years on the Armitage Rescue Squad. She and the young man in the back of the rig were paid, while Remmick was a volunteer. The combination of volunteer and paid responders was fairly common in the semi-rural areas of Pennsylvania.

"How many CPR calls is that for you now?" Remmick asked.

"I dunno. Maybe 50?"

"This is why I joined, to save lives."

"OK," she said with a smirk.

"Really."

"OK."

He examined her dark face. "I don't like your tone."

She turned to him now. "My tone? What are you talking about? All I did was agree with your sorry ass."

Remmick had gone through a period of defensiveness when his fellow EMTs found out about his past. While he didn't wear a sign around his neck, he never denied it if confronted.

"Sorry," he said. "I'm still not sure, you know--"

"When someone's fucking with you?"

He grinned. "Yea."

"You'll know it when I fuck with you. The past is the past. I think you're basically alright for a middle aged ex-con."

"Um hm. Did anyone ever tell you that Tiffany is a very common name for the snooty white girls of Ardmore?"

"You need some new material, felon."

Remmick studied the road ahead. "I know."

Later, Remmick sat at one end of his couch while Beulah sat at the other, eyeing him up, skittish and nervous. Between them sat Maggie, dressed-down in sweats and fuzzy socks, munching cheddar Goldfish out of a small bowl. CNN was on with the sound low.

"So, you think the guy was dead before you even started?" she queried.

"Yea. Sudden cardiac arrest. All the shocks in the world won't help."

"And the wife?"

"But I don't think she was surprised."

"And you?"

He turned his face away from CNN and looked at her. "Me?"

She nodded slightly while crunching a Goldfish. His face broke into a knowing smile as he reached over and took her hand and held it. They sat that way for a while, watching Wolf Blitzer.

Chapter 3 - Dark Passengers

Bill Klemmer pushed his shopping cart down the produce isle of the ShopRite. He had decided to forego his morning shower, opting instead to spray the remainder of a can of deodorant onto his body. He walked down the aisle with a cart that had one squeaky wheel. He wore the same sweatshirt and parka he had on at the fire scene more than twelve hours ago. His bare belly peeked out from under the sweatshirt at his beltline. He reeked of Old Spice and smoke. His hair was perfect.

Strolling up to the tomatoes, he felt an itch and reached into his pants, scratching his butt violently, getting most of his hand well up into the crack. His entire body jiggled as he dug his hand up there and scratched. After what seemed like forever, he withdrew his hand and used it to search for the perfect tomato, touching one after another, looking for one that wasn't too ripe, or too young. He picked them up, squeezed them, tossed them slightly, then put them back onto the pile. He finally selected two, then moved on to the lettuce. His cart wheel squealed and his hand reeked as he fondled one head of lettuce, then another, then another.

He soon became aware of a faint vibration near his left arm pit. He withdrew his phone from the inside pocket of his parka.

"Hi," he said.

"There will be another job for you tonight," said the familiar voice.

"Already? Where? What time?"

"It'll be a beauty."

"You gonna tell me where and when?"

"Later. I'll call you later." And the phone went quiet.

Klemmer looked at the phone, annoyed. He stuffed it back into his pocket, whipped his cart back to the produce isle and headed towards the salad bar.

He passed an elderly woman shopping for tomatoes.

Karen was annoyed that she had to juggle the schedule to accommodate the resignation of the Saturday anchor, Wendell Hobbs, a lightweight reader who came from QVC with no journalism chops whatsoever. She was glad he left but pissed that she now had to go trolling for someone to work on a Saturday with three days' notice. On top of that, she was given a pile of vouchers for freelance jobs that had gone unpaid for a couple months due to the forgetfulness of the assignment desk people. At the top of the pile was a voucher with a handwritten Post-It note from Roy Strickland to pay the individual immediately. While it was unusual for the general manager to care about a freelancer getting paid, she assumed this particular photographer got pissed enough to actually get him on the phone to complain.

She got up and walked around her cubicle to the assignment desk to speak with Nancy.

"What's the deal with the freelancers?" she asked. "No one's passing these vouchers up the ladder."

"I know, sorry. They get tossed into a pile and forgotten."

Sikorsky held up the top one. "See this? Handwritten, pissy note from the GM. Who is W. Klemmer?"

"He shoots overnight stuff. He got the good flames on Aramingo Avenue early this morning, the video I showed you? He's a semi-regular. Always gets there before everyone else. I mean, always."

"Spread the word to everyone on the desk. When you fill out a voucher, it has to get to me within 24 hours, so I can sign it and send it upstairs. Capisce?"

"OK. Sorry."

Karen ambled back to her cubicle, sat down and picked up her phone. She dialed the three digits to Roy Strickland's office.

"Mr. Strickland's office," came the disciplined voice of Lori, the GM's assistant.

"Hi, Lori, it's Karen. Is he there?"

"Hang on, please."

Karen was put on hold, but only for a few seconds.

"Hey, Karen," came Strickland's voice.

"Hi, Roy. I'm sending an intern to the business office with this Klemmer voucher. What's so special about him?"

"He called me and gave me a raft of shit about not getting paid. I had no idea we were this behind. These freelancers help keep us competitive, which I don't have to tell you."

"Yea. I had a talk with the desk. Shouldn't happen again."

"OK."

"What's the latest on the news director search?"

Strickland let out a sigh. "I'm looking through another batch of résumés. I'll let you know."

"Bye," she said and hung up the phone. She had a feeling Strickland was paying her lip service, that he wasn't interested in a quick hire, that he was actually happy with her being in charge and that she would die with her computer screen locked on the vacation schedule. She leaned back in her chair, which creaked threateningly, locked her hands behind her head and stared across the newsroom at nothing in particular. She had an idea, and it was ridiculous.

Wednesday turned into Thursday, day turned into night and the temperature was back down into the upper teens. Cold like this wasn't just about physics. It was winter's middle finger.

Huddled deep under a stinking, microfiber comforter, Klemmer lay in a fetal position on his sagging bed. His hair was not in order. His feet, still in the socks he'd worn early Tuesday and then all day Wednesday, peeked out from under the covers. He stirred ever so slightly, inhaling, then exhaling loudly. He sensed calm and warmth, finding himself in Wildwood, New Jersey, on a white beach heated by the summer sun. He stood on the beach naked, as people walked by him without noticing. Out on the ocean, he saw a tall ship with billowing sails and a skull-and-crossbones flag flying high above it. On the deck he spied a man with a patch over his eye and a hook for one hand, waving a sword in his other hand. Racing up on the beach behind him came a fire engine loaded with firefighters, wearing breathing packs and helmets. They jumped off the rig and ran past him, ignoring his nakedness. They waded into the ocean, dragging a hose behind them, then trained the hose towards the pirate ship, which was now on fire. In the sky he spotted a single-engine plane dragging a long banner which read MURRAY'S SMORGASBORD $5.99, MARGATE. He began walking along the beach and looking down at himself. His stomach protruded so far he could not see his own genitalia without craning his neck. And when he finally saw down there, his genitalia were gone. Only smooth, hairless skin remained. His breathing came more rapidly as fear welled up in him. He began to run along the beach because the firefighters were chasing him. He began panting. People on the beach were now stopping to stare. The faster he ran, the more difficult it became. He felt someone behind him getting closer and closer. He was now panicked and running for his life. Suddenly, a hand touched his neck and squeezed it making him turn to see who it was. It was his mother, laugh-screaming like a banshee with wide, bloodshot eyes and spittle flying through the air.

He shouted "No!" thrashing himself awake. He heard the echo of his own voice resonating in his room, followed a few seconds later by his alarm clock. The sound of the rhythmic beeping further rattled him. He looked at the display--2:14 AM. He caught his breath and remembered. He looked around the room. Everything was as he left it.

Soon, he was back in the Camry, bundled up in his parka, marking 26 hours in the same clothes. He took Kelly Drive along the east bank of the Schuylkill River into center city, past Boathouse Row and the Art Museum, down the Ben Franklin Parkway to 21st Street where he turned right. He cruised along 21st Street towards Chestnut. Upon reaching the intersection, all was dark, cold and quiet. He pulled over into an illegal spot at the corner of 21st and Chestnut and waited.

Huddled under a cool, clean, down comforter on a 100% cotton, 600-threadcount fitted bedsheet, Bud Remmick listened to his wife's rhythmic breathing. He couldn't believe how fortunate he was to have her next to him. Memories of sleeping fitfully on a hard, one-inch thick pad with a scratchy, polyester blanket under his chin were still vivid. The smell of bleach returned to him some nights. The cold loneliness of administrative segregation was never far, but he could will it away by moving closer to Maggie under the comforter and, usually, fall back asleep. He slipped into his recurring dream of sitting in the library at the Kaleidoscope Network, surrounded by police and the pert young librarian with the aftermath of a catastrophe just feet from him. Dust swirled over the wreckage of the ancient metal bookshelves, now a tangle of misshapen and rusted steel intermingled with magazines and books. Next to his feet on the floor, a puddle of vomit. Sticking up out of the rubble--a human foot wearing a brown shoe. Remmick's heart raced and his breathing became shallow. Sickening fear welled up as the anticipation terrified him. A bloody hand emerged from the debris, then another hand. They moved books away from a dark spot that became larger and larger, big enough for a head to poke through like a crowning newborn. And there it was, a head, slipping through a bloody gash in the debris, covered in dark red blood as one accusing eye opened and stared at Remmick.

"No!" he shouted and thrashed awake. His eyes popped open. The echo of his own shout still resonated. Maggie snoozed away, next to him, oblivious.

He settled back into his pillow, willing his vital signs back to normal. He stared up into the darkness. He would never completely shake that part of his past, even in bed with his wife, and every day of his life as he looked for a job, volunteered as an EMT or walked down the street, wondering if someone would recognize him or his name.

There was a flash and a second later, an explosion that shook the Camry and startled Klemmer. The source was up ahead maybe 50 yards. Smoke emanated from a structure. He looked at his phone to see the time--3:12 AM. He maneuvered his body to get out of the driver's seat, slammed the door and headed back to the trunk. He opened it and fished his camera out of the trash that was piled there. He closed the trunk and started making his way to the source of the smoke. His tortured waddle brought him ever closer to the scene of what was evidently a post-explosion fire.

Klemmer looked around. No fire equipment yet. He approached and aimed his camcorder at the fire, which was gaining momentum. He stood in the same spot, unmoving, holding the shot steady, focusing on the source of the flames which appeared to be a first floor window

Sirens could soon be heard and Klemmer was aware that he had gotten there well before the fire department. This registered briefly as a concern, but it didn't register for long because he was getting prime video of a breaking story that no one else would have.

Again.

Chapter 4 - Position Available

The mood in Strickland's office was neither jolly nor moribund, but one of nauseous expectation. Roy sat at his desk. Karen sat on one of the two upholstered chairs facing it, holding her Phillies mug which she had just topped off. Strickland was staring at his computer. She knew what he was staring at. Strickland's phone rang.

"Yes? OK, send him in."

He replaced the phone on its cradle and shot Karen a look which she interpreted as one of dread. She returned a look of eye-rolling amusement. They both stood as the door opened and in walked a blast from Karen's past.

"Bud Remmick!" she exclaimed and greeted him with a hug that lasted quite a while. "You are looking really good." She broke off the hug and turned to Strickland. "Roy Strickland, Bud Remmick."

Remmick made his way across the worn carpet towards Strickland's desk. The general manager had moved out from behind it and met Remmick with a handshake and a smile. "Very good to meet you. Have a seat, Bud."

"Thank you both. Good to meet you too, Mr. Strickland. Karen, I swear to god, you haven't changed, seriously."

"Bullshit. I've aged 10 years doing this fucking job, which is why you're here."

"Call me Roy," offered Strickland. "I appreciate you coming in, Bud. Karen thought this was worth a conversation."

Remmick sensed wariness in Strickland's voice and noted the immediate disclaimer that *Karen* thought this was worth a conversation. "Well, I'll admit, Karen's call came as a surprise." He shot a glance her way. "No, it shocked the shit out of me."

"Ha, I see your vivid use of the King's English hasn't changed," she said with a nervous lilt. "God knows, we never talk like that around here, do we Roy?"

"Right," Strickland said with a half-grin. There was an iciness about him that Remmick could feel. Karen sensed danger and jumped in.

"Well, let's talk about it," she said. "Yes, it was my idea to call you, Bud. I know you from our past life together here at Channel 7. I thought we always worked well together. You always had great instincts and could write and had a fabulous way with the staff. We're missing all of that at the moment."

Strickland looked somewhat wounded by her remarks but kept with the program. "We need a news director, Bud," he said. "Karen thinks you are an excellent candidate."

The words were still surreal to Remmick. The irony was palpable.

"But *you* don't think I'm an excellent candidate, do you Roy?" he said. "In fact, I think you've Googled me and have my entire life story right there on your screen."

A look of alarm crossed Strickland's face briefly. He glanced at his screen, then back at Remmick. "As a matter of fact, I have been doing my due diligence, yes."

"No worries. I'd do the same thing if a convicted felon applied for a job in my newsroom."

Strickland sat up straighter in his chair, evidently relieved that Remmick had put it out there. "Yes, well," he began, and was interrupted by Karen.

"I think we have a case here of a person who has done his time and paid his debt," she said. "I think what happened was a one-off. And Bud is here to tell us what's changed since then, right Bud?"

Strickland's eyes remained locked on Remmick. He was studying him, but wasn't sure what he was looking for. He'd never had a killer in his office before.

"What's changed," Remmick said. "I've been out of prison for two years. I'm 50. I served every minute of my sentence. I never lied to anyone about what I did. I never denied responsibility. I also showed no remorse." He looked at Karen, then back at Strickland. "I still don't. That was a problem for the parole board and I understand that it may be a problem for others. So be it."

Neither Strickland nor Karen made a sound, their eyes riveted on Remmick.

"My time at Kaleidoscope was good, busy but good. It was different than local, of course. The commute was brutal. The guy I worked for--" Remmick stopped talking.

Karen's look of worry became more intense. Strickland never changed his expression.

"I was stupid and angry," Remmick continued. "I might still be a little stupid, but I've gotten considerable help with my anger. I go to meetings, therapy. I quit drinking. I became an EMT, a volunteer. I rediscovered my wife. Today, the only thing I'm angry about is my dog, Beulah, who requires certain rituals before she relieves herself outdoors."

This was the ice-breaker Karen was waiting for. "Dog shits in my house *once*, she's gone."

This elicited an actual smile from Strickland, whose attention was focused on his computer screen. The chuckles died down.

"You pleaded guilty to involuntary manslaughter," said Strickland without looking up from his screen. "Some said your four-year sentence was a gift. The New York Times reported your lawyer got you a referral for a shrink to testify that--"

"It was an affidavit," corrected Remmick. "He never actually showed up in court to testify. I know the details, Roy. What's your question?"

Strickland looked up from his screen and said, "I just wonder--"

"If I would ever kill again? Isn't that what you wonder?"

Karen's smile had evaporated. Her face betrayed pain, maybe embarrassment.

"Yes," answered an expressionless Strickland.

Remmick nodded and said, "That's fair."

There was an uncomfortable silence for a few long seconds, then Remmick spoke again.

"I'm a different person now," he began. "My wife helped me. A few people trusted me when I got out and they helped me. My old prison superintendent gave a recommendation to the rescue squad I joined, god knows why."

"Yes, he called me, too," said Strickland. "He says you deserve my trust."

Remmick looked down at the floor with a grin and a slight nod. "That is surprising. How did he--never mind."

Strickland's demeanor became softer. He relaxed his brow, took his eyes off his computer screen and looked a little less frightened. "We don't have any policies that forbid us from hiring felons. We do background checks and drug screens, like any employer, but we retain final say over who gets hired. Understand, this is a first for me, and it would be a first for this workplace, hiring a person who has killed, and not just anyone, but a news director, for Christ sake. Saying it out loud makes it even stranger."

Remmick had no response. He just looked at Strickland.

Karen had been wringing her hands, watching the back and forth.

"I hear your concerns. I respect them. I'm sure Karen has told you how things worked last time I was here. The newsroom was solid and the employees were happy. While hiring me would be a leap of faith, I can say with confidence that if you took the leap, you wouldn't be sorry."

Strickland stood and said, "I appreciate that, Bud. I think Karen and I need to talk more about this and I want to bring a few more people into the conversation. We will be in touch very soon." He extended his hand and Remmick shook it. Remmick faced Karen and they hugged once more. He turned towards the office door and walked out.

"Did you see who just came in?" asked Reginald of the small group gathered at the assignment desk.

"Bordon Remmick," said Nancy, the assignment editor. "The killer himself."

"He used to work here, right?" queried noon producer Rita, a wiry, red-headed young woman in her 20's who had trouble standing or sitting still.

"Yea, ten years ago or something," said Reginald. "I think Karen worked with him."

"What's up with that?" snapped Rita. "No news director to kill around here."

"Where's he been?" asked Nancy.

"He got out of jail a couple years ago I think, then nothing," said Reginald. "Maybe he's making birdhouses in his garage."

"His wife got a county job out in the sticks," said Nancy. "I remember reading something."

Karen emerged from the elevator and walked towards her cubicle. There was a din of voices around the assignment desk, so she walked over. "What's going on, kids?"

"You know what's going on," said Nancy with a sly grin. "Bonding with old friends?"

"Yes, you could say that."

"Anything you'd like to share?" asked Rita.

"Yes. My lower back is killing me from that crappy chair and I need a diet Pepsi. Who would like to grab me one from the machine?"

"C'mon, Karen," said Reg. "We know you used to work with him. What was he doing here?"

"Visiting," she said curtly, then turned her back on the group and walked to her cubicle.

The Schuylkill Expressway, the essential, legendary and completely despised highway that connects a large chunk of Philadelphia with the western suburbs, hasn't changed, thought Remmick, as he cruised westbound at about 40 MPH in heavy traffic. He passed the West Conshohocken exit, site of the former Inn of the Four Falls where he and Maggie had been to Kathy and Rick Sutcliff's wedding years ago. The Inn was now an office complex but the "Conshohocken Curve" was still in place and the roadway still bottled up with traffic for no apparent reason. The Expressway was the most direct way to the Pennsylvania Turnpike's northeast extension, the road to Armitage.

Remmick did not feel good about his visit. The general manager viewed him skeptically. Remmick felt eyes following him as he walked the newsroom perimeter to get to the elevator. The place had changed since he was there, new carpet, rearranged desks, new computers and every employee appearing to be 18 years old. It would be a culture shock to return to Channel 7 now.

Yet, he sensed the wave of warmth projecting from Karen. He was certain they would work just fine together, regardless of the stranger-in-a-strange-land feeling that would surely permeate.

Chapter 5 - Temporary Insanity

One of the few cathode-ray-tube television sets still in existence in the Commonwealth of Pennsylvania sat in Lillian Woodruff's living room in Armitage. On any given overnight, that TV was tuned to the Discovery Channel, perhaps reruns of *The Deadliest Catch*, or *Dirty Jobs*. Lillian was up on this particular Thursday night at 1:48 AM, sitting in her broken recliner, dressed in a polyester kimono, eating Lucky Charms with 1% milk out of a Hello Kitty bowl about five feet from the TV screen. Her bare feet revealed gnarly toe nails. The rest of her 64-year-old body showed her no mercy--sagging breasts, arthritic right hip, a skin tag dangling from the left side of her neck and rippled thumb nails inherited from her father.

A clamshell cellphone on the recliner's right armrest lit, vibrated and blared the voice of Joan Jett shrieking *I Love Rock and Roll*. Lillian placed her spoon back in the cereal bowl, picked up the phone and flipped it open.

"Yea," she said, eyes never leaving the TV screen.

"351 Arnold Place, altered mental status," announced a bored sounding man.

"K," came her barely one syllable response and she flipped the phone closed. She put the cereal bowl down on the overcrowded end table and got up, padding to the credenza against the living room wall upon which sat an old, white phone with numerous speed dial buttons. Well, it was white at one time. She reached with an extended index finger to begin dispatching EMTs to the call on Arnold Place, her white phone being the time-tested Armitage EMS Overnight Dispatch Center. Lillian, a former volunteer EMT, grudgingly accepted her retirement role as night dispatcher for the handful of EMS calls the Armitage Rescue Squad answered in a given week. Each button on the speed dial had the name of a squad member written next to it in pencil--first name, last initial. Posted on the wall above the credenza was the weekly duty schedule. She peered at it and began by pushing the third button.

Less than two miles away, an iPhone came to life with the synthesized sound of an old-fashioned telephone. It was loud enough to scare the hell out of Remmick, who was dead asleep in bed next to Maggie. He set the ringer to maximum volume, making sure he would wake up on the nights he was on call. He reached over, peered at the small, lit screen to see the TALK button and pushed it as he picked up the phone and held it to his one exposed ear. "Yea"

"You awake?" asked Lillian.

"No."

"It's your friend at 351 Arnold again."

"Oh boy. What's he doing?"

"I didn't get that, only that he's altered. No lights or sirens, OK?" Lillian was annoyingly concise, as always.

"OK, on the way." He hit the red button and put the phone back down on his night table. He already had his underwear, socks and t-shirt on. He rolled out of bed, stepping right into his duty pants which he pulled up while standing up in one motion. His boots came on next, a 60-second operation in the dark, followed by his job shirt, embroidered with his name at the pocket, the squad's patch on the right upper arm and the PA EMT patch on the left. He clunked down the dark stairs, grabbed his EMT coat on the way out the door, fumbled with his keys and climbed into the Lumina for the quick ride to the squad building. Less than five minutes later, he and Tiffany were motoring in the ambulance to 351 Arnold Place.

"I don't need this shit tonight," said Tiffany, who looked slightly the worse for wear.

"You alright?"

"Girls' night out," she said with some effort. "On a Thursday night."

"Your hair is, a little--"

"Do not speak to a black woman about her hair at two in the morning."

Remmick said nothing further during the 1.7-mile drive to 351 Arnold. The ambulance pulled up to a scene of darkness and eased to a spot behind the lone police cruiser in the driveway. The two of them got out to see what was happening. They were greeted by a police officer wearing a plain, black baseball cap and wielding a cellphone. His Glock was strapped to his hip and he wore a heavy vest. Remmick recognized him.

"Hey, Francis," he said to the very young cop whose vest said simply *Police*.

"Good morning, Bud. Our friend here has been asking for you."

"Eulis wants me?"

"Yea. I guess you're pals now." The officer's tone was one of vague annoyance.

"Great. A fan."

"Mr. Packer is holding himself hostage. He says he has a gun and he wants to kill himself. I really don't want to go down there and have to shoot him. County SWAT is on the way, but they're still gearing up. Might be another twenty minutes. And the troopers are on a bad accident on the turnpike, so you're stuck with me."

Remmick shifted from one foot to the other. Tiffany rolled her eyes, then yawned. This would make the third time they had been at this address in the past couple weeks. Each time, Eulis was transported to Mercy Psych. Each time, he spent 72 hours there, then was sent home.

Remmick went to the side compartment of the ambulance and pulled out a beat-up bullet proof vest. The officer looked at him. "What do you think you're doing?"

"I knew I might need this one day," said Remmick. "Guess this is the day."

"First off, that's a piece of shit. Second off, I can't allow you to do *anything* before SWAT gets here."

"He's not a bad person. He's off his meds again, that's all. This is a medical call as far as I'm concerned."

"I appreciate that. On the other hand--"

"I'll be alright."

"He didn't have a gun the last time."

"Have you actually seen a gun?"

"I don't have to see it."

Remmick slipped off his EMT coat and slipped on the bullet proof vest, secured it around his midriff, then put his EMT coat back on and zipped it up. He turned to Tiffany. "Do you have anything to say, Paramedic Shaw?"

"Don't get your ass shot off."

Remmick's blank expression broke for a moment as he quipped, "This takes community service to a whole new level."

"This is on you," said the officer. "You're putting me in a hell of a spot." Francis looked at his watch with some urgency. Still no sign of SWAT.

"OK, let's get this over with," Remmick said.

The two of them began making their way to Eulis Packer's front door. It was a short walk, maybe thirty yards down the driveway. His front door had a small, bare lightbulb shining just above it. As they got closer, Francis ran ahead, then secured himself just to the right of Eulis's door as Remmick trod the last several steps. He found himself at the door, and then knocked.

"Eulis? It's Bud Remmick."

"Bud Remmick?" came a voice from inside. "Is that Bud Remmick?"

"Yes, sir. You asked to see me?"

The door opened six inches and a thin, black man's face appeared at the opening. Remmick remembered from his prior visits that Eulis was 62, had a history of bi-polar disorder and was on Seroquel and Xanax. Eulis's face registered instant recognition and broke into a smile. "Yes sir, you are Bud Remmick."

"Last time I checked."

This elicited a snorty chuckle from Eulis who opened the door wider. "You can come in."

"I'll stay right here, if that's OK."

"Are you afraid of me?"

"Well," replied Remmick, eyeing up what looked like a pistol Eulis held in his right hand. "You're the one with the gun. I sure don't want to see either of us get hurt tonight."

Eulis had the gun pointing haphazardly towards the floor, his finger nowhere near the trigger. It looked like a black revolver. It had a bright orange cap on the tip of the barrel.

"How would you feel about putting that down on the table over there?" asked Remmick.

"Since the last time you were here," said Eulis, "I looked you up. Thought your name was stuck somewhere in my brain. I was right. You killed that guy."

"Yes."

"You did time."

"Four years."

"And now, you're all better?" Eulis had a look of wonder on his face. Remmick was both fascinated and terrified by this line of questioning.

"Um, well, better than before, I guess."

Eulis smiled. "That is a mother fucking non-answer, Mr. Bud. *Better than before.* What is that?"

Remmick stood with his arms at his sides, his eyes moving from the gun to Eulis, back to the gun and back to Eulis.

"Death by bookshelf," said Eulis with a wry grin. "Unique, if I may say."

"It's not a résumé-builder."

"I need to know why you did it."

Remmick stopped breathing for a moment--the question he was never quite able to answer. His heart rate picked up, his breathing became more rapid and it got warm. "I guess I went crazy."

Eulis's brow got tight. "Shee-it. I read that bullshit online, man. Temporary insanity. Like, I'm going crazy right now, for just a little while. Is that how you mean it, Mr. Bud? Crazy, then not crazy later on? Conveniently crazy, is that it?" His tone had grown more belligerent as his voice hit an edge that made Remmick more nervous.

"I got angry and snapped," Remmick said. It was an admission he never said out loud. "It just--happened."

Eulis tilted his head to the side while continuing to study Remmick for another few seconds. "OK. That's what I thought." He looked down at the plastic gun in his hand, then back up at Remmick's face. He laid the gun gently down on the coffee table several paces into his living room. "It's just a toy."

A wave of cool air wafted across Remmick's face, a phantom breeze of relief.

"I need to go see the doc," said Eulis with quiet resignation.

"OK. Can I walk you out?"

"Uh huh," replied Eulis. He stepped into a pair of slippers in front of the chair that sat next to the coffee table, stood for a moment looking at Remmick, then nodded and trudged towards the front door.

"We're coming out, Francis," announced Remmick over his shoulder. "No weapons. Everyone be nice."

He and Eulis walked out the door together as the officer appeared with his pistol in hand, pointed towards the ground.

"This is a little surreal, Eulis," said Remmick.

"Yes. But I'd rather not be dead."

"Amen."

Francis assisted Remmick in guiding Eulis to the outside wall of his home where he was ordered to place his hands and spread his legs for a pat down. It was done quickly. Eulis was compliant. There were no handcuffs, no DOWN ON THE GROUND shouts. Rather, Francis put a hand on Eulis's right arm while Remmick did the same to his left and they walked him slowly to the ambulance. Remmick stepped up into the rig first, helping Eulis in.

"Stretcher or bench seat?" Remmick asked.

"I think stretcher. I could use a rest."

Francis appeared at the back double-doors of the ambulance and addressed Remmick. "You need someone to ride along?"

Remmick looked at Tiffany, sitting in the driver's seat, and asked, "Do we need someone to ride along?"

"Don't look at me. I'm just a bozo on this bus."

"No. We're good," Remmick said to Francis, who was now being joined by a phalanx of police in black uniforms, helmets and large rifles. Francis backed away while closing the rear double doors. Vehicles now pulled up next to the ambulance and Remmick heard new voices as he strapped Eulis lightly onto the stretcher. He sat back on the bench and put on his own seatbelt. As he did so, the rear double doors swung open again and an unfamiliar man appeared.

"Hi. Is everything squared away here?"

"All good, " said Remmick.

"Do you require an escort?" asked the man, evidently a SWAT officer with lieutenant's bars on his collar.

"Nah, he's fine. The gun was a toy."

Eulis was lying in a fetal position, snoring.

"Um, alright," responded the SWAT lieutenant, looking annoyed. He closed the doors again.

Tiffany pressed the gas and the ambulance pulled away at a leisurely pace.

Remmick looked out the scratched ambulance window from the bench where he sat, then turned his attention to Eulis's chart and began writing. A cold night under an overcast sky yielded no death or destruction this time.

"What a night, huh?" he said to no one in particular as he gently felt for Eulis's radial pulse.

30

Remmick noted the time, 3:41 AM, as he climbed back into bed as stealthily as he could. Maggie stirred.

"Anything interesting?" she mumbled. "I didn't hear a peep on the scanner."

"Remember that guy, Eulis, altered mental status, who we took to the hospital a couple weeks ago?"

"Hm, I guess."

"Tonight he threatened to kill himself. Had a toy gun. He asked for me."

Maggie raised her head in the dark and eyeballed her husband. "Say what?"

"So, we had a chat. All's well. We took him to Mercy Psych."

Maggie continued staring at him for another few seconds, then turned away from him and settled back in. "Good work," she mumbled. "Another life saved."

Remmick's eyes were wide open, staring straight up at the ceiling. He had just condensed an hour of anxiety, adrenalin and fear into three short sentences, the TV news version.

"Still got it," he said under his breath, in the dark.

Chapter 6 - The Heat Gets Hotter

Later Thursday morning, after the sun rose and the working world got its act together, a man who looked to be in his early 40's, wearing a navy-blue uniform and a white hat representative of the Philadelphia Fire Department, could be seen on a small TV monitor on Karen Sikorsky's desk, adjusting a microphone on a podium. It was Lieutenant Chuck Rafferty, Public Information Officer, preparing to speak. Karen watched on the dedicated transmission line the station had to Fire Headquarters for occasions like this.

"Good morning," began Lt. Rafferty, who looked confident and relaxed, his ruddy face taking command of the TV space. The medium-wide shot showed the backs of the heads of reporters gathered in the seats before him. "I have updates on two recent fires that required significant manpower to control."

Karen sat at her computer, pausing from her mundane management duties to type notes into a Word document.

"Within the last two days, we've had multi-alarm fires at the former Grunwald Company warehouse on Aramingo Avenue and a four-story mixed use building on 21st Street near Chestnut in center-city. I'm happy to say no one was injured in either fire."

Karen was typing madly on her keyboard, even though she could play back any portion of the news conference on her computer at any time. Old habits.

"The Fire Marshal has returned a disturbing report. The cause of each fire appears to be arson."

Karen reached over to turn up the volume a hair.

"In each case, the source of ignition was traced to a corner of a room near a window. In those corners were the remains of what appeared to be rags and plastic packing tape, the type used to bind boxes for shipment. The rags were taken to the police forensics lab and found to be soaked in linseed oil."

At that, Karen stopped typing. "Oh, man."

"Rags soaked in linseed oil and then packed tightly into a container, generate heat and can self-ignite."

"Nancy, are you listening to this?" shouted Karen to the assignment desk.

"Yep. What's linseed oil?"

Rafferty continued. "Those who remember the Meridian Plaza fire in 1991 will remember that fire was caused by rags soaked in linseed oil stuffed into a box during a construction project on an upper floor. That was an accident, but we lost three firefighters."

"Is this spontaneous combustion he's talking about?" asked Nancy out loud.

"Yes," answered Karen. "I'll never forget the video of them removing those bodies."

"The Fire Marshal believes it is not a coincidence that each of these two fires was caused the same way," Lt. Rafferty continued. "In cooperation with the police, we are actively looking for an arsonist."

"Damn," said Nancy from her desk. "Lead story."

"Fuckin' A," agreed Karen. "Will Harvey be ready to go for the noon show?"

"I'll make sure," said Nancy, who began dialing the cellphone of Harvey Jameson, the Channel 7 reporter at the news conference.

Karen barked at Reginald, the associate producer. "We need file of the 1991 Meridian Plaza fire. Can you get it in time?"

No videotape shot before 2000 had been digitized, which meant Reginald had to go to the so-called "tape archives," a closet down the hall from the elevator containing metal shelves holding cardboard boxes labeled in black marker by year and containing old 3/4-inch tape cassettes from the U-Matic days of video technology. Most lay helter-skelter inside the boxes with crude, hand-scrawled labels containing one or two-word slugs and, hopefully, a date. Reginald stepped into the closet and scanned the boxes for one marked 1991. It was there. He lifted it down from a shelf just at eye level. Inside was the usual mess of tapes, which he began pawing through.

At the assignment desk, Nancy had Harvey on the phone and they traded information.

"Let me talk to Harvey," said Karen.

"Sure. Let me transfer him to you."

Karen's desk phone rang just seconds later and she snapped it up. "Hey, Harvey."

"Hey," he responded.

"Do you remember that Meridian Plaza fire he was talking about?"

"No, I wasn't in Philly then."

"It was terrible, tragic, stupid. Everything possible went wrong. Three dead firemen. It burned for hours."

"They tore that place down some years ago, right?"

"Yep, ostensibly because it was unsafe but I always thought they did it to erase the memory of that job."

"So, these new fires, these are going to hit home for the Fire Department."

"You bet. I can't remember the last time since Meridian Plaza that we had any fire caused by spontaneous combustion, for god sake. It's like a *Mythbusters*."

"OK, " said Harvey. "Let me get on with this."

"Bye," said Karen and hung up her phone.

Reginald now appeared, brandishing an old video cassette. "Found it," he announced and marched it over to an ancient U-Matic playback machine that had been rigged up to a Mac for the infrequent task of converting analog video to digital. It had to be done in real time, so with the clock ticking towards noon, Reginald cued it up to a spot that showed a lot of smoke, did some clicking on the Mac screen, hit PLAY on the old tape machine sending it into the Mac where it was converted to an MPEG 4 file. He dubbed off about two minutes' worth. He clicked a few more times, sending it to the video server where it was stacked for the noon producer to insert into her rundown.

A lead story breaking ninety minutes before show time injected energy into the newsroom--mad typing at computers, paper scripts printing, the producer shouting last minute changes to the director and having a quick discussion with Harvey about his liveshot.

Karen was reading scripts, weeding out clichés as quickly as the kids wrote them. She counted four uses of the word "blaze" in one piece of copy, and eliminated all traces of "devastation" and one of the two uses of "tragic" from Reginald's Meridian Plaza sidebar.

"All the copy's in now," shouted Karen towards the producer.

Armitage was close enough to Philadelphia to have Channel 7 and the other Philly stations on cable. Bud had rolled out of bed late and had already gobbled down most of a bowl of instant oatmeal, with

Beulah watching cautiously, when he sat down in front of the living room TV with his coffee and switched it on at 11:59 AM.

"Coming up, arson is blamed for two Philadelphia fires in two days," barked the tease for the Channel 7 noon news. "Also, new hope for impotent men: Does a coffee a day lead to bedtime play? Join us at noon!"

How little has changed, thought Remmick as he scraped the last of his oatmeal from inside the bowl, licked it off his spoon and washed it down with his coffee. He looked at his GI Joe mug and thought, "a coffee a day." He glanced down at Beulah who was staring at him. He gave her the finger.

In his stinking bedroom many miles away, Bill Klemmer was attacking a corned beef special on rye as he sat on his bed, watching Channel 7. He wiped his hands on his sheets, picked up the remote and turned up the volume.

"Good afternoon," announced anchor Pamela Whitehead. "Our top story at noon, Philadelphia police seek an arsonist who they say started two big fires in two separate parts of the city within 48 hours."

Klemmer's mouth stop chewing and his eyes grew wide as Whitehead voiced-over Klemmer's video. "Fire officials say this fire two nights ago at an abandoned warehouse on Aramingo Avenue, and this fire early Wednesday morning in center city, were both intentionally set."

"Shit," spat Klemmer through a mouthful of corned beef.

"A Fire Department spokesman says the fires were started by rags soaked in linseed oil packed in boxes, a known cause of spontaneous combustion," continued the anchor, who then paused for a sound bite.

"It was like a time bomb," Rafferty said. "The box could be set down in an inconspicuous place, the actor could walk away and the fire would ignite minutes or hours later with no one anywhere near it. The center city fire was accelerated by a propane tank left open."

Whitehead appeared back on screen. "Philadelphia detectives and the Fire Department's arson unit have launched a joint investigation."

Klemmer dropped the rest of his sandwich onto his bed and scrambled off the mattress, pulling up his briefs as he rolled onto the floor. He started tossing sheets and papers, looking for his cellphone. Seconds later, he had the phone to his ear.

"You are a disgusting pig," said the voice at the other end. "You are a fat piece of shit worthy of nothing. Don't you dare call me and complain about your miserable life."

Klemmer was accustomed to the verbal abuse, but this was a bit more virulent than usual. "I don't know why you're so mad," he said. "I just asked you a question."

"And I will not answer. All you need to know is what I tell you. You can do whatever else you want but when I want something, I expect you to accomplish it."

Klemmer shifted from one foot to the other and looked sullen. "OK."

"Fucking right it's OK. I don't care what they're saying on TV. I know all about it, obviously."

Klemmer had turned down the sound on the TV so he could talk on the phone.

"You just keep on following my directions and keep your mouth shut, and everything will be fine, forever and ever. Copy that?"

"Yes, copy."

"Good. Now get on with your pathetic so-called life and don't call me again. I'll call you." There was silence now. Klemmer looked at his phone, looked at the silent TV, then wandered over to the desk in the corner. He picked up a framed photo of his father, a handsome man in his time.

"You didn't tell me what should I do," he said to the photo. His eyes welled up.

Chapter 7 - New Beginnings

It was a no-brainer for Remmick. Not so much for Maggie.

"I need this," he said as they sat on their couch, nursing diet Pepsi's and sharing a bag of popcorn. "*We* need this."

"No, we don't," she said. "We sit here each night, yelling at the TV, making fun of the giggling, idiot local anchors, the banal writing, the ignorant condescension. Do you really want to be part of that again?"

He crunched hard on a handful he had stuffed into his mouth. Beulah followed every move with her eyes, hoping for a handout. Anderson Cooper was on CNN with his political panel. Remmick didn't answer Maggie right away. The painful truth was, they needed the money.

"We're still into Arnie for almost a hundred K," he said. "He single-handedly made it possible for me to be here today and not rotting in prison. He found the right shrink who swore to the right bullshit. Hence, the right prison sentence for my stupid ass."

There had been little communication with Arnold Shapiro, Esquire, since Remmick got out of jail, only his monthly emailed account statement. The Remmicks were able to pay him a couple hundred here and there, never the full monthly payment. Arnie didn't complain. He and Bud had history going back years to the night at McGlinchey's pub in center city Philadelphia where they met. Yet, there was a chasm between them now, another byproduct of Remmick's incarceration, a split that seemed to have more to do with Maggie than money.

"I think Arnie's a snake," said Maggie. "I think he was all ready to move in on the grieving wife of his own client who was conveniently in jail. I don't trust him. I wish we didn't owe him."

"So, you're making my point for me. I don't totally share your opinion of Arnie, but I would love to have this debt off our backs. That's not gonna happen as long as I'm answering 911 calls for free and hanging around here in my underwear."

She put her arm across his shoulders and pulled him closer to her. "You really want to drive almost two hours to Philly each day? That piece of shit Lumina will never survive."

He recoiled in mock horror. "Please! That car has only 175-thousand miles on it. It's not even near the end of its second life."

"I give that bitch two more trips on the turnpike before she goes tits up."

There was a knock on their door, an unusual occurrence since they hadn't made any friends in the neighborhood. Remmick put down his soda, stepped into his Skechers and made his way to the door. He glanced through the peephole, then opened it.

"Hello," he said to his new next-door neighbor. "Come on in."

"How are you? I hope I'm not interrupting anything."

"Nah, we're just hanging. Maggie, this is Les, our new neighbor. We met the other morning."

Maggie got up from the couch and walked over, offering her hand. "Nice to meet you, Les."

"And you, Maggie."

"When did you move in?"

"Six days ago. Still got boxes everywhere. Just started the new job also, so I'm a little stressed."

"Well, if you need anything."

"Actually, the reason I'm here is to get a little guidance on trash."

"Ah, yes. You moved from a world of municipal trash collection?"

"Yea. Never had to find my own trash hauler before. One of the charms of Armitage."

"We use Waste Management. But there's also Wilson Hauling and Trash Masters."

"I should use Trash Masters just because of the name."

"They're the most expensive of the bunch."

Bud stood silently with his hands in his pockets.

"OK, I'll think on it," said Les, who then became quiet, leading to an awkward silence in the room.

"So, how do you like the neighborhood?" asked Bud.

"OK, I guess. I haven't ventured out much, except that morning when you and I met."

Bud grinned and glanced at Maggie. "I had on my Beulah-poops-in-the-yard outfit."

"Ah, I'm sure you were charmed," Maggie said.

Their new neighbor smiled, looked down at the floor and kicked an imaginary rock. Another awkward silence ensued.

"Actually," he began, "there's another reason I came over. Hope you don't mind."

"Not yet," said Bud with a slight edge to his voice.

"After we spoke the other day, it occurred to me that, um--"

Remmick looked at Maggie. Their eyes locked for that moment.

"Your name rang a bell," said Les, whose eyes raised up from the floor and turned towards the Remmicks. "And so, you know, I wasn't sure whether--"

"You weren't sure whether it was OK to ask me if I am that guy?"

Les nodded.

"Why don't you have a seat, Les," Bud said. "Would you like a beer?"

"Sure."

Maggie disappeared into the kitchen. Bud sat on the couch and Les sank into a chair that was caddy-corner. Bud's demeanor morphed into one of quiet amusement. Maggie returned in less than a minute with a Corona for Les and another diet Pepsi for Bud. She then took a seat next to her husband.

"What would you like to know, Les?"

Les took a long hit on his beer, then placed the bottle on the glass coffee table, folded his hands and looked Remmick in the eyes. "I'm sorry, I guess I--"

"What would you like to know?" persisted Remmick.

"You are the Bordon Remmick who killed his boss, right?"

"Yes."

"You did time in New Jersey, a few years?"

"Yes."

"And now," began Les, looking down at the floor again, "you're out." Les looked up from the floor.

"Yes, I'm out, and ready to kill, kill, kill again."

Les's half-grin grew cold and remained frozen on his face as his eyes moved from Bud to Maggie, back to Bud. Both Remmicks were smiling at him, relaxed smiles of kids sharing a joke.

Les dropped his head, exhaled loudly, then looked back up at them. "You're messing with me, aren't you?"

Bud and Maggie laughed simultaneously. "No, gosh, Les," said Maggie through a toothy smile. "He's serious."

"I guess you get this all the time."

"Actually, no," said Remmick, also smiling. "No one's ever asked me if I am that killer guy." He and Maggie traded glances again and the laughter subsided. Les looked slightly less uncomfortable and elected, at this point, to hold his tongue. Instead, he lifted his Corona to his lips.

"To be honest, Les, this conversation reminds me of one I had just yesterday in Philly. A job interview."

Les nodded.

"I don't wear a sign around my neck, but I don't deny it if asked. If it comes out, it comes out. I would rather there not be any misunderstandings."

Les nodded again and said simply, "OK."

"So, what else do you want to know?"

"You pushed bookshelves onto him?" he blurted out. "Really?"

"Really."

"Never heard that one. In all my years--" He stopped in mid-sentence.

Remmick waited for the sentence to complete, but it didn't. In the split second that he realized Les had stopped speaking, he noticed his haircut for the first time, and that he was clean shaven. And his eyes, always hard at work.

Les realized the jig was up. "I'm a cop."

"No shit," said Remmick, acting as though he knew all along.

"State police. Transferred from Trevose. My boss and I didn't get along, so he sent me out here, the sticks. No offense."

"Hey, I didn't get along with my boss, either," announced Remmick, wide-eyed with the affected joy of a psychopath. "I guess I should have transferred, too."

Les stood at that point. "Maybe I should go home before I say more stupid shit."

Maggie and Bud stood and waited for Les to move first. He sidled away from his chair and made his way to the front door.

"Hey, it's been a hoot," chortled Bud as he extended his hand to Les. "Glad you came by."

"Really?"

"Really. Nothing like transparency."

Les gave each Remmick one final glance and said, "Good night."

Bud closed the door, then turned to look at Maggie. She shrugged, then motioned to Beulah to follow her out the kitchen door to shit in the yard.

"I don't have time for your blubbering," were the words Klemmer heard as he clasped his phone between his ear and shoulder. "It's as though I haven't taught you anything."

"You've taught me everything," said Klemmer in a shaky voice as he squeezed a large amount of Bosco into a glass of milk, then stirred it with a tablespoon. "I just don't know what to do. I don't want to go to jail."

"You don't have to do anything. Just follow the program. Stop being such a crybaby."

Klemmer sniffled as he grabbed the chocolate milk and sat down on the edge of his bed.

"Your work has been outstanding. As long as you do what I say, nothing bad will happen."

"OK."

"I will have another job for you, maybe tomorrow."

"Can't we take a break?"

"No."

Klemmer slurped his chocolate milk and felt like crying again. "I don't want to."

"I don't care what you want. Do what you're told!"

"Alright! Stop yelling at me!" He slurped the last dregs of his beverage, put down the glass and wiped his mouth with his sleeve.

"You'll hear from me soon. Good night."

Klemmer sniffed a final sniff and sat down on the bed and reached over to the TV and said, "Good night, dad."

Chapter 8 - Our New Boss

The excitement in the Channel 7 newsroom rivaled that of the day Frank Rizzo showed up to meet and greet the staff when he acquired his talk show at the radio station down the hall. Rizzo's sheer presence filled a room. The former Philadelphia police commissioner, two-term mayor and unabashed Number One Philadelphia Italian-American, managed to command respect and awe, even among his many enemies.

You couldn't say the same about Bordon Remmick, a medium sized, slightly overweight German-American who wore his first suit in a decade like an 8th grader at a middle school graduation. His time in prison etched away at his looks, leaving those to guess his age baffled--55? 60? Older? Given the legend that had grown around him, there was still a sense of awe as he walked off the elevator with Karen, paused a moment to make eye contact with some nearby newsroom employees, then walked into what would be his new office.

"Here we are," said Karen as they turned on the light in the small room. The ceiling fluorescents popped on all at once revealing a drab and sexless office equipped with several flat-screen monitors sitting side by side on a long credenza, a large metal desk that looked like it had fallen down a flight of stairs, a flat screen monitor on the desktop and a couple of upholstered chairs that had also seen better days.

"OK," said Remmick, looking around the room.

"I don't use it," said Karen. "I sit in the newsroom."

"When was the last time anyone used it?"

"Your predecessor, nine months ago."

"Yea?" Remmick said with a raised eyebrow. "Is he stuffed in a drawer here?" He opened one of the credenza drawers. It contained a rack for hanging files, but no hanging files.

"There's money in the budget for new office furniture, I'm told. Strickland's assistant will take care of it. Just tell her what you want."

Remmick walked behind his desk and pulled out the chair. It glided effortlessly on quiet wheels and didn't appear too grungy, so he sat down. He opened the drawers. The center drawer contained a handful of paper clips and two rubber bands. The others were empty.

"Can you do me a favor?" he asked Karen. "Please ask the newsroom folks to come in and bring some chairs with them."

"You haven't been here five minutes. Don't you want to--"

"I'm good. Please."

Karen smiled and turned to leave.

"You come back too, right?" Remmick said to her.

"Yes, of course."

"What's that?" asked Reg as he walked up behind Nancy, whose attention was riveted on her monitor. She was watching what looked like some kind of hearing.

"Early release hearing at King's Pointe Correctional Facility, two years and eight months ago," she said. Her eyes never left the monitor.

Reg pulled up a chair and sat next to her, moving closer to the monitor. NJDOC was superimposed in small white letters onto the lower right corner of the screen, just above the date and time. "Remmick!" he said in hushed wonder. "How'd you get this?"

"Freedom of Information Act," she replied. She turned up the volume as the man in the witness chair began speaking.

"I am John Ungar, Superintendent of Kings Pointe Correctional Facility. I support early release for Mr. Remmick. In his time here, he has participated in all assigned activities according to prison regulations. He suffered a near-fatal, unprovoked attack at the hands of another inmate and has been recovering from that injury. He has expressed regret for his crime."

"Next is the chairman of the parole board," explained Nancy.

"Thank you, Superintendent Ungar. The next person to speak is--"

"Excuse me, sir."

"Yes, Mr. Remmick?"

"I think I can save you and all these folks here some time."

"Yes? How's that?"

"May I speak?"

"Yes, Mr. Remmick. What would you like to say?"

"Um, I, ah, I need to say something now."
"Go ahead."

"Check this out," said Nancy, drawing Reg's attention to the figure seated in the front row dressed in a gray jump suit.

"I appreciate you all coming here. I appreciate the superintendent's words about me. I don't know why he said them, but I appreciate it. Once, back in the newsroom, I remember watching a Pentagon news conference and heard a general answering questions about some military issue, don't remember what. A reporter asked him a question he didn't know the answer to. Instead of just saying 'I don't know', he said, 'I have not achieved clarity on that issue.' I thought that was the most bureaucratic sentence I'd ever heard. Wordy and precise. Cold. I've been thinking about that answer lately. When you don't know answers that you should know, it really does come down to clarity. Achieving clarity. It's a precise description of the process of understanding. Achieving clarity, the second to last step in achieving truth."

Nancy and Reg were spellbound.

"Contrary to what Mr. Ungar told you, I do not regret killing that fucking maggot who abused, threatened and assaulted a perfectly good human being. His exercise of power and control over Hilde Schimmel terrorized her. He blackmailed her for months. She couldn't fight him. And when she tried to leave, he tossed her into a glass table. She gave herself to him, but he wanted more. She didn't know how to give more. So, she got out the only way left to her."

"She killed herself," said Nancy. Reg looked at her, then back at the screen.

"Therefore, I'm glad he's dead. Four years in jail has been a small price to pay for erasing Ronald Morone from the planet. EVERYBODY GOT THAT?"

Nancy and Reg looked at each other for a moment. The board chairman spoke again.

"Well, Mr. Remmick, I see we've come full circle. Does anyone have anything to add?"

The tape was silent.

"We're adjourned."

Nancy clicked STOP.
"Damn," said Reg.
"Our new boss."

Bud sat behind his ratty desk as newsroom staffers, one by one, rolled chairs into the office and made places for themselves facing him. He knew the sooner he overcame the initial jitters of introducing himself, the better for everyone. He didn't know these people, but he was pretty sure they knew him.

Whispers subsided and nine people sat before him plus Karen who stood by the open door. As she swung the door closed, Bud said, "No, leave it open." She complied.

"Good morning," he said to the room with a smile, his hands folded on the desk before him. "As I'm sure you know, my name is Bordon Remmick. I've accepted the position of News Director and I'm looking forward to working with all of you." He sat silent for a moment, looking at each face, one by one. The room was absolutely still.

"It wasn't all that long ago that I sat where you are sitting. I hated the morning meeting at Kaleidoscope more than having needles in my eyes."

This elicited quiet giggles from several in the room.

"I'd like to meet each morning only with Karen, the assignment editor--Nancy, correct? --and the chief technician. Is that person here?"

A hand raised, fourth from left, back row. "Gordon Richardson here," said a 40-ish man, medium dark skin with a mustache and shaved head.

"Great, Gordon. Nice to meet you. Most days, the assignments will be obvious. Some days, they won't. But we don't need a cast of thousands to figure that out."

By now, the elephant in the room was squealing loudly. Remmick flashed a knowing grin and nodded his head ever so slightly.

"Yes," he said. "I am that guy." He scanned the room, looking for reactions. There were only fixed stares. "I'm not going to waste your time by retelling that which I am sure every one of you knows very well. I will only say that I made mistakes in a past life and I paid for them. I'm still paying for them. My life is an open book thanks to the internet and honestly, I haven't found much about me online that isn't true. As the professional, curious news people you are, I'm confident you know my whole story. I ask you for the benefit of the doubt. Judge me by what I do, not by the past. Fair?"

He didn't count the nodding heads, but it appeared that all agreed.

"OK. And now, I owe you this one opportunity to ask me whatever questions you want. After this meeting, I don't want to hear them again. So, who's first?"

He scanned the faces, some looking nervously at each other, some still riveted on him. There was still no sound emanating from any corner of the room.

"Well, let me go right to the top of *my* list of Frequently Asked Questions."

Dead silence continued. He picked up a Sharpie that was on the desktop and held it to his mouth like a microphone.

"Mr. Remmick, do you think you might ever kill again?" His question, posed to himself, made Reg's eyes grow wider, which Remmick found amusing. He turned his body to the opposite side, grasped the Sharpie with the other hand and answered himself. "That is not my intention, no. However--" He paused and glanced at those gathered in the room and could see them lean in towards his desk. He resumed. "Who knows what evil lurks in the hearts of men?"

The wiry red-head squirmed in her chair, looking anxiously around at the others. She tentatively raised her hand, then immediately lowered it. Remmick looked her way, raised his eyebrows, then looked away.

"Relax, people. No reason this can't be fun." His broad smile elicited relieved sighs and a couple random chuckles. "My door is always open, folks. I'm looking forward to going to work. Class dismissed."

Karen had been standing at the door the whole time as the staff filed out, pushing their chairs ahead of them.

"That wasn't funny," said Reg in a whisper to Nancy as he followed her out of the room.

"Who knows what evil lurks in the hearts of men, for Christ sake?" said Roy with arms crossed.

"The Shadow knows," said Karen through a toothy smile. "Eventually, one of the children will figure it out."

"I doubt any of them has a clue about 1930's radio."

"Oh, come on, Roy, he was messing with them. You should've seen the looks on their faces."

The two sat in Strickland's office at opposite sides of his desk, munching on a couple of salads.

"He broke the ice. He will have them eating out of his hand in another couple weeks, you watch."

"Sorry, I'm still not with the Remmick-Is-A-Standup-Guy program yet."

"I know. As I said, give it time."

There was the usual, hushed buzz of voices in the Capitol briefing room, a ritual none of them looked forward to. The reporters sat in the same seats each time, waiting for the hulking mass of so-called humanity named Thomas Franklin to stroll into the room and hold court. And when he did, the buzz halted immediately. Franklin strode in with large steps that made dull thuds against the ancient hardwood floor. He was not a beautiful man. His square head, thin hair and massive neck inspired comparisons to the comic book Thing. His thinnish lips and round face squeezed out words that sounded crooked and insincere at every turn. Yet, he always smelled good, a pimpish fragrance that summoned an image of Harvey Keitel in a taffeta dress.

"Thank you all for coming," said Franklin as he stepped up to the podium and launched his monthly news conference. "Of course, you should be thanking *me* because without me, you'd have nothing to report on, am I right? Go ahead, what's your question?" He pointed to a young man in the front row.

"Governor," began AP reporter Jesse Stinson, "yesterday you were quoted in the Philadelphia Daily News as saying, and I'm reading here, 'Teachers are constantly sucking on the hind tit, begging for more money, whining about classroom size and programs we can't afford. Their union needs to get them to buck up and shut up.' Do you regret saying any of that?"

"No, I don't."

Stinson and the others waited for more. There wasn't any. "A follow-up then, Governor. Are you saying teachers are a burden on society?"

"I think I was clear enough. Next question."

"Governor, Jennifer Kruthers, Fox 29. Do you think that kind of language is helpful at a time when public schools in Philadelphia are barely surviving? Many of the teachers there are doing heroic duty—"

"I know about the Philadelphia public schools. You're right, they're barely surviving. But the taxpayers are tired of bailing out that district. Let them go charter all the way for all I care. I understand they are in contract talks now with the union. Good luck with that. Yes, over there."

"Pat Regalman, Pittsburgh Post-Gazette. Sir, we've learned that you are on a mission to replace a number of established government employees with your own choices. Your opponents are calling it a patronage whitewash. Care to respond?"

"When I ran for Governor, I promised to put competent people into important positions to serve our citizens. There's no patronage here. I don't like that word. I have my eye on people who I know are competent and yea, I know some of them, so what? Why would I surround myself with people I don't know?"

"Sir, a follow-up. We also learned that the Democrats oppose this effort to, um, put people you know into these jobs. They've said they will actually eliminate those jobs before letting you—"

"Let 'em try. Man, you guys are making me work over here. In the back."

"Governor, Melanie Rogash, Channel 5 News. Do you have any comment on the recent revelation that Bordon Remmick, who you once called a psychopath, is now working as a TV news director in Philadelphia--Channel 7 to be exact?"

Franklin pondered the question for a moment. "No, I wasn't aware of that. Christ, I wonder who *he* knows?"

"He worked there in the past, before his prison—"

"So, this is America, where a crazy person who kills someone gets out after doing, what, a couple years in jail? Seriously?"

"Four years, to be exact," said Rogash.

"And then goes back to work like nothing happened? That's a fu—that's a disgrace."

"Governor, Max Welltower, KDKA. Do you agree with the president that sanctuary cities are—"

"So, he's out and working among the humans again, eh?" said Franklin. Welltower stopped asking his question and the rest of the reporters went silent. "That's a friggin' joke."

Welltower tried another tack. "Governor, the Democratically controlled legislature has the votes to cut those jobs in the upcoming budget. How do you expect to defeat their majority?"

"That was a good man he killed," said Franklin. "Ronald Morone was a model conservative, god-fearing and a patriot. When that sick bastard--" He caught himself and stopped cold. The reporters waited for the sentence to complete. "We're done. Have a nice day." Franklin turned and walked away from the podium, leaving his security detail and chief of staff to scramble after him. The reporters continued shouting questions.

Chapter 9 - Dead or Alive?

The former Margaret Schlossberg enjoyed government work. There was a certain order to it, though things took way longer than she was used to. Livingston County had its share of older residents--aging baby boomers, established residents who were born and raised there and quite a few New Jersey expatriates. Back in Ardmore, her meals-on-wheels program was a microcosm of the senior world, a couple hundred clients with families who cared about them to varying degrees. Most of them appreciated not having to worry about food and cherished the daily visits from volunteers. At the County, Maggie had a staff, department heads and her very own bureaucracy. She had a budget. She had a boss, three of them, actually, the County Commissioners who met in public twice a month, and a local senior advocacy group that made a pest of itself at those meetings. But it was a job she was comfortable in, good at and happy to have, all things considered.

She sipped her coffee and picked at a blueberry muffin when her intercom buzzed. "Line one for you," came the voice of Angela, her administrative assistant.

"Who is it?"

"Wouldn't say, just 'a friend'."

Maggie picked up the phone. "Hello?"

The replying voice was familiar, but unexpected. "Hi, Mrs. Remmick. This is John Ungar, New Jersey Department of Corrections. How are you?"

Maggie held her breath for a moment. "Wow. I'm fine, I think."

"So, you remember me?"

"How could I forget? Your kindness back in the not-so-good-old-days was huge."

"It was an opportunity to help you out a little."

Ungar, the superintendent at King's Pointe Prison during Bud's incarceration, had made it possible for Maggie to see Bud after his injury and vouched for him at his early-release hearing. Of course, Bud disavowed Ungar's testimonial, reaffirmed his lack of remorse for the killing and served every last minute of his sentence as a result.

"How's he doing?" asked Ungar.

"Fine. He's just starting a new job in Philly. And he seems to like the EMT thing."

"Yes. I spoke to his captain at the rescue squad a while back."

"Bud told me. And you also spoke to his new boss. Thank you again. I don't understand why you have a soft spot for him after the way he acted towards you, but I appreciate it. I think Bud does too, he just doesn't know it."

"I saw some of myself in him, I suppose. Glad it's been working out. I always admired how you stuck with him, even during the worst of it."

"Thanks."

"I work in Trenton now, Department of Corrections."

"No more day to day prison drama?"

"No. More political drama now. Which is the reason for my call."

"Do tell?"

"My boss and your boss talk a lot. And my boss can't keep a secret."

"This would be the Governors of Pennsylvania and New Jersey you're referring to?"

"Yes. The boys like each other, despite the public pissing matches. And my boy likes me, for some reason. But your Governor has a bit of a hard-on for your husband and this has led to pointed questions about you."

Maggie felt suddenly invaded, like a looting was about to take place. "Me? What did *I* do?"

"Specifically, his concern revolves around your government job. How you got it. Who didn't get it. Why the wife of a convicted felon--"

"Fuck me!" shouted Maggie in a voice loud enough for Angela to peek her head around to look through the open door. "For real?"

"Yes. I'm not sure how far he is taking it, but Governor Franklin has taken an interest in you, and not in a good way."

"Christ, I saw the open position on the state employment website. I emailed my resume. They called me. They interviewed me. I got the job. End of story."

"I'm sure that's the--"

"No one ever asked me about my husband, my name, nothing," she spat. "Fucking political hacks!"

"Yes, correct. Except this political hack's reach over hiring and firing is impressive and disturbing."

"Just when I thought it was finally over," Maggie said, her voice shaking. "Bastard!"

"I didn't mean to ruin your day, but I thought I would share, in case you wanted to, I don't know, make plans."

"Plans? My only plan up until now was to microwave my soup."

Bud sat at his desk, alone in his office, tapping on his keyboard, trying to teach himself the newsroom software called NewsCache. One of his three monitors was tuned to CNN with the sound off. The late morning anchor was chatting with one of the many political panels CNN seemed to have in storage. The lower third news ticker contained stories about a mudslide in California, the latest outrage from Washington and another harangue from the North Korean dictator.

Using a carefully aimed remote, Bud turned on the far-left monitor, which was already tuned to Channel 7. One of the few remaining soaps on network television was on. There were a few hours until the next newscast.

Outside his door, he heard the sounds of men's voices and the shuffling of feet. He got up and went to the door and took a step out, gazing to the rear of the floor where the editing stations were. Two young men were tossing a football across the room, changing positions as though practicing passing and receiving on the move. Seated at one of the edit stations was a young woman who was staring intently at her screen. Suddenly, the errant football left its planned trajectory, hit one of the hanging fluorescent fixtures and ricocheted down, landing with a crash on the woman's computer monitor. She let out a scream at the same moment Remmick shouted, "Hey!"

The two men and the woman looked up at him and froze.

"Really?" shouted Remmick. "Are you guys in need of something to do?"

The young man closest to Remmick said, "Uh, no, um. Sorry!" He looked over at the woman who was still recovering. "Sorry, Lydia. Really sorry."

"Come here," shouted Remmick. The two men made their way towards their new boss. Remmick stood with his arms folded as they arrived and stood before him.

"What's your name?" Remmick asked the skinny, white one.

"Louis," he answered timidly.

"Louis what?"

"Carmichael."

"Louis Carmichael. And you?"

"William DeLore," replied the stocky black one.

"And you guys do what around here?"

"Shooter-editors," replied DeLore. "When we're not on lunch, that is."

"Do me a favor," said Remmick in a tamer voice. "Practice somewhere other than indoors, OK?"

"Sure, OK," Carmichael quickly agreed.

"Lydia," Remmick shouted to the woman.

"Yes?" she replied.

"Is it broken?"

"Cracked. No picture."

Remmick took on a dire visage with a tilt of the head that signaled the end of all life.

"See that?" he said with mock exasperation and a slow shake of the head. "A precision instrument, gone." Those monitors went for less than a hundred bucks.

"Jeez, we're sorry," offered Carmichael for the third time.

"I know you are," replied Remmick, maneuvering himself between the two men so he could put his arms around both their shoulders, then pulled them close to him. "But here's what I'm gonna do. I'm gonna chalk this up to a first day memory that I'll have forever. Because I'll remember both of your names. Forever."

"OK," said Carmichael. DeLore said nothing.

"OK," confirmed Remmick, removing his arms from their shoulders. "Now fuck off." The young men didn't need a second invitation.

Remmick placed his hands in his pockets and made his way to the newsroom. People were eating at their desks. TV monitors were tuned to various programs. Remmick looked around to see if he could remember names. There was Nancy, the assignment editor, a generic white woman, maybe mid-20's with shoulder length brown hair. Several desks away was the show producer, the skinny red-head, Rita, wearing a white and red striped top with short sleeves that revealed epic tattoos on her left arm and tight, red pants. At the desk a few feet away from her was the associate producer, Reginald, a young black man wearing a tie with a busy black and blue pattern over a black shirt. Remmick knew none of their last names. Anchor Pamela Whitehead and weatherman Roger Caffrey were chatting at a desk in the far corner. Remmick's eyes snapped back to Reginald, who was staring at him.

"Hello again," Remmick said to him and walked in his direction.

"Hi."

"Reginald, right?"

"Yep. Reg is good."

"Good to meet you again. How long have you worked here, Reg?"

"Almost a year and a half. Started as an intern, then got hired after I graduated."

"Outstanding. So, I shocked you back there, huh?"

Reg looked befuddled for a moment. "Uh, what do you mean?"

"Back in my office. I thought your eyes were going to bug out of your head for a moment there."

Reg was embarrassed and looked down at his keyboard. "Sorry."

"You don't have to be sorry. I was trying to be funny."

Reg said nothing but looked warily at Remmick, who now pulled up a wheeled chair next to his. Remmick knew he was making the young man uncomfortable.

"This may sound presumptuous," said Remmick, "but I sense you still have questions."

Reginald looked up from his keyboard and trained his eyes off to the side, avoiding eye contact.

"I said I'd never answer those questions again, but I'll make an exception in your case," said Remmick.

Reginald turned his head to face Remmick. Their eyes met.

"How could you do that?" he asked Remmick in a low voice. "Kill that guy?"

Remmick was both surprised and pleased by the young man's directness.

"I didn't plan it. It was an emotional time. I'd just lost a co-worker. I was a pissed-off guy back then. Anger issues." He stopped for a moment. "I snapped."

"Are you sorry?"

"Maybe you should get your hands on the video of my early release hearing."

"I've seen it."

"Then you know the answer."

Reginald looked away for a moment, then turned back to Remmick. "*But if you do not forgive others their sins, your Father will not forgive your sins.* That's in the Bible."

"That ship has sailed. I don't expect forgiveness."

"Then you won't end up in heaven."

"That's OK. I have a reservation at the other place, up front by the band." Remmick stood and started wheeling his chair back to the desk from which he stole it. He turned his head and said over his shoulder, "The one I like is, *There but for the grace of God go I.*"

"That's not in the Bible."

"It's in mine."

Bill Klemmer drove the old Camry at about 50 on the Expressway, careful not to pass his exit. He had gotten a call from Channel 7 that his check was finally ready. Instead of waiting for it to show up in the mail, he decided to go get it. His oversized elbow hung out the window and the wind blew through his hair, which he had treated with new product. He glanced at himself in the rear-view mirror. He put on his blinker and veered onto the exit lane, getting off the Expressway and on to City Avenue. Channel 7 sat atop a hill overlooking the Schuylkill River and the Manayunk neighborhood of Philadelphia. The station was built in the 70's as film was being replaced by video tape. Three-hour film processing was replaced by instant playback. Two-person photography crews were replaced by "one-man bands". The age of ENG, electronic news gathering, changed everything, as "live" became a marketing mantra and a new toy for news directors, consultants and advertisers. The viewers, of course, simply came along for the ride.

Decades later, Channel 7 was a shell of its former self, regularly killed in the ratings by its two main competitors and fighting an uphill battle to remain a relevant force in the Philadelphia news market. Equipment was aging and manpower was diminishing. Yet, it had Bill Klemmer, whose loyalty was linked to his father, a life-long viewer who later shot video for Channel 7. The younger Klemmer pledged to sell video only to Channel 7, a small competitive edge enjoyed by the station.

The Camry pulled into the Channel 7 parking lot, an aging asphalt surface pock-marked with ragged potholes and faded lines. Klemmer parked as close to the back door as he could, hauled himself out of the car and waddled to the door. He opened it and approached the security guard, a woman in her 50' with a pale white face, bright pink lip gloss and a uniform that encased the top half of her body to the point of bursting.

"I'm William Klemmer, here to pick something up?"

"From whom?" the guard asked.

"Nancy at the desk."

"Hang on." The guard picked up her phone and dialed four digits. "Nancy? A William Klemmer is here for you?" She paused, then hung up. "She'll be right down."

Klemmer stood with his hands in his coat pockets, waiting. About one minute later, Nancy appeared at the double doors leading from the stairway behind the guard station.

"Hi, Bill," she said. "Here's your check. We're sorry for the delay in payment."

"It's OK. We appreciate it."

"Sure. We?"

"Me and my dad," he said, concluding their short interaction. He turned and walked back out the way he came. Nancy and the guard watched him walk to his car through the glass door.

"Who's he?" asked the guard.

"Freelancer. He's good."

"He'd better be good at something because he smells to high heaven."

Nancy chuckled, then turned and went back through the door to the stairway back up to the newsroom. As she walked toward her desk, her new boss was bending over her chair, playing with one of her police scanners.

"Hi," she said.

"Oh hi, Nancy," Remmick replied. "Reminds me a little of home."

"Why's that?"

"I have a scanner. Not nearly as interesting as listening to Philly, I'm afraid."

"Who do you listen to?"

"My rescue squad, the local cops, state police, volunteer fire. I'm an EMT in my town."

"Is that right? What town and when on earth do you have time to do that?"

"Armitage, Livingston County. I do one duty shift a week and help out on weekends when I can. I wanted to volunteer somewhere when I got out and they had a need for ambulance responders. I couldn't get work so I had plenty of time to take the EMT course. It was a no brainer."

"That's awesome."

"It's so immediate, you know? One minute your cellphone beeps, five minutes later you're in someone's living room, helping them. I had no idea I would like it so much."

"That's great. So, you *save* lives now."

Remmick's look turned ice cold. Nancy had no follow-up as she readjusted her scanner.

"Did we straighten things out with that freelancer?" Remmick asked.

"Oh, yea. We sometimes forget to move the vouchers up to the second floor and their payments get delayed. We're working on that. He's up to date now."

"And this guy is who?"

"Bill Klemmer. He works overnight jobs for us. I thought he was a loner but apparently he works with his dad." Nancy had taken her seat at the desk and adjusted the volume on the scanner Remmick was playing with.

"OK. See you later."

As he walked back towards his office, he passed Karen's cubicle and saw her watching something on her monitor. He took the seat next to her.

"I'm trying to figure out your newsroom software, NewsCache," he said.

"Oh, you mean NewsCrash? It's shit," she said, paying more attention to her video monitor. "We've had it for three years and it's never worked right. The station bailed on the support contract because it costs, you know, *money*. So, it's kind of every man and woman for themselves now."

"Who's the newsroom expert?"

"A combination of Reg McKnight and Gordon Richardson."

"Has it ever gone down at the worst possible moment?"

"You mean like an hour before a show? Oh yea."

"So, what's Plan B?"

Karen looked up from her monitor, stood and motioned for Bud to follow her. They walked the length of the floor to a closed door behind the edit stations. She opened it to reveal a caged-in storage area with a combination lock. Behind the cage were what appeared to be the last seven typewriters still in existence in the western world.

"Holy shit," said Remmick. "Olympus typewriters?"

"Plan B."

"This is a big check," Klemmer said into his cellphone, holding it with one hand and the steering wheel in the other. "They owed a lot."

"Put it immediately in the bank," said the voice.

"I'm on my way there right now."

"Your next assignment will be tonight. Listen carefully."

Klemmer navigated the Camry up the Roosevelt Extension, making his way back home while listening to instructions. He guessed he'd need a nap if he was going to be up in the middle of the night again.

"Can you help me?" Remmick asked Gordon in his most pathetic voice as he stood at Gordon's office door. "NewsCache is baffling."

"They don't call it NewsCrash for nothing," said Gordon with a smile. "Let's take a look."

The pair walked the short distance from Gordon's office to Remmick's. Both sat down behind Bud's desk and stared at his computer.

"I read the online manual," said Remmick. "It made my head explode. The software is supposed to do everything right? Word processing, rundowns, video playback and stacking. And it feeds the prompter, right?"

Gordon looked at him and grinned. "It never actually did all that. All they use it for now is word processing, the rundowns and script printing. The prompter and video functions are done by another system which also happens to suck."

"Nice. Sounds like a good place for the new News Director to start."

"It's gonna cost money, man. Both systems need to be replaced by one that does it all."

"I get it."

"What else have you been doing on your first day at school?"

"Well, after my epic welcome meeting this morning, I moseyed around the newsroom, making a pest of myself. Visited with Karen and some of the newsroom kids."

"You need to keep an eye on Nancy. She's a good kid and smart, but tends to forget the system around her that depends on communication. And, she has a little attitude."

"I got that. She made good on a late payment to a freelancer, a guy named Klemmer."

"Sure, Bill Klemmer. Our full timers run into him from time to time when they're out late."

"He's apparently quite a hot-shot. He and his father."

"Sorry?"

"That's what Nancy said. Klemmer and his dad."

Gordon moved his eyes away from the computer screen and stopped typing for a moment. "Well, that would be a good trick since Klemmer's dad has been dead a couple years now."

Chapter 10 - The Will to Act

"This comes directly from the top," the Major said to the Trooper. The Trooper, Lester Noble, was incredulous. "From the Colonel?"

"No, the top," replied the Major. "Governor Franklin."

"Excuse me sir, why does the Governor care--"

"Are you questioning an order, Trooper?"

"No, sir. Sorry, sir."

"Good."

"It's just that, well, I'm sure you're aware--"

"That they are your next-door neighbors? Of course, I'm aware. That was the whole point of your relocation to Armitage, son."

"Well, that's news to me, sir. I had no idea I was here for this purpose."

"Sometimes, the communications pipeline is inefficient. And that, Trooper Noble, is regrettable. But it changes nothing."

Lester was in shock. He shifted in the already uncomfortable chair that faced his supervisor's desk. He was appreciative of the housing assistance at the time, never once suspecting that he was being manipulated. Major Brian Harcourt, as the nameplate stated, sat before him.

"What am I supposed to be looking for?" asked Lester.

"Anything that could be considered unusual behavior."

"That's pretty broad."

"Exactly."

Lester was feeling nauseous. He was trying to remember if spying on your neighbor was a lecture he missed at the academy.

"Any more questions, Trooper?"

"No sir."

"Then, carry on."

Bud arrived home after his first day on the job in a state of exhaustion. He thought he kept up a good facade for the staff, but realized he had a lot to learn. The two-hour drive at the end of a long day was just the icing on the cake.

Maggie's car was in the driveway. She would always beat him home, of course, since she worked only 20 minutes away. He trudged through the front door, threw it closed, tossed his coat onto the chair and spied Maggie on the couch staring into space holding a rock glass containing ice cubes and a clear liquid.

"Oh my," he said. "Breaking out the vodka."

"It's my third."

"I see," he said, sitting down next to her and giving her a peck on the cheek. "What's the occasion?"

She turned her head and looked him in the eye. "Are you ready for this?" Her face was etched in pain, her brow was a knotted mess.

"What?"

"Apparently, the mother fucking Governor of Pennsylvania is none too keen on me having this job. He is concerned that a government job has gone to the spouse of a convicted felon."

"The Governor of Pennsylvania?"

Maggie nodded, her eyes locked on his, amazed at hearing the words spoken out loud.

"Who says?" asked Bud.

"An old friend. John Ungar."

"What? My old prison warden?"

Maggie nodded again, this time with her mouth open. "He called me today from his new job in Trenton to tell me this. He's tight with his Governor, Hale, who told him that Franklin has made me his personal mission."

"That's unbelievable. What, why--"

"I didn't get more details. I was in too much shock to ask."

"And this is because of me?"

Maggie just nodded.

"What did *I* do?"

Maggie looked at him with an annoyed sneer.

"I mean, lately?" he added.

"I put a call in to the County Commissioners. Their staff director, the woman who hired me, Marjorie what's-her-name. I don't know if I should start to advocate for myself, act like nothing's wrong or jump off a building."

"You've heard nothing official?"

"Nothing. The first I heard any of this was from Ungar."

"Well, maybe *he* got it wrong. Unless you hear it from your boss, I wouldn't go crazy."

His reassuring tone did nothing to remove the pained look from Maggie's face. "It never occurred to me that--"

"That my name would fuck you up?"

"Yes."

"I'm sorry."

Maggie raised her glass to her lips and guzzled what was left. Then, she resumed staring into space.

Dusk had fallen on the northeastern United States, and from northern Delaware to New York City, the temperature sank to the upper 20's. It was fully dark by 6:30. Rush hour traffic was still a factor, though rush hour in Armitage was more like a rush half-hour. The worst of the traffic was on route 80 at the Pocono exit.

In Philadelphia the Schuylkill Expressway was as predictable as ever, bunching up traffic almost its entire length from Girard Avenue into south Philly. Cars moved at 30 miles an hour, then stopped, then resumed at 40 miles an hour, then 20, then 50 for a tenth of a mile and so on. Among the infinite makes and models of cars packed onto the highway was the 2005 brown Camry driven by Bill Klemmer. He was tailgating the Chevy Equinox in front of him, slamming on the brakes each time he saw the tail lights illuminate. Klemmer's destination was the Vine Street Extension, the part of the highway labyrinth that connected Center City Philadelphia. He was way early for tonight's mission, but he had been restless at home, thinking about the fires and avoiding further unpleasant conversations.

There was fear in his heart and a knot in his stomach. This one was far more dangerous than his last two projects with a higher risk of being caught. But his orders were unequivocal, stern and threatening: "Do this or I will come down on you like a dump truck full of bricks," he'd said. "Stop whining and shut your mouth!" The verbal abuse was always part of the equation. It got worse after his mother passed, as though Klemmer had something to do with that. His mother, a shrew in her own right, spent her adult life angry at all males, thanks to an abusive father who later abandoned her and her mother. Evelyn Klemmer showed both her husband and son nothing but scorn over all of life's little setbacks, blaming them in some way for each of them. Later, as Alzheimer's disease took its toll, she became combative, violent, always reaching out at Klemmer from her sickbed, grabbing his hair and clothing, screaming about the dishes not being done, throwing her tissue box at him.

"She hates you," his father would say many times. "She hates you just for being you."

Yet, he cried when she died. She was his mother, after all. His father, on the other hand, was almost joyful while turning bitter at the same time. Klemmer did not understand his behavior in the least, but adapted to it to survive.

As though his car were on autopilot, Klemmer found himself exiting the Vine Street Expressway at 15th Street for the drive south, below Lombard, below Federal. He was eyeing his GPS to see how much farther it would be to the small side street south of Federal where he had been told to go. He was only a few blocks away, but it was not even 7 o'clock. He would have to find a place to park and nap.

The 6 o'clock news was history and most of the day shift had gone. Only Nancy remained. She was tidying up the desk and was in the process of handing off to her evening counterpart. Gordon Richardson had his jacket on and his briefcase in hand as he walked up to the desk. "Have a good night," he said.

"Thanks," replied Nancy. "I'm outta here in a couple more minutes."

Gordon turned to leave when he remembered something he had meant to ask Nancy earlier.

"Hey, question," he said, turning back to face her. "You saw Bill Klemmer today?"

"Yea, we owed him money."

"Did he tell you something about his father?"

"Yea, something like, me and my dad appreciate it."

"OK. You know his father died, like two years ago."

Nancy's eyebrows raised momentarily, but then lowered as she pulled on her parka. "No, I didn't."

"Yea. Wonder why he said that?"

"Maybe he was talking about the memory of his father." Nancy seemed unconcerned.

"I guess. See you tomorrow."

"Bye."

"Stop it!" bellowed Bill Klemmer to no one. He had nodded off in the car as he had planned. He had not planned on having yet another horrible dream. His mother, face drawn and haggard, grabbed his hair and tugged on it. The more he fought, the more she pulled.

"Stop it! Stop it!" he yelled, this time waking up with a start. He didn't understand where he was. He was not at home in bed, but sitting in the front seat of his car with his coat on. He peered through his foggy window, looking for a landmark. He was utterly confused.

"Get it together, you fat fuck!"

"Shut up!" shouted Klemmer, shaking his head as if to knock the voice out of it. "Shut up!" His breathing rate increased and he was sweating. He finally started remembering--waiting for 2:00 AM to arrive, Federal Street at Worman Place, vacant lot. He looked at his Casio--1:52 AM. He tried to remember why 2:00 AM was so important. Oh yea, not before 2:00 AM because he doesn't get there before 2:00 AM, usually. Dad knew. Dad had photographed here before, so he knew. There was supposed to be a tent made of a blanket and a couple broom sticks. It was there. Had he missed the guy going in?

Klemmer's head became still as his breathing slowed and he got his bearings. His video camera was on the seat next to him. He reached over to check the battery when he saw movement out of the corner of his eye through the foggy passenger side window. He reached over with his hand to clear a spot and peered out the window to see a man dressed in dark, hooded parka and sweatpants lumbering past his car. He dragged one leg and was saying something to no one. Klemmer couldn't make out the words. He watched the man slowly drag himself towards the homemade tent. He was going home.

In the cold, dark space that was his unlit backyard, Lester Noble was fiddling with the camera he had just bought at Target. The box said it was wireless and battery powered. He was on his side of the fence that separated his apartment building from the Remmicks' little house and hidden behind the thick honeysuckle bush. He attempted to place the camera inside the bush, hidden enough so it wouldn't be seen, yet with a clear line of sight to record video of whatever happened in the Remmicks' backyard, and maybe more. Lester didn't feel good about it, but he was able to set aside his reluctance in favor of self-preservation. He needed this job.

There was a smartphone app that Lester would use once he got the camera in a good spot. Fortunately, the wireless network in his apartment provided enough signal for the camera to work. He clicked various settings on the app until he saw the picture. It was skewed about 30-degrees. He walked back towards the fence and reached into the bush to adjust the camera angle, watching on his phone. The picture straightened up. He went to SETTINGS again and turned off the blue indicator light on the camera so no one would see it shining through the bush. He took a final look at the app and saw a clear view of the Remmicks' side door and yard. No activity. It was 1:00 AM.

The homeless man had been inside the lean-to for a good half hour and Klemmer's breathing sped up again. He was scared. He was cleaning off all his fogged-up windows with tissues now and looking out of all of them in a 360-degree circle to make sure no one else was around.

"I'll show you who's useless," he said out loud. He started the Camry and eased it forward. He turned right onto Worman Place, his eyes riveted on the makeshift tent in the vacant lot. His speed was maybe five miles-an-hour as he turned the wheel to the right to ease the Camry off the street and up over the curb, first the front wheels, then the back. He navigated towards the tent, heading towards the point of no return. He aimed the car at the pair of legs sticking out. He turned the wheel to bring the car closer. He slowed down, estimating how much he would have to maneuver the car to bring the right tires directly over the length of the body lying under the tent. When he was about twenty feet away, he gave it some gas and the car headed without hesitation towards the feet. Klemmer felt a slight bump as the car's front tire ran over the feet then up onto the legs, and up over the buttocks and back of the man. He next felt the rear tire travel the same path, becoming elevated as it struck the feet, then legs. The car slowed to a near stop and Klemmer knew he was coming up onto the head. He gave it some gas and felt the front tire run over the hump, then heard a sickening pop, the sound of a melon cracking open. The front of the car was now taking down the tent as the rear followed the same path, running over the man's head. In another few seconds, the car was traveling a smooth path without obstacles and Klemmer knew it was over.

The Camry did not hesitate as he hit the gas, steering the car out of the lot, down over the curb and back onto Worman Place. He did not speed away but kept driving, turning right onto 16th Street and into the night.

"Fuck you," he said to no one. "Fuck you."

Chapter 11 - Controlling Interests

Thursdays are for survival, past the hump of Wednesday but still short of Friday. Thursday is a day to suck it up and move forward. In the spirit of sucking it up, Bud looked at himself in the mirror and was displeased. He had gotten down to 240 pounds while incarcerated, one of the few prison achievements he was proud of. Now, he was back up to 270. At five-feet-ten, it was hard to pull it off. He had traded his eyeglasses for contacts, which gave his wearied eyes no place to hide. He remained clean-shaven as he had in jail, but was now contemplating a beard. Maggie said it would just make him look older. While his hairline had receded over the years, his close-cropped brown hair seemed to add youth, even with the gray at the temples. Bud concluded as middle-aged white men go, he wasn't the worst specimen, but there was room for improvement.

Gazing into the mirror, Bud's eyes wandered down his neck, down his chest and torso and landed on the pink scar on his lower right side, the three-quarter inch souvenir of his close encounter with a jailhouse shiv that almost ended his life.

"I really am sorry," where the words that still bounced around inside his head, the words of cellmate Levon Samuels as he plunged the shiv into him. Bud had passed out from the blood loss, then woke up in the hospital. He never saw Levon again, but started seeing a lot of John Ungar. He didn't know why Ungar had taken an interest in him. He'd visited him twice in the hospital, made a special accommodation to let Maggie visit him shortly after his return to King's Pointe and finally, of course, said what the parole board wanted to hear. At the time, he didn't understand why Ungar cared.

Maggie walked by the open bathroom door and doubled back after seeing Bud staring at himself in the mirror. She stopped to stare, too.

"It's getting annoying, answering the same questions over and over again," he said to her reflection.

"I know."

"I guess the buzz is still fresh. Those kids at the TV station look at me like, I dunno, they're scared or pissed or both."

Maggie approached him, watching in the mirror, wrapping her arms around him from behind.

"And Les, our new neighbor. Do you know what his last name is?"

"What?"

"Noble. Les Noble."

Maggie smiled. "Really."

"I'm hoping he's *more* noble. That was an odd little visit."

"The novelty will wear off. You have to expect that when you first meet people."

"Yea, people," he muttered. He grabbed Maggie's hands and gently pulled them away, turned to face her and kissed her un-glossed lips. She was dressed and waiting for the mirror.

Bud went to the bedroom and got dressed, then made his way to the living room and glanced at the wall clock--6:55. He tried to be on the road by seven each morning to get to the newsroom a little before nine. There was usually a phone call in the car with Nancy about the news of the day, the noon show, any other issues. The morning drive to Philadelphia was somehow less taxing than the drive home. The 20-ounce coffee helped and most days there was also a breakfast sandwich for the ride. The latter had to go, Bud realized, if he were ever to get back down to a fighting weight of 240.

The best part of the drive was the Northeast Extension of the Pennsylvania Turnpike, a recently repaved, boring roadway. The worst part was the Schuylkill Expressway, a rush hour travesty with no redeeming qualities. The morning traffic report on KYW could have been a recording, replayed day after day, detailing the eastbound backups heading into the city, past Girard Avenue to the Vine Street Extension, an endless loop of motoring despair.

Bud's exit, City Avenue, came well before the downtown congestion. He always felt relief upon his arrival, getting out of the car in the Channel 7 parking lot, stretching his legs and feeling his bladder about to burst. This was his new life.

There was activity at the assignment desk when Bud entered the newsroom. Rita and Reg had joined Nancy at her computer and were viewing video which showed flashing red and blue lights.

"Good morning," said Bud cheerily as he walked towards the group. "What's up?"

Nancy looked up from her screen. "Crime scene video, just came in. Homeless guy killed overnight in south Philly."

"Killed? Like, murdered?"

"He got run over, apparently while sleeping in his little tent," offered Reg.

"Head crushed," said Rita tersely while swaying back and forth.

"Hit and run," added Nancy. "No suspects, no apparent witnesses. Cops won't say whether it was done on purpose because they don't know."

Remmick watched the video for a few seconds. Yellow crime scene tape surrounded what appeared to be a couple of blankets propped up with sticks. A blue tarp extended out from inside the tent, evidently covering a body. Red and blue lights flashed in the dark. "Is this Klemmer video?"

"Uh huh," replied Nancy. "The other stations are all over the scene now, but we seem to be the only ones with night video. Klemmer was on the ball again. I guess there wasn't much radio chatter, so the other stations got there late."

Remmick continued watching the video, which now showed a man in a jacket and tie, probably a detective, lifting up the blue tarp and nosing around inside the makeshift tent. "When did Remmick drop this off?"

"I dunno, hours ago," replied Nancy. "It sat at the guard station downstairs until Regina came in at eight. She brought it up."

"So, who are we assigning?"

"I thought Ricciutti."

"Who?"

"Jim Ricciutti. Veteran reporter. He's got good face recognition among the cops."

Remmick nodded in agreement. "OK."

"If it's gettable, Jim will get it. Reg will back him up with phone calls."

Remmick nodded again. "Is this the noon lead?"

"So far, I think so."

"OK," said Remmick. He looked over towards Reginald. "Anything from downtown?"

"No. They're canvassing local businesses and homes to see if anyone might have surveillance video. That's it."

Remmick nodded, then shuffled back towards his office. He peered into Karen's cubicle. No one home. He glanced towards Gordon's office. Door closed.

He opened his own office door and stepped inside. There was a musty smell as the fluorescents came on with their bluish buzz. He walked over to his desk, dropped his coat onto a chair next to it and sat down. He wondered if this is what Ronald Morone did each morning when he came to work before he killed him.

A hundred miles away, Maggie Remmick hung her coat on the hook behind her office door and placed her 16-ounce, 7-Eleven coffee on her desk. The Wawa was closed this morning due to a renovation which Maggie deemed unnecessary and inconvenient. She sat down at her desk and saw the flashing red light on her phone indicating a message. That'll wait, she thought, while I sit here for a few minutes, drink this coffee and think about the best way to get meals delivered in Mt. Pocono today without Jules, my best volunteer, who had the nerve to move out of the state after inheriting a half million dollars from his recently departed father.

Maggie always arrived before anyone else. She got a lot of work done between eight and nine o'clock each morning. Since her conversation with John Ungar however, she felt different. Vulnerable. It was not a good feeling and she tried to wipe it out of her soul by shaking the New York Times open. But the blinking red light annoyed her and compelled her to act. She picked up her phone, dialed her PIN and retrieved this message:

"Hi, Maggie. This is Marjorie Cutler at the Commissioners' office. Give me a call when you get this message. Thanks." Silence followed.

"No, I won't give you a call," said Maggie in a dark whisper as she hung up and snapped her Times back open to the National section and a story about millennials moving back home with their parents.

The sound of the head cracking kept Klemmer awake.

"I hope he was asleep," said Klemmer out loud while staring at the ceiling. "I hope he didn't feel anything."

"What the fuck do you care?" replied his chief tormentor. "You did what you were told, that's all that matters."

Klemmer continued staring at the ceiling and the voice quieted. He turned his head to his night table and looked at his watch--8:21AM. He didn't remember sleeping but he did remember a dream. He was having more trouble lately, figuring out whether he was dreaming or not. His cloistered life left little personal space. He had the assignments and all they entailed and the edgy voice of his father, never letting up, never allowing him a moment's peace.

Sunlight tried to sneak in through Klemmer's shaded bedroom window but only a small shard peeked through a hole in the filthy shade. He knew it was the morning after he had committed murder. He knew everything would be different now.

His cellphone buzzed on the night table. Someone was calling, but he elected to ignore it, instead wiping away tears.

Bud got back into the habit of reading the Philadelphia Inquirer, the city's only decent newspaper, a ritual that was part of his morning read-in that also included the Daily News and the New York Times. He also read all the desk notes from the night before, which could include everything from news items that were explored to complaints about the sogginess of the Chick-fil-A sandwiches from down the street. His attention was riveted by an article buried in the B section detailing Governor Tom Franklin's lament over the impending layoffs of state employees.

"It is regrettable," quoth the Governor, "that the Democrats from Philadelphia and other eastern districts of our great state have voted their politics over their consciences. It is their short-sightedness that is causing these layoffs."

Remmick went on to read how the Governor's grand scheme to shift his own people into various jobs was derailed by legislators who, according to the Inquirer, sought to eliminate the jobs totally instead of allowing him to stack them with political hacks. The jobs were already populated by non-patronage employees, regular people, as reckoned by the Inquirer, who were now at risk of being laid off for the sole purpose of denying Governor Franklin venues to take care of his political friends. Those supporting the elimination of the jobs were mostly from Philadelphia and the suburbs, Democrats with an institutional hatred of Franklin, his Republican agenda and his history of political patronage. Their official line was, of course, it's all about balancing the budget.

The wheels turned in Remmick's addled morning brain as he wondered what, if any, impact this would have on Maggie. Was it a coincidence that the rumblings she'd heard from Ungar came as Franklin was seething about this? Would he use Maggie's job, a position under the control of county politicians, to take care of one of his asshole buddies?

Four years in prison had not dulled Remmick's instincts or his cynicism. He started feeling a familiar sensation at the back of his throat, a tightening of his airway muscles and quickening of his breathing. It was, as he had learned from his sponsor, his "anger aura". He recognized it right away, a giant step of progress made in the past two years as he learned to come to grips with feelings and intentions that had brought him to disaster in the not-so-distant past. It was that old black magic, primal emotion struggling to escape, that he had to handle on a daily, sometimes hourly basis.

As if on cue to defuse a ticking time bomb, Gordon stuck his head into Bud's office. "Good morning," he said.

"Hi, Gordon. Happy fucking Thursday."

"Jeez, you've been here just a couple days and you're already in the spirit of things."

"Yea, well, some things never change, I guess. What's going on?"

"Nothing. Quiet, I guess. Everything OK?"

"Pennsylvania partisan politics are not OK."

Gordon was a man nonplussed by cryptic statements without context. His expression went unchanged. Bud persisted.

"My wife's job in Livingston County may be in jeopardy because of our nitwit Governor."

"Really? But she doesn't work for the State."

"No, but she works for a county governed by hardcore Republicans who appear to have their noses firmly up his ass. I'm thinking he might have her fired to make room for one of his pals, except if these Dems have their way, they would eliminate the job altogether."

"Hm. That is messed up."

"The hate is palpable."

"Speaking of messed up, something's been bugging me." Gordon's right turn to a different topic was also annoying. "Your freelancer Bill Klemmer. You know the name?"

"Yes, he's been cleaning up on breaking news in the middle of the night."

"He told Nancy yesterday that he and his father thanked her."

"And you told me you thought his father had passed away."

"Oh, I don't think it, I *know* it. I used to see him in the street all the time, shooting for various stations. He was a fixture in this town, first in the film days, then ENG. I don't go all the way back, but I remember him well enough. And when he had his heart attack and died, it was kind of news."

"OK. And?"

Gordon looked at Bud, frustrated. "Never mind."

"He's probably just keeping his father's memory alive. You know, like my grandmother is looking down on me right now and telling me to stop complaining, be happy I have a job, a wife, etcetera."

"I guess I am the only person bothered by this. I will take my obsession elsewhere."

"Don't obsess. It takes the shine out of that bald head."

Gordon smirked, flipped Bud the finger, and walked out. Bud watched him with amusement as he walked back to his office and closed the door. Yes, Bud liked Gordon Richardson.

When Klemmer woke up again, it was 10:43 AM. He sat up and pivoted his body so he was sitting on the edge of the bed. He reached over to his night table, grabbed his cellphone and looked at the voicemail indicator. One message from an unfamiliar number. He clicked the PLAY button and listened on speakerphone.

"Hello Bill, this is Gordon Richardson at Channel 7. Can you call me when you get a chance? Thanks."

A Red Alert sounded in Klemmer's head. *Why is Channel 7 calling me? They never call me. What's wrong?* He decided to ignore it, but didn't delete it. *Maybe nothing's wrong. Maybe they are calling to compliment me on my amazing video.*

His phone started vibrating in his hand. Another call from the same number. *What does he want?* He made a sudden, strategic decision and clicked TALK.

"Hello?" he said without energy.

"Hi, is this Bill?"

73

"Yea."

"This is Gordon Richardson at Channel 7. I left you a message earlier this morning."

Klemmer's eyes sank to the floor. "Yea."

"How are you?"

"Fine."

"Listen, I have a question for you. Um, not sure how to ask this."

Klemmer sat still in his underwear on the edge of his bed.

"I knew your dad. Worked with him in my days as a photographer."

Klemmer said nothing.

"The other day, you told Nancy Winstead that you and your father appreciated the check."

"Yea," said Klemmer in a weak voice. "So?"

"I was sure your dad passed away a couple years ago. Am I mistaken?"

Klemmer's mouth dropped open. His eyes were glassy. He struggled to form words. "I--I," he grunted. Then suddenly, "You are mistaken!"

"So, I'm sorry, what--".

Klemmer pushed the red HANG UP button and dropped the phone on the floor. His hand shook.

Maggie was sorry she returned Marjorie Cutler's call. She now sat in her office, on the other side of a pathetic looking desk, something assembled out of fiberboard and cheap hardware reminiscent of the desk Maggie had in her college dorm. Government infrastructure at its finest. Cutler was a formal looking woman of about 50 with black hair wrapped in a bun and a navy business suit with a white collar buttoned right up to her throat. She wore little make-up, a dull shade of pink lip gloss and no jewelry. Maggie's instant, one-word analysis of her was, "handsome." Her desk held a multi-line telephone, a laptop computer, a can containing some pens, a framed photograph of a dog and her business card holder. The woman appeared to be experiencing discomfort just sitting at her desk.

"Thanks for coming in," Cutler said. "Something's up."

Maggie said nothing.

"I shouldn't be telling you this, but it is irritating, so I will. I got a call from Governor Franklin's chief of staff yesterday, inquiring about you."

Maggie stared at her.

"Seems they are interested in your most recent performance evaluation."

Maggie now stirred in her chair. Knowing the answer to her own question, she asked it anyway. "Why?

"He wouldn't say. However, it's no secret the Governor is shopping his people around because he's so very loyal to his political hack friends and he has apparently promised some of them jobs, regardless of their experience, competence or temperament."

Maggie was afraid her worst fear was about to come true.

"I believe he is targeting your position. The chief of staff, Morris Gilder, wouldn't say so because he is a weasel. I know him from a previous life. He is an impotent little putz who should thank god every day he has any job at all, let alone the Governor's messenger boy."

"So, I am out of here?"

"Oh, no, no, no. See, those boys in Harrisburg are playing a little game. This is the intimidation portion of the game. They swing their dicks around, hoping to knock down the Legos here in the counties where they have people who owe them."

Maggie was impressed. Her boss had balls.

"You, Mrs. Remmick, are a find. You are the best thing to happen to your agency, maybe, ever."

Maggie almost smiled. Instead, she felt emotion welling up behind her throat.

"I told little Morris that your evaluation was buried in a corrupted Word file and would take some time to retrieve due to the ancient computer infrastructure we are dealing with thanks to his boss's tight-assed and clueless assessment of our IT needs. This made him go away for now, though I don't think he liked my tone."

Maggie swallowed hard and breathed deeply. "I don't know what to say."

"You don't have to say anything. I'm not sure how much juice this bullshit has, but I plan to mount a defense if they try anything. I don't want to lose you."

"I am really grateful for that," Maggie managed, fighting back tears. "I like this job."

"And the job likes you. Unfortunately, politics has been a way of life around here for decades. Personally, I despise politics. I like getting things done and I don't like being toyed with. I am not easily intimidated, which accounts for how I've survived here for 25 years."

"I didn't know much about you before this meeting, but now I think I'm in love."

Cutler rolled her eyes. "Charming, of course, but save your love for the end game. This is just the beginning. You can go now. I thought you should know what's going on."

Maggie stood and extended her hand. "I can't tell you how much I appreciate it."

Marjorie Cutler stood and shook Maggie's hand. "Keep your head down and do your job. I'll be in touch."

Maggie offered a weak smile, turned and walked out of the office. Cutler sat back down and turned her attention to her laptop screen.

"Video is everywhere, as you know," Reg told Karen, who had called him into her cubicle to discuss the south Philly homeless man death. "Looks like they got some. A parking lot at 15th & Federal behind a beer distributor has a 24-hour surveillance camera. Cops are reviewing the video as we speak."

"Can we report that?"

"My source says we can report they are reviewing surveillance video from the area, but not this specific location. The owner wants to keep his business out of the media."

Karen was impressed that young Reg actually had a "source."

"He wouldn't say when they'd be done," he added. "I'll call periodically to check."

"Good work. Keep us honest on this, OK?"

"Yep," he replied and walked back to his desk.

Karen had arrived at work at ten this morning, late for her, but Bud had told her to sleep in, that he was glad to deal with the administrative crap she'd been handling for the past nine months and that she deserved a little slack. Yes, she thought, I do. She had poured her coffee into her Phillies mug and microwaved it on high for sixty seconds. She sipped gingerly, having heated the mug to the temperature of molten lava.

It had only been a few days but she liked having Bud around again. She was reminded of their first stint together years ago when Channel 7 was in its glory days, number one-rated with money for a helicopter and endless field trips to locales across the country, even overseas. Today, the mantra was to make a profit, keep the station above water at any cost. The result was a poorly paid staff, failing equipment and a bargain-basement News Director with a prison record. Roy Strickland, another holdover from the glory days, toed the company line by keeping costs down, a feat that resulted in the station's survival, the sad new baseline for success.

Much of the nuts and bolts of the station's budget fell upon Strickland and the station's business manager. But newsroom operational costs fell squarely on Remmick's desk. It was the part of his job he was learning to hate. The tasks of sifting through invoices, purchase orders, vouchers, time sheets and vacation requests were dealt with only briefly in his pre-hire chats with Roy and Karen. As he found out, the reality of these tasks sucked.

In response to concerns expressed by Karen about freelancer payments being delayed, Bud fished out a voucher from one pile of papers. The voucher was easy to see because it was pink. He studied it and saw it was made out in the name of W. Klemmer and was for this morning's video of the homeless man hit-and-run. The payment would be $200. Bud winced when he saw the figure. Sounded high for one job, but he wasn't sure what the market demanded these days. He picked up his phone and dialed.

"Mr. Strickland's office," answered the cheery voice of Lori.

"Hi, it's Bud Remmick. How are you?"

"Good, Bud. He's not in the office at the moment."

"My question is actually for you, Lori. I want to get a record of all payments to freelance photographers for the past, say, year. Is that possible?"

"Probably. I'll see if the business manager can generate that for you."

"Great, Lori, thanks. I appreciate it."

"Ok, I'll be back to you, Bud. Talk to you soon."

Chapter 12 - Politics as Unusual

John Ungar sat at his desk, pushing paper from one spot to another. He was bored out of his mind and actually missed prison life. As superintendent of King's Pointe, he was a big fish in a small, dysfunctional pond. Here, he was just another cog in a large machine that had something to do with corrections and a lot to do with politics. His long climb up the ladder to Deputy Commissioner of the New Jersey State Corrections Department had taken him from Union County Sheriff in Elizabeth, New Jersey, to Graterford Prison in Pennsylvania, to King's Pointe and finally here, a solid oak desk with a Cross pen and a Dell computer with a 20-inch flat screen monitor. The screen was devoid of actual work and instead displayed a photograph of himself at the Cherry Ridge shooting range in Riverdale after winning a trophy in a pistol competition. The picture was taken six years ago when he had more hair and less around the middle. Ungar, divorced with a son at Villanova, had gotten proficient with his Beretta PX4 Storm, a semi-automatic pistol whose 40-caliber hollow-point rounds had what gun enthusiasts liked to call "stopping power." He could easily snap off three shots in rapid succession at a target 20 feet away and always create the tightest grouping of all competitors. During his career in law enforcement and as a civilian, he had never fired either in self-defense or in the line of duty. He was permitted to carry as a state official, a privilege not afforded the average New Jersey citizen.

As he stared at the photo on his screen, he also saw his reflection, way less hair, thicker mustache, pock-marked skin left over from his adolescence. His eyes were calmer.

He had a 1:00 PM appointment with his immediate boss, the Corrections Commissioner, who had just returned from a trip to Pennsylvania where he had accompanied his boss, Governor Hale, to a conference of corrections officials from across the northeast. Trends in corrections, confinement and rehabilitation were on the agenda at the conference, which featured the head of the German prison system as keynote speaker. Pennsylvania Governor Franklin was also there and shared a table with the New Jersey contingent.

Ungar found it laughable that there was a discussion about "trends in corrections" when it was apparent to him that cost and containment were the only important factors in most American prisons and that progressive attitudes about rehabilitation, solitary confinement and other hot button issues were unwelcome. On the other hand, he'd spent a lot of time in an office the past year and thought maybe he was simply out of touch. He did concede, for example, that since his days at Graterford, attitudes towards violence by prison personnel against inmates had changed for the better. His own experiences, along with his breakthrough white-light moment during the Graterford riot almost a decade ago, had changed his own thinking. Leaving anger at the door turned out to be a lifesaver for him, a revelation he owed, in some small measure, to Bud Remmick, thanks to a chance encounter in a lavatory at Graterford years ago.

Ungar was a Corrections Officer at the time. It was the night of the only prison riot he'd ever experienced. Trouble had been brewing for weeks and exploded in violence and murder. One corrections officer was killed. Among the news people who showed up at the prison was a Channel 7 producer named Bud Remmick, his photographer and an intern. Ungar played back the event in his mind as he stared at his image on the computer screen.

Remmick opened the door and hoped the urinal would be right there. Instead, his arrival froze a violent scene-- a man in a uniform had just landed a booted kick against the head of another man who was on the floor, face down, hands cuffed behind his back. The man on the floor didn't move. Blood flowed from his nose. The uniformed man's foot was now parked on the neck and he locked eyes with Remmick. Sweat dripped from the tip of the man's nose, onto the body beneath his foot. Remmick followed the path of the sweat drop from the foot, back up to its source. His eyes stopped at a small pin attached to the guard's white collar. It was gold in the shape of a tiny magic wand with a gold starburst attached to the end.

Remmick's head unfroze and his eyes clicked back to their original purpose-- scanning the room to find a place to piss. As his eyes scanned, the uniformed man's eyes followed his. Remmick made his way quickly and quietly to the urinal, his pants unzipped and penis halfway out well before he got there. The relief was instantaneous and overwhelming. He stood there for what seemed an eternity, not daring to even glance over his shoulder. He finally zipped up and turned to the same scene that greeted him as he walked in.

The guard stared down at the inmate he'd been kicking. The inmate was still breathing. Remmick looked at his own face in the mirror, turned once more to look at the guard, who kept his head down. No words were spoken. Remmick then turned to the door and left the bathroom, walking the way he came, back to the visitor's room.

The information Ungar had extracted from the handcuffed inmate was key in flushing out the conspiracy behind the riot and finding the weapon that had been used to kill the corrections officer. It played heavily in the decision by Ungar's bosses to promote him. Remmick had evidently never told anyone about what he'd seen in the bathroom. Ungar only assumed this because he continued to be employed at Graterford, was never called up before a disciplinary board and continued to be promoted. The inmate whose head he had kicked died a short time later in an attack by a rival gang.

The revelation that a stranger had seen him venting his naked anger on a handcuffed prisoner changed everything for Ungar. He felt, somehow, grateful that his most vile, primal emotion had been exposed. He had never physically abused anyone. He ruminated over it for months, even years afterwards, grateful that the one person who witnessed his behavior had not ratted him out, leading to a self-examination that changed his life. Later, at King's Pointe, he had assumed Remmick would eventually catch on that he was getting some slack from him. He never did.

So, keeping a line of communication open with Maggie Remmick seemed like a constructive pursuit. And it couldn't hurt to have a friend in a government position, even in another state.

Ungar logged off his computer and rose from his desk to make his way to his one o'clock meeting to hear about new trends in corrections.

Remmick had wandered from his office, down the main hallway and saw the door to Pamela Whitehead's office wide open. He peeked in and saw her sitting at her computer, studying the screen. The anchorwoman was tall and blond, perhaps in her early 30's, striking brown eyes that had penetrating power in contrast to a pleasant, almost peaceful smile.

"Pamela, Bud Remmick," he said as he approached her desk with his hand extended. "Very nice to meet you."

She looked up from her screen and flashed that smile, putting Bud immediately at ease. "Hi, glad to meet you, Bud. Welcome to our little circus."

"Thanks. I just wanted to say hello, if I'm not interrupting something."

"Nah, I'm pricing ceiling fans on Amazon. Don't tell the boss."

"OK, I won't," he said with a grin. There was one other chair in the room, which he placed himself in. It faced her desk. "How long have you been at Channel 7?"

"Almost six years."

"And? Are you still feeling the love?"

"Uh, well, not so much lately. But I'm kind of beyond expecting love, being satisfied with just having the job."

"I like you on TV. I don't expect you to be going anywhere unless it's your choice."

An almost palpable relief could be seen in Pam's demeanor. "Well, that's nice to hear, thank you."

"Of course, I'm just the News Director so it's not just up to me. But Karen tells me Strickland hasn't been known to micromanage the talent."

"Well, just in the two minutes you've been in my office, I sense an exponential improvement over your predecessor. And I don't mean Karen, she's a doll. I mean the prick who was full time ND months ago."

"Yea, I've heard things," said Remmick, recalling anecdotes from Karen about ex-News Director Andrew Kenner.

"One day, just before they shit-canned him, he was sitting in that very chair, stared at my chest and said, and I quote, 'Nice rack.' I gave him a kind of cross look and said something like, 'is that something you would tell your wife?' He looked at me like I was offending *him*."

"Did you ever tell anyone? That's actionable, of course."

"Nah. I knew that in his little cartoon-loop brain, he was trying to be wry and funny and collegial. I should have said something to someone, I guess. But Karma caught up with him. They fired him the following week. We all just assumed it was because the station was in the ratings shitter. No one was sorry to see him go."

"I hope that as time goes by, you would feel comfortable reporting something like that to me. There's no room for that kind of bullshit in my newsroom."

Pamela studied him for a moment, letting those words sink in. A few too many seconds passed and the room became uncomfortable.

"What?" he asked.

She averted her eyes, looking a bit embarrassed. "You talk a good game."

"Ah, cynicism. Sign of a good reporter."

"I sat through the same sexual harassment Power Point as the guy who placed a dildo on my desk chair for my birthday, and the other guy who posted Penthouse centerfolds in his cubicle back there in editing, blathering about free speech. And of course, Kenner, who also talked a good game when he wasn't complimenting my rack."

"I guess you'll have to judge for yourself whether I'm just another asshole male." He got up from his chair.

"Wait, I'm sorry. I didn't mean to lump you in with those guys."

"It's OK. I gotta get back to the kids running my newsroom." He paused for a moment and pondered whether she had any idea whom she was talking to, then said, "I'll see you on TV."

"OK," she said and watched him walk out. She felt a small pang of regret, but it passed.

As he walked up the hallway back towards his office, Remmick was transported back to the last time he saw Hilde Schimmel, his Kaleidoscope employee and friend, as she cried in his office, face battered after a close encounter with Ronald Morone more than seven years ago.

One second, he was looking down at some paperwork sitting on his desk. The next second, his door suddenly closed and Hilde sat in the chair against the wall at a 90-degree angle to him. He was startled by her sudden appearance.

"Hey," he said.

She stared straight ahead for a while, then bowed her head.

"I said no," she said in a small voice.

"No to what?"

"No to Ronald."

Remmick looked at the bruise under her eye, wicked and purple, blotched onto the perfect canvas that was her face.

"And he did that?" he asked, pointing.

She nodded almost imperceptibly. "At my place, last night. I told him I didn't want to anymore and he could tell whoever he wanted about me."

She raised her eyes to Remmick's, her chin aquiver and tears welling up.

"But he didn't care," she said, sobbing. "He said he owned me and he would never go back to life without me."

Remmick didn't say a word. He believed it all too easily.

"When I got up and told him to get out of my apartment, he whipped around and backhanded me. I think I went halfway across the room, knocked against the glass coffee table on the way down."

Remmick urgently wanted to go to her, but he resisted.

"He said I had it coming. He said he just wanted to love me and how could I do this to him. I couldn't talk, I was shocked. I couldn't get off the floor." She touched her cheek and winced. "Then he just left."

"Did you call the cops?"

She shook her head.

"Why the fuck not?"

"I drove myself to St. Luke's emergency room, told them I fell, went back home and took a shower and went to bed."

The anger of that moment, and the events that followed, were with him every day. It took the conversation with Pam, however, to recall the workplace abuse that made the nightmare all too real for Hilde, less so for Pam perhaps, but still a reality she had to deal with. He was troubled that these feelings came back to haunt him in such a stark way, and he felt the anger aura welling up again.

The chubby fingers that usually clutched a small video camera now caressed a KelTec P-3AT pistol. Built for the budget-minded and not at all elegant, the P-3AT was designed for concealed carry and peace of mind, not so much for accuracy. Its short grip was too small for Klemmer's beefy hand, but it was what he could afford. The six-round magazine was certainly cute, but he figured if he ever needed more than five bullets in a close encounter, either he or the other guy would be dead anyway. The .380 round made it a glorified pea-shooter.

Klemmer wasn't sure what to do with his pistol. He had obtained the carry permit some months earlier, a simple process in Pennsylvania. As he pawed the pistol now in his bedroom in front of his dresser mirror, he considered the power it represented. The loaded magazine lay on the dresser. There was no bullet in the chamber. He pointed it at his reflection, clicked the trigger several times. He waved it in the air, aiming at various objects in the room. At one point, perhaps out of boredom, he pointed it at his own head and gazed at his reflection. He didn't pull the trigger.

Klemmer was lost. He had killed someone. He had no power now and desperately sought some kind of upper hand. The brief conversation he had with Gordon Richardson rattled him. *Yes, you are mistaken, asshole.* Since that conversation, father had been quiet, no phone calls, no name calling. No assignments. Klemmer fondled the pistol, stared at it lovingly and felt the beginnings of an erection.

A hundred miles away, Trooper Lester Noble had removed his SIG 227R from his holster while approaching a car he had stopped on 611 just north of the Mt. Pocono Municipal Airport. The car, an older model Honda Civic, was doing 80 in the 65 zone. Upon running the tag, it came back stolen. He called for backup, which was a good ten minutes away. He decided to approach the vehicle. He held his pistol in his right hand, down by his side and behind his leg, out of sight for the moment. Approaching the car from the right side, his eyes were riveted on the driver, the sole occupant. The closer he got, the more it became apparent that the driver was barely able to see over the steering wheel. He was a young man, very young.

"Hi," Noble said through the open passenger window. "Turn off your engine, please. You know why I pulled you over?"

The driver looked to be no older than 16, if that. He clicked off the engine and turned his eyes to the steering wheel. "Yea."

Noble eyeballed the interior of the car, looking for weapons, drugs, anything that didn't belong. He sniffed a few times. Nothing. "How old are you?"

The driver still stared straight ahead. "Fourteen."

"Fourteen. I clocked you doing 80 back there."

"Really?" said the young man with a half-grin.

"Step out, please. I don't suppose you have any ID on you?"

The boy shook his head. Noble walked around to the driver's side as the boy got out.

"OK. Turn around for me. I'm detaining you for the moment until I figure out what you're doing driving a stolen car." Noble deftly applied handcuffs to the boy's wrists and led him to the back seat of his Charger.

"I didn't steal it," the boy blurted out. "I told him I was taking it."

"You told who?"

"My step-father."

"What's your name?"

"Jimmy Jackson."

"OK, Jimmy Jackson. I need to talk to your step-father."

"He's a dick. He'll beat the shit out of me for this."

"You know you're not old enough to drive, right?"

"I do it all the time. No one cares."

What followed was a brief negotiation during which Noble obtained a phone number for the step-father. Meanwhile, his backup arrived and pulled behind his Charger. Twenty minutes later, the boy's step-father arrived looking none too pleased. After an exchange of words, Jimmy Jackson was transferred to the other cruiser for transport to the county jail with the step-father following in his pick-up. Noble felt badly for the boy, but once the car was reported stolen, it was in the system and the boy and his step-father would need to see a judge.

As he watched the other trooper drive away, Noble settled back into his Charger and tapped on his computer screen. He didn't want to do the report now. What he wanted to do was go back to Trevose where he knew people. He missed his friends. He grudgingly started typing his report while listening to music on his phone. He double checked his body camera, making sure he'd turned it off after the Jimmy Jackson affair was terminated.

Later, following an otherwise unremarkable shift, Noble pulled into his driveway and exhaled deeply. He glanced at the Remmick home. No cars yet. He got out of his F-150, fiddling with his phone as he did so. He called up his wireless camera app to check the image from the back yard. There it was, in all its 1080P glory, showing the Remmick's side door and back yard. He went to the recordings and saw several sequences in which one of them let the dog out, then back in. There was at least one recording of Bud walking out the door into the yard, but he was fully clothed this time. Noble figured that since Bud had a new job, his days of wandering around outside in his boxer shorts might be over. So far, that seemed to be the case.

Chapter 13 - Sources Say

Young Reg McKnight was positively perky. Karen saw a gleam in his eye and a grin that made him look even younger than his 22 years. It was a dress-down day, so he wore his version of casual-- olive green cargo pants with a long-sleeved khaki shirt and Timberlands that added an inch to his height. He stood in Karen's newsroom cubicle.

"So?" she asked expectantly.

"My source says they got video of the incident. A car doing the deed and a license plate."

"From that parking lot camera?"

"Yup."

"And they got a hit on the plate number?"

"Yup."

"But of course, they wouldn't tell you who the car is registered to."

"Nope."

Karen was rightly impressed with the young man's work. "Who's your source?" she asked, point blank.

His brow furrowed. "Do I have to tell you?"

"It's Rosenstein, isn't it?"

No reaction.

"Isn't it?" she pressed.

Reg's eyes widened and he threw his hands into the air, surrendering.

"I knew it."

"How?"

"Reginald, there are very few cops in Philadelphia who confide in the press anymore. Since that last corruption blow-out two years ago, which came about only because the Inquirer is still a good paper, the FOP lawyers put out the word, no more sourcing for reporters. Capisce?"

"Huh? Cuh-PEESH?"

"Except for Lieutenant Tyler Rosenstein in homicide, all the good old boys and gals who liked to see Truth, Justice and the American Way play out on TV have clammed up."

"So, I lucked out and made friends with the only cop who gives it up for the press?"

"Basically, yes. And I am duly impressed."

Reg couldn't help smiling.

"So, what can we actually report?" she asked.

"Only that the investigation is continuing to make good progress. Anything more and he's afraid it'll tip off the owner of the car."

"He wouldn't give you a description of the car, I suppose?"

"Uh, uh."

"So, if we go on and report that sources say police have video of the incident and have a license number."

"It'll be Rosenstein's ass."

Karen nodded, then added, "Does he know you're black?"

Reginald's eyes narrowed. "I don't know. I never mentioned it. Why?"

"Tyler is a dedicated and honest cop who happens to be tremendously racist. He would never admit that, of course."

"I believe you. When did you guys become such pals?"

"Another life, years ago. Very boring. Time to go to work. I'll be looking for your script."

"OK," he said and bounced off towards his desk.

A burgundy Chevy Impala sat in a legal parking space on the 600 block of Brill Street in a tired neighborhood of row homes in the city's Lawncrest section. The street was one-way and so narrow, one lane of traffic could just about fit through next to the single lane of parked cars. Of the 80 homes on the block, two were boarded up, several were in severe disrepair and the rest attempted to keep up appearances in the face of epic neglect. The post-World War II housing was disintegrating. People who could afford to live here couldn't afford much in the way of upkeep other than a few plastic patio chairs and some paint on cast iron railings.

In the driver's seat of the Impala sat a large black man with a round face and close-cropped hair wearing ear buds and nodding to music. Next to him sat a less ample white man with red hair and a serene, pale face whose eyes were riveted to the screen of his phone. The larger of the two shifted uncomfortably in the Impala's narrow seat, reaching down his right side to adjust the firearm attached to his hip.

"It keeps getting caught in the seat belt thingie," he complained, while his partner continued tapping away on his phone.

"If you wore a shoulder holster like I told you," said the redhead, still looking at his screen.

"Yea, I know. I don't want to hear it again."

The mobile radio mounted on the center console was the only clue that this was a police vehicle. The few residents of Brill Street who were walking about in the cold, accustomed to seeing random cars containing random people, paid no attention.

"Breaking your balls is my greatest joy in life," said the passenger.

"I am here to serve. But I would appreciate it if you would fuck off now."

The radio crackled to life. "Fifteen Two-B, status report," said a female voice through the tinny speaker.

The driver picked up the microphone and clicked the button. "No activity."

"Very well. You stay awake there now, Brick."

"Ten-four." He replaced the mic onto its holder.

"I hate stake-outs in the cold," said the redhead.

"Yea, but I'll talk with her anytime. She's a hottie."

"You're old enough to be her father."

"And you, Shawnie, are a buzzkill."

Anyone eavesdropping would never guess that Brick Perryman and Shawn Maguire were partners, let alone friends. They were partnered after joining the Homicide Division almost ten years ago. The ensuing love story was epic.

"Thank you for farting, again," complained Brick.

"The closed environment and the heat make it seem worse than it is. It was a stealth bomb. Let me see that picture again."

Brick cracked his window and handed him the laser-printed enlargement of a driver's license photo. Fuzzy, faded color with poor resolution, the image was of the registered owner of a certain car spied leaving the scene of a murder the other night.

"That's one fat boy," said Brick.

"Yup."

"William Klemmer, 675 Brill Street," Brick read from the bottom of the print.

"Wha'd he do again?"

"Possibly ran over that homeless guy the other night. He's the registered owner."

"And what are we supposed to do?"

"Knock on his door, ask him what he knows."

"But it's so nice and warm in here, especially after that last fart, isn't it?"

"You are a charmer. How about we get this over with?"

"Fine," said Maguire who stuffed his phone into his pocket and opened the passenger side door. Perryman opened his door and fanned the contaminated air out of the car with his two hands. A few seconds later, they were walking towards 675.

The street was in disrepair with large portions of asphalt missing and so many cracks in the curb it sat in pieces like a puzzle. It was quiet, noonish and cold. Neither man spoke as they walked up the steps leading from the cracked sidewalk to the front door of 675, ten steps divided into two flights of five. All the homes on the block were built so the basement windows were above street level to accommodate coal deliveries back in the 40's and 50's. It meant the first floor was elevated, thus the steps.

Seeing no doorbell, Maguire opened the exterior screen door and knocked loudly on the inner door. It was always a crap shoot, knocking on someone's door. About a minute passed with no response. He saw a crudely mounted surveillance camera pointing at them. He squinted at it, produced his badge, held it up and said, "Police."

"I don't see that Camry," noted Perryman after looking over his shoulder at the line of cars parked on the street.

Maguire knocked again. They waited again. Still no response. "Let's go around back, see if it's parked in the driveway."

They walked back to their Impala, started her up and made the short drive from the front of the house to the common back driveway shared by all the homes on the block. They stopped at the rear of 675 and saw no Camry.

"Let me try once more," suggested Maguire. He got out of the car while Perryman stayed put. Maguire knocked loudly on the back door and waited another minute. Still no response. He walked back to the Impala and climbed back into the passenger's seat.

"Well, then. Is it lunch time?"

"Perhaps so," said Perryman. He picked up the microphone and said, "Fifteen 2-B to dispatch. We're clear from our location."

After a short pause, the familiar voice responded, "10-4, hon."

The Impala drove up the remainder of the driveway, took a right onto Bingham Street and disappeared into the drab sprawl of northeast Philadelphia.

At almost the same moment, Bill Klemmer's phone started vibrating in his pocket. He was at the Right-Fire Shooting Range off Torresdale Avenue firing .380 rounds through his little pistol. Almost none of his shots hit the target. He exhausted his six rounds and put the gun down to retrieve his phone. The vibration signaled a notification that one of his home surveillance cameras had detected motion, triggering a recording. This usually happened each day when the mail carrier arrived, but he checked it anyway. He scrolled through the recordings until he found one that had been made only minutes ago at his front door. He clicked on it and watched the playback. Two men he didn't recognize were knocking. They waited. Then one looked straight at the camera and held up a badge and said, "Police.". He heard the larger black man say, "I don't see that Camry," and Klemmer's blood ran cold and he launched into a panic, almost dropping his phone onto the concrete floor and backing away from the gun port. He started making his way towards the door, eyes darting and almost blinded by fear.

"Hey," yelled a man wearing a yellow vest and a name tag. "Aren't you forgetting something?"

Klemmer looked at him like a madman. It was the range master pointing at Klemmer's pistol and ammo, which he had left in the port.

"Sorry," babbled Klemmer as he stuffed the phone back into his pocket. He returned to the port, picked up his range bag and used the other hand to sweep the pistol and remaining ammo into it. He zipped up the bag and hurried away. The range master watched Klemmer leave, then looked back at his port, noting the port number and the time.

"Rosenstein, you amaze me," said Karen to a police lieutenant of her acquaintance. "Your heart of gold turns to coal at the drop of a hat."

"Sticks and stones," replied Rosenstein, whose mellow 51-year old voice projected through the telephone and hit Karen's ear like maple syrup. "If I tell you, it will not be a good thing for any of us, mostly me."

"What if I promise not to put it on TV?"

"Then, what's the point? Reporters report, as I've learned the hard way."

"When did I ever fuck you over? Huh? When?"

"Never. But what about your little Schwarzer pal, Reginald what's-his-name?"

"He's a good kid. You have nothing to worry about. If he fucks up, he knows I'll kill him. And how did you know he was black?"

"Please, who do you think you're dealing with? I can smell 'em a mile away."

"You haven't lost your Hitler Youth cachet."

After several seconds of silence, Rosenstein said, "So, if it's not going to be reported on TV, why do you want to know?"

"I want to be in position when you guys bust whoever this is. Murdering a homeless man is still murdering. It'll be a significant story and I want it first."

Karen could almost hear the gears churning in Rosenstein's warped head.

"It's a good thing I like you," he said. "And we'll always have the Winslow Motel."

"Oh man. That was a one-off, and you know it."

"You absolutely can NOT report it. You absolutely can NOT repeat it to anyone. Do you get the meaning of the words NOT and ANYONE?"

"Yes, Tyler."

"And you can't move until I say so."

"Yes, Tyler."

There was quiet on the phone again. Karen listened carefully, as she knew it would come now.

"The registered owner is a William Klemmer, 675 Brill Street, Philadelphia, DOB 9/23/86."

Karen's next breath was delayed. She felt a sudden nausea. She blinked hard and shook her head back and forth, then one word escaped: "What?"

Chapter 14 - TGIF, Maybe

Bud and Maggie sat at a table for two at Rum Sally's, Armitage's best excuse for casual dining and drinking. It was 8:43 Friday night and the after-work crowd was being joined by the looking-for-love crowd. Maggie nursed a double vodka on the rocks while nibbling on Ultimate Nachos. Bud grudgingly sipped yet another diet Coke while picking at some fried calamari.

"We're the oldest people here," said Bud, glancing around.

"You only think that. You're surrounded by kids all day, everyone else is turning in to them."

Both had ordered burgers and fries, a meal requiring no imagination.

"I'm exhausted," said Bud to a ring of squid on his fork. "I can't even tell you what actual work I did. Between the drive and trying to make friends and the paperwork and the computer system--they call it NewsCrash--I don't think I made any actual news decisions all week."

"Don't complain. At least you've just started, so it's too early for them to be plotting your demise."

"How'd it go with that Marjorie woman?"

"Great. She's on my side."

"Really."

"Yea. At first, I thought she was a bit aloof, but she's a player. She said Franklin and his apes are rattling their cages to see what they can shake loose in the Counties. Here's a quote: *'I don't like to be toyed with.'* She said she'll fight for me."

"Damn. Sounds like love."

"That's exactly what I told her. I told her I loved her."

Bud stopped chewing and stared at her. Maggie downed the remains of her vodka, smacked down her glass and grinned a stupid grin. "Goddam right!"

As if choreographed for the moment, the server arrived with their burgers--medium for Bud, rare for Maggie.

"Can I get you anything else," the sincere young man asked.

"Yes," said Maggie. "A new job."

"We're good," chimed in Bud. "Thanks."

The young man smiled and walked away as the couple began navigating their plates, the fries, the ketchup.

"Today, I chatted with Pam Whitehead, the noon anchor," Bud said with his mouth half full of burger. Maggie glanced at him, consumed with her meal, as he asked, "What would you do if a male co-worker sat down in your office, stared at your chest and out of nowhere said, 'Nice rack'?"

Maggie pondered for a few seconds then said, "I would tell him to watch his fucking mouth, kick him in his sack and report him, in that order."

Bud dipped a fry into his ketchup and took a bite. His mouth formed a little smile as he looked into Maggie's eyes. "That's my girl."

"Why?"

"Pam had a close encounter with my predecessor and that's exactly what he said to her. But she didn't report it to anyone."

Maggie took a large bite out of her burger and nodded in acknowledgement. "Welcome to the world of #MeToo. But he got fired eventually."

"It reminded me of the Kaleidoscope days, Hilde and all. I started getting angry again." Bud shifted uncomfortably in his chair. "But I walked it off."

"Good boy. There are a lot more Ronald Morone's in the world. You can't kill them all."

His hand froze while dipping a french-fry into ketchup. The moment the words escaped her mouth, she regretted it. "Christ, Bud, I'm sorry."

He resumed manipulating his fries and his ketchup for another couple seconds, then lifted one into his mouth. His eyes met hers. She could see he was wounded. She reached for his other hand but he pulled it away. He said nothing and continued eating, averting his eyes to his plate. Once again, as if his Higher Power controlled timing, his cellphone buzzed in his pocket. He wiped his hands on his napkin and reached for the phone. The number was Karen's cell. He clicked IGNORE and put it back in his pocket.

Maggie stole occasional glances his way. He didn't look at her or speak to her the rest of the meal.

Klemmer was sitting on his bed dressed in Hanes white cotton briefs and a formerly white t-shirt in the middle of the mattress, rocking. He held his little gun like a toy, waving it around from time to time, exhaling with guttural sounds, inhaling like an asthmatic. At random intervals, he dropped the pistol on the mattress, grabbed his hair with both hands and continued rocking severely. Then he would reclaim the gun, wave it, point it, click the trigger, all the while rocking forward and backward.

"I am not a loser," he said under his breath from time to time, looking at the pistol with energy and purpose each time. "You are mistaken," he repeated to no one. "You are mistaken."

He reached over to the night table and grabbed a handful of bullets out of a SpongeBob bowl. He clumsily loaded them into the magazine, one by one, then snapped the magazine into the pistol. He racked the slide, advancing the first round into the chamber. He stopped rocking now and gazed at the gun with new respect.

"You could end it right now," said the taunting voice.

"You are mistaken," said Klemmer, staring blankly at his weapon.

"You don't have the balls to use that thing."

"You are mistaken," replied Klemmer, a glaze in his eyes as he rocked again holding the gun carelessly in his right hand.

"Who are you going to use that on, boy? Huh?"

"I'm not telling you," he replied, aiming the pistol at his image in the mirror, feeling his large hand closing onto the tiny grip. Suddenly, a shot snapped his hand back, shattered the mirror and a small amount of urine escaped into his underwear. Tiny glass pieces flew off the mirror into the air and the sound seemed to echo for an eternity. Klemmer saw his eyes wide in a mirror segment. He was still holding the gun. He dropped it onto the bed, now fearful of its power. The hot shell casing landed on his thigh, giving him a small contact burn. He was spooked by the discharge of the gun.

Did he pull the trigger?

Back at the Remmick homestead, Bud sat on the couch with Beulah. In an uncharacteristic show of affection, Beulah licked his hand. He petted her and sank into the couch. As he did, she sat up straight and licked his right cheek. He wondered to what he owed this display of affection.

Maggie came into the room in her sweats and started laughing. "Oh, my."

"See, she does love me."

"I'm not even going to tell you where that tongue just was."

Beulah gave Bud several more licks as he sat staring at the wall. After a few more licks, he pushed the dog away and she hopped off the couch and ambled into the kitchen. He gave her a nasty look which she, he imagined, wore as a badge of honor. He picked up his phone to retrieve the voicemail message Karen had left him earlier. Maggie sat down next to him and picked up the TV remote and began surfing. Bud had gotten quiet with the phone to his ear. Maggie glanced over at him and saw his eyes and mouth both wide open. Her eyes were fixed on his now. After another few seconds of silence, Bud removed the phone from his ear, clicked one button, then another, and put it back to his ear. He said nothing to Maggie, who was now more than curious.

"What's up?" she asked.

"Karen," he said into the phone. "I just got your message." His eyes wandered around the room as he listened to the phone. Maggie was getting anxious.

"And what are we doing about it?" asked Bud. He sat in silence, listening to Karen. After about a minute he said, "Jesus Christ." He pushed a button on his phone and dropped it onto the coffee table.

"What? What?" Maggie implored.

"It's like the gods are saying, 'This is your penance, asshole.'" He looked at Maggie and began to find his words. "It appears one of my freelancers may be a killer."

Maggie raised her eyebrows but said nothing. Instead, she got up from the couch, walked into the kitchen and poured herself a vodka. She grabbed a diet Pepsi out of the fridge, then brought both into the living room. She sat down heavily next to Bud and handed him his soda and said simply, "It's been a hell of a week."

Chapter 15 - Reality TV

The Saturday, 4:23 AM call would never have worked back in his drinking days. There was that time he was manager on call at Kaleidoscope when a plane crashed into an Indiana corn field at 3:30 AM and he had to get on a conference call to figure out coverage. He was still drunk, but had to absorb details of the story, recall which reporter and crew were available in which cities and get them on flights. He'd hoped his slurred words would be written off as sleepiness and not drunkenness.

On this Saturday morning, he was cold sober but near-comatose when his cellphone rang at 4:23.

"Nose bleed, 8-year old male," said Lillian, "1942 Richmond Street."

"OK," Bud replied and dragged himself into response mode, pulling on his clothing and shoes, trudging down the steps, picking up his EMT coat and trotting out to the Lumina. Four minutes later, he was in the ambulance, driving Miss Tiffany, who was surprisingly awake and perky.

"I can't imagine my mother calling 911 for a nosebleed," she said. "Actually, my mother wouldn't have called 911 for anything short of decapitation."

"Yea, mine believed in Vaseline and Vicks VapoRub for everything."

"How's the new job? You gotta drive to Philly every day now?"

"Yea. After one week, I'm already sick of the drive. The job itself is interesting. Lots of curious young folks who knew all about me before I even walked in the door."

"Uh huh."

"They spent the week eyeing me up, wondering who I was going to kill next."

"Have anyone in mind?

"Real funny."

After a drive of about six minutes, they arrived at 1942 Richmond Street, an unremarkable house in a neighborhood of rundown, one-story single-family homes. They approached the front door and knocked.

"EMS," shouted Bud.

After less than a minute, the front door opened and a short, dark skinned, dark haired man dressed in sleeveless undershirt and sweatpants stood looking at them. "No, no, is OK," he said while waving his hands.

"Someone here called 911," said Tiffany. "Is there an emergency?"

"Is OK," the man said. "OK, OK. Ya no está sangrando."

Bud and Tiffany looked at each other.

"Can we come in for a minute?" asked Tiffany, pointing to herself and Bud, then gesturing towards the inside of the house.

"Sí, sí."

They walked into the living room, a small space crammed with old furniture, no carpet on the hardwood floor and a very large TV. Perched on the floor with legs crossed and manipulating a gaming controller was a boy involved in the action on the screen.

"This is him, el Chico?" asked Bud. Tiffany looked at him. He shrugged.

"Sí," said the man.

Next to the boy on the floor was a pile of crumpled tissues, each with a spot of blood at the wadded end. Bud started filling out a patient care report. Tiffany approached the boy and knelt down next to him. "Hello," she said. The boy never took his eyes off the screen. She looked at his nose. No bleeding. She did a visual once-over of his body, most of which was exposed since he wore only a pair of shorts. No apparent injuries. The boy was preoccupied and in no obvious distress. "You had a nose bleed?" she inquired.

"Yea, but it's all better now," the boy answered in perfect English. "It just does it sometimes."

"Anything else bothering you?"

"Nah."

"Nombre?" Bud asked the man, pointing at the boy. Using the few Spanish words he thought he knew, Bud managed to do a sketchy report with basic information. Since the bleeding had stopped and the boy was in no apparent trouble, he checked off NO TREATMENT REQUIRED. He refrained from speculating on why an eight-year old boy would be up at 4:30 in the morning playing video games, opting only to report what he saw. Satisfied that the crisis had passed and the father had simply panicked at the sight of his son's bloody nose, Bud and Tiffany left.

Back in the ambulance, Bud was in the driver's seat. Tiffany pulled out her phone and pushed one button. "Hi, Lillian. No transport, no treatment."

"Language barrier, right?" Lillian asked.

"Yea, little or no English. But my partner here muddled through. Did you know Bud speaks five whole words of Spanish?"

"Peachy. I'm going to bed now. The paid dispatchers are on the clock."

"Bye."

"Do you feel like getting breakfast?" Bud asked.

"Yes, indeed. I want to hear all about you getting the stink-eye at your new job."

Armitage's other restaurant was a Denny's, newly renovated, open 24 hours and staffed by a variety of minimum-wage employees who wore silly uniforms with name tags. It was 5:03 AM when Bud and Tiffany sat down at a clean table for four. Several other tables were occupied by single parties. The fluorescent lighting was rude. There was music playing through ceiling speakers, pop songs that Bud didn't recognize. Tiffany studied the menu.

"Feels like huevos rancheros," she said, closing her menu, placing it neatly on the table.

Bud continued looking at his menu as the server sidled up to their table.

"Good morning. Coffee or juice?" she asked in a way-too-perky voice.

"Both please," replied Bud. Tiffany nodded in agreement. "We can order. I'll have a western with American cheese, rye toast."

"Huevos rancheros, please," said Tiffany.

The server made quick notes on her pad, smiled and said, "OK."

"Guess I'm up for the day now," Bud said glumly. "During the week, I'm in my car by seven on my way to Philly. Thank god for Saturday."

"I will be going back to bed. Then, back up for my Saturday shift."

"You are a true public servant."

"Not really. I like the overtime. I'm not working other jobs like the other paramedics, so I take it as I can get it."

The coffees and juices came. Bud eyed his coffee with love.

"Can I ask you a personal question?" Tiffany ventured, stirring the creamer into her coffee.

"Sure, if there's anything left to ask."

She took a small sip of coffee. "Did it change you?"

But paused before responding. "I guess."

Tiffany waited for more. "That's it? You guess?"

He gazed at her with weary eyes as he formulated a more adequate answer.

"I consider myself lucky. There are probably very few people who can say they did just four years for killing a man. I had a good lawyer. I wasn't a career criminal. I wasn't--"

"Black," she jumped in.

"And as victims go, Ronald Morone wasn't exactly a sympathetic character."

"I guess lucky is one way to look at it. What about God?"

"I had visits from the prison priest. He peddled the notion of God's will and wondered why I thought I could take a man's life, the way God can."

This captured Tiffany's interest.

"I told him to take God with him on the way out of my cell." Remmick flashed back to that exact moment, the day he was released.

"If you're here representing the same God who let Ronald Morone walk the face of the earth to beat his wife and drive Hilde Schimmel to kill herself, then get out of my sight and take God with you."

He stared into his coffee and Tiffany snapped him out of it. "Hey, no worries, I was just asking."

"I appreciate my wife more. I appreciate the parts of myself rooted in good. I'm grateful I didn't die when my cellmate attacked me. And, I'm grateful for you."

Tiffany smiled and fluttered her eyelids at him.

"Do you want more compliments?" he asked with a look of mock interest.

"Hell, yes."

"You are non-judgmental in a judgmental kind of way."

"Alright."

"You are assertive and very good at your job."

"Yes."

"Yet, you're not bossy or self-absorbed. You care. You put up with my shit and you haven't judged me."

"*Hell* yes. I deserve a medal."

He grinned and started working on his omelet, which arrived during the Q&A.

"As white males go, you appear trustworthy," she said. "I don't trust hardly anyone, especially white people."

Tiffany was transfixed by her breakfast and Bud remembered his omelet and both got to it.

Still reeling from the news about Bill Klemmer, Karen decided to sleep on it. She didn't feel much better about it when she climbed out of bed on Saturday morning. As always, her elderly gray and white cat, Griffin, lay in a neat ball at the foot of the bed, unperturbed by her movements. She stepped into her ancient slippers and padded down her stairs to her kitchen where a pot of coffee had magically made itself at exactly 7:30 AM. She fetched a *Visit Cape May* mug out of the cupboard, filled it with coffee, tossed in two sweeteners and some half-and-half and trudged into her living room. She sat down in the armchair her ex had cherished. She never moved it or reupholstered it. It felt like home just the way it was. She sat staring at nothing, allowing the coffee to warm her. Karen lived in Upper Darby, a suburb just west of Philadelphia in Delaware County. It was a community once steeped in history and tradition that of late had become a haven for drug dealers and associated crime, being in proximity to some bad West Philly locales.

She had almost regretted her conversation with Lieutenant Rosenstein since it burdened her with perilous information. She also second-guessed her decision to tell Bud, but felt she owed it to him as news director. And if it turned out that Bill Klemmer was indeed the driver of the car in question, there would be way more shit headed their way. The police would want to know what knowledge, if any, the station had of the crime. Was he working with someone on the inside? And worst of all--

Karen froze with her coffee mug halfway to her mouth, as her mind wandered to the most treacherous possibility of all.

At almost the same moment, about a hundred miles away, Remmick lay in bed, supine with his eyes searching the ceiling. As predicted, he couldn't get back to sleep after the nose bleed call and now he was tortured by his conversation with Karen. The cogs of his brain chugged along, trying to process it. He first had to replay the chat in his head to make sure he wasn't dreaming it. He began to play out the ramifications. After a minute of that, his eyes became very wide.

"Christ," he said under his breath. He turned to look at the clock on his night table-- 7:56 AM. "Oh well, if she's not up now, she will be." He scrambled out of bed, more awake than before, and made his way to the living room where his phone was charging. He unplugged it, touched a single button and held it up to his ear.

"My, up early on a Saturday," came Karen's voice after two rings.

"Yea, sorry. You're awake?"

"Yes."

"I just had a horrific thought."

"Me too."

"What if," he began, paused, then repeated, "What. If."

"This isn't the first time?"

"Yes. What if this isn't the first time?"

Silence on the phone lasted a number of seconds.

"Karen?"

"I'm nauseous."

They each stared into their respective dead zones, awestruck by the notion.

"I can't even--imagine," began Karen.

"Those arson fires, which we just happened to get exclusive video of?"

"Oh my god. No fucking way."

"No fucking way," he agreed.

At that moment, Beulah peed on the living room rug.

"No fucking way, bitch!"

"Why am *I* a bitch?"

"Not you, my stupid dog."

"Crapped on the floor?"

"Peed. Right in front of me."

"Mercury Retrograde, man."

"That's a myth."

"No, it fucks up the universe."

"Is that even real?"

"Yes!"

They both stopped and reset.

"If I didn't live two hours away," Bud said.

"Oh, forget it. It can wait until Monday."

More silence, more seconds ticked by.

"I'm going in," he said.

"Me too. See you in a couple hours."

Maggie heard Bud moving around and talking on the phone. She feigned sleep while he got dressed and gave her a peck on the cheek before leaving. She figured it was a crisis that got him up and out of the house on a Saturday, but didn't inquire about details. Based on their brief chat last night, she figured it was serious.

She had finally been able to fall asleep after a fitful few hours of ruminating about her job. Maggie had shown herself to be a strong woman, able to overcome unexpected obstacles including a husband in jail and the accompanying economic hardships. As always, it was the things out of her control that bugged her. She had taken to reciting the Serenity Prayer at times like this at Bud's urging, but after a while it was just words. She was heartened at having a champion, Marjorie Cutler, who seemed to assert some control over the politics of her office. Yet, how much influence did she really have? Politics sucks, Maggie thought as she rolled out of bed, stood on the floor, scratched her head with both hands and walked towards the kitchen.

The brown Camry was packed with trash bags full of clothing. The trunk contained a metal lock-box that held the video camera, several unopened SD memory cards, the pistol, several boxes of .380 ammunition, the fake Channel 7 ID and an envelope of cash. Driving the Camry carefully towards the Tacony-Palmyra Bridge, Bill Klemmer was sleepless, frightened, and clueless about where to go and what to do since learning the police had been to his home.

"I'll be fine," he said out loud, being careful to stay within the speed limit and to not run any of the camera-equipped red lights on the Roosevelt Boulevard. The plan was to live out of the Camry until the heat was off. But he didn't know when the heat would be off. He wasn't sure how the police were led to his home. Did someone see his car that night? Maybe someone got the license number. Oh, probably someone had a camera going, he concluded. In any event, he was certain his car had been made, and so keeping it in motion was the thing to do. He had no hard target, so he decided to drive to New Jersey. Taking the Tacony-Palmyra would put him onto route 73 southbound into New Jersey, destination unknown.

Chapter 16 - Bugging Out

The last time Bud got cozy with a police source was several years before he left Channel 7. He was an associate producer, hot on the trail of the horrific murder and dismemberment of a baby boy in northeast Philadelphia. Police had already arrested the mother, Tanya Morshevitz, who had admitted killing baby Max, dismembering him and scattering his body parts in Neshaminy Creek. Follow-up calls were required to figure out why she did it and, if possible, how she did it. Bud's primary source was Captain Leonard Reese, whom he had known since his days as a homicide lieutenant. Bud had established a relationship with Reese based on the lieutenant's inflated ego and evident belief in a free press. Reese became a confidential source for many stories, but he was always careful not to compromise an investigation or endanger his job. This usually meant the information Remmick obtained only went so far.

In the Morshevitz case, Remmick called Capt. Reese the day after the body parts were discovered.

"Why did she do it?" Remmick asked.

"I'm not concerned with motive," Reese responded.

"Where did she do it?"

"Hang on, Bud, I got the DA on the other phone. Can you hang on?"

"Sure, Len."

"OK. Keep your ears on."

Remmick heard Reese place the phone down on his desk while picking up another phone. He began talking in a loud voice.

"Mr. Allenby, good morning," said Reese cheerily. Remmick knew the name, Assistant District Attorney Richard Allenby. "Yes, I just heard back from the sergeant who visited Tanya at the lockup. Yes, she confessed. She couldn't take the baby's screaming any more. She smothered him with a pillow, then took him to the kitchen sink and cut him up. She said God told her to do it."

Remmick breathed quietly.

"She put the body parts into a cooler and drove out to the creek. She thought better of dumping the cooler and scattered the pieces around instead. Then she went home."

Reese's explanation was punctuated by pauses as he listened to the assistant DA's questions.

"No, the husband wasn't home and had no clue. He's pretty much in shock at the moment. OK then, let me know if you need anything else. Bye."

Remmick heard the phone being hung up and Reese picked up the receiver again.

"Sorry, Bud, had to deal with the DA. So, are you all set?"

"Yes, Len, all good. Sorry to bother you."

"No bother, be good." Both hung up.

Now, a decade later, Bud sat with Karen in his office at Channel 7 on a Saturday morning, nursing coffees and Egg McMuffins. He appreciated Karen's trust in him, sharing the information she'd received from Lieutenant Rosenstein. But now, the question of the hour: what to do with it?

"We're supposed to just sit and wait?" he asked.

"Yes. I know, it's unacceptable."

"How do you know this Rosenstein?"

"We've known each other a long time. Let's leave it at that."

"And how do you know this Klemmer dude?"

"I don't. I wouldn't know him if I tripped over him. I've processed his vouchers but never laid eyes on him."

"Gordon knows him. Or I should say, he knew his father."

"I guess he's been doing work for us the past few years."

"Two years and nine months," replied Bud, reaching for a stack of papers on his desk. "I asked office services to print me out all of our freelancer buys for the past couple years. Those with W. Klemmer's name begin two years and nine months ago."

"Why'd you do that?"

"I thought $200 per job was a little steep. Turns out everyone else charges $100."

"How many jobs has he done for us?"

"Since he started, forty-one."

"Jesus. Is it possible?"

"What, that he caused each job, then photographed it? I don't know. But since we're not supposed to know the cops are onto him, there's nothing much we can do with this information, is there?"

"Oh, I don't know about that. It might be helpful to Rosenstein, if he'll promise to keep *his* source quiet. Ya follow?"

"Yes. You get one, you give one. Do you think we should tell Strickland?"

"Hell no. Need to know basis."

The Tacony-Palmyra Bridge was in his rear-view mirror. Up ahead was nondescript real estate and the four-lane highway that was Route 73. It passed through the communities of Palmyra, Pennsauken, Maple Shade, Marlton, then merged farther south with the Black Horse Pike on the way to the Jersey shore. It occurred to Klemmer that he might have bathing trunks stuffed into one of the plastic bags in his back seat, forgetting that it was February and about 28 degrees outside. He had a couple of good childhood memories of the beach at Beach City--Maxon Pizza, Jill's Arcade, the Wonderama Pier. He wondered what it would be like to live under the boardwalk, swimming by day, eating hot dogs and freshly cut french-fries by night and Kohr's ice cream any time he wanted. Thoughts of the boardwalk reminded him of money and he had an urge to count his. He pulled over onto the shoulder, looked into his rear-view mirror, got out and headed back towards his trunk. He opened it and went to the lock-box, opening it with a key on his keyring. He withdrew the bank envelope and grabbed the wad of bills inside. He stood counting it by his open trunk as cars sped by. A brisk wind picked up the corners of the bills, forcing him to hold on to them tightly.

After a laborious few minutes of counting against wind gusts and icy temperatures, he came up with a total of $6,100 in hundred-dollar bills. It was everything that was in his savings account and everything but $100 in his checking account.

He stuffed the cash into his pants pocket, tossing the empty envelope to the road. As he looked back up, he saw a police car pull up behind him, lights flashing. At the same moment, he instinctively grabbed the pistol out of the lockbox and stuffed it into the right pocket of his parka. The police officer emerged from his vehicle.

"How you doing?" asked the officer as he walked towards Klemmer.

"Good," Klemmer replied. "I heard a noise coming from back here, just pulled over to look."

"I see. So, do you need a tow?"

"Nah, false alarm," Klemmer replied. He decided to leave the trunk open so as not to arouse the officer's suspicion.

"Can I see your license, registration and proof of insurance, please?"

"Oh, sure. It's in my glove compartment."

"OK. I'll get it."

Klemmer watched the officer open his passenger door, then the glove compartment where he found the plastic pouch that held his credentials. Klemmer wasn't worried. He had no drugs, no alcohol and the pistol was in his pocket. The officer walked back towards his cruiser.

"Sir, just stand right there while I run your info, OK? Anything I need to know?"

"No," said Klemmer with a forced smile. He watched the officer return to his cruiser and get inside. He could see from a distance that the cop did something with his computer and picked up a microphone.

It occurred to Klemmer that if the Philly cops had come to his home, his vehicle info must be on NCIC by now and that this Jersey cop would see it. His eyes were locked on the cop, looking for any signs of alarm on his face or sudden movements. Klemmer's right hand found its way into his parka pocket and fondled the pistol. What seemed like an eternity ticked by, but less than two minutes later the officer got out of his cruiser in an almost leisurely gait and approached Klemmer, holding his credentials.

"OK, sir, you're good to go," she said and handed the documents to Klemmer. "But do me a favor and pick up that piece of paper you just tossed on the ground. No littering."

"Oh sure, sorry."

"Have a good day," said the officer as he walked back to his cruiser.

Klemmer watched the officer drive away, then closed his trunk. He exhaled a breath of profound relief. He made his way back to the driver's seat, started up the Camry and proceeded to merge from the shoulder back into traffic, still with no firm destination.

"I come bearing gifts," Karen said into her cell phone.

"Oh yea?" queried Rosenstein with suspicion.

"Yea. By the way, sorry to get you on a Saturday."

"Why should you be any different? I haven't had a life in 23 years."

"Would it interest you to know that William Klemmer has done 41 video jobs for Channel 7 in the past two and a half years?"

A couple seconds of silence passed before Rosenstein answered. "It might."

"It might because?"

"Because he might have had this bright idea before, to do a crime, then videotape it."

"Something like that. But you know, lieutenant, innocent until proven guilty, etcetera."

"Yes, of course."

"And, if anyone asks where you got this info--"

"I came up with the idea all by myself. Then, as part of our investigation, I called Channel 7 to confirm how many jobs Mr. Klemmer has done."

"Excellent."

"It's pretty amazing that you picked this moment to call me. We just got a call from the Pennsauken police. That's New Jersey."

"No shit."

"One of their cops encountered our friend on 73 this morning. He was pulled over on the shoulder checking out a noise coming from the rear of his Camry."

Karen's mouth dropped open and her eyes grew wide. "And??"

"And, our BOLO printout was sitting on their dispatcher's desk," Rosenstein answered with a tone of disgust. "She didn't enter it into the system until well after the encounter. So, the cop had no idea we were looking for him. The dispatcher caught it later while typing it into her CAD system and remembered the cop had called in the same license plate."

"Once again, human error disrupts the digital universe. OK, so everyone in New Jersey is balls-to-the-wall looking for our boy now, right?"

"I guess so."

"Jeez, those guys could fuck up a wet dream. Why don't you get off your butt on a Saturday and get over there and kick some ass?"

"I just might. But not until I finish eating these pancakes."

And the phone went silent.

Klemmer was careful to stay just at, or just above, the speed limit as Route 73 became the Black Horse Pike. It wouldn't be long now before he would be at the shore. The question before him: Which shore town should he go to and what should he do once he got there? The Jersey Shore, in the dead of winter, wasn't much fun.

He continued to replay his encounter with the police officer, almost giddy that he wasn't challenged for anything more than littering. The pistol remained in the pocket of his parka and the cash in his pants pocket, both items he considered essential in the event he had to make a quick escape.

"I got it all, baby," he said out loud to no one. The voice of his father had remained silent since he embarked on his journey. "Fuck you people. Fuck all of you."

He caught himself doing 68 miles an hour and quickly reduced his speed.

"No time to be dumb. You are mistaken, motherfucker, if you think I am dumb."

Anger had been building as Klemmer's loneliness became more profound. He had no one now. Even his father's verbal abuse would have been welcome. He had carefully carved out a solitary life for himself and his father over the past couple years. The downside of choosing to be on his own, he now realized, was abject loneliness. And the combination of abject loneliness and anger was as toxic as could be.

Klemmer craved pizza from Maxon's. He could taste it. Thus, he decided Beach City was his destination, a dry town, family-oriented with blocks of clean beach and a vibrant board walk. He remembered staying at a motel as a little boy, but couldn't remember the name or its location. No matter, he thought, there are a ton of motels in Beach City. The thought of sunny skies, the smell of the surf and the feel of warm sand on his feet made him smile. Now, he couldn't wait to get there, regardless of a high temperature of 28 degrees.

As he traveled south on the Black Horse Pike, police departments across New Jersey received a stop-and-hold request for a brown

2005 Toyota Camry, PA tag 48Z5779 registered to a William Klemmer of 675 Brill Street, Philadelphia.

Bud and Karen finally went home. There was nothing more to do at the station.

Saturday evening in the Remmick living room was highlighted by reruns of "ER", the background for the listless ritual of eating pizza on the coffee table. Neither Bud nor Maggie had much to say, but the pizza was decent.

In Upper Darby, Karen had stripped down to sweatpants and her Associated Press t-shirt and watched *Aliens* on Cinemax for the one millionth time. She loved the character of Ripley and fancied herself to be the newsroom version of her. She soon fell asleep in her recliner with Griffin purring in her lap.

The Remmicks were in bed by 11 PM. Light from the street sneaked in through the half-opened blinds creating a comforting aura in the room. Bud's eyes were open. Maggie's weren't and she was slipping into a rhythmic breathing that signaled impending sleep. Bud turned towards her supine body and moved her hair gently away from her forehead and kissed her there. He then kissed her lips. She smiled faintly but still said nothing. He propped himself up on his right arm while his left hand deftly made its way down her stomach, creeping with a light touch to the elastic band of her pajama bottoms. His hand found its way inside and moved lightly just above her pubic hair.

"May I help you?" Maggie asked with a little grin.

"Yes," Bud replied, inhaling and planting a real kiss on her lips. She kissed back, turned her body onto her left side to face him and started moving her right hand over his naked back.

Chapter 17 - Going Both Ways

It always felt strange to Les to be off on a Monday. But he still got up at 6AM, made coffee and checked his phone. He poked a couple icons that launched a video.

"C'mon, drop it," said the voice on the video.

He was sitting in his sparsely furnished living room, dressed in workout pants and a State Police t-shirt, gazing at his phone.

"Drop one for me," came the plea with an edge of desperation. The male voice was that of his next-door neighbor. "Don't be a bitch. Shit for me, right now."

In any other universe, Noble would have been amused by the sight of a man, in this case Bud Remmick, dressed in boxers and a parka, pleading with a dog to shit in his yard. Under these circumstances, however, he felt guilty and dirty and now, given the subject matter, stupid.

"Alright!" shouted Remmick joyfully as Beulah now assumed the position and completed her mission.

"Compelling," Noble muttered under his breath. He fast-forwarded through the video which ended shortly thereafter with images of Remmick opening the kitchen door to let Beulah back in, then going inside himself.

Noble took stock of the video evidence he had compiled so far: a pants-less Remmick begging his dog to shit, numerous openings and closings of the kitchen door to let the dog out and back in and one instance of Remmick walking in the yard while talking on his cellphone.

Noble dropped his phone on the couch next to him. He pointed the remote at his 55" TV and clicked it on. The screen came to life, still tuned to the E! network where he had watched *Botched* the night before. His apartment had a couch, the TV, the table that held the TV, a small kitchen table with two chairs and his bed. Almost two weeks after moving, he hadn't done any decorating, hadn't made any friends or even explored Armitage.

Noble, the product of a black father and white mother, had a look of ethnic ambiguity that sometimes worked for him. Other times, it did not. He found a certain level of tolerance in the State Police, which was hurting for minority troopers. Too often, however, that tolerance gave way to expressions of racism--no overt epithets, no utterance of the N word, but coded phrases that patronized or subtly insulted him. He found it particularly true here in the sticks. Back home, he was comfortable with friends whom he came up with, first in high school, then the academy and later at his barracks. Many had common acquaintances to the point where it seemed like everyone knew each other.

His transfer to the Poconos was sudden and unwelcome. It followed an unpleasant encounter with his Captain over Noble's level of "production", the Captain's euphemism for the number of tickets written by a trooper in a given month. Noble found himself giving warnings more times than his boss liked. His boss had to answer to higher authorities who clamored for tougher traffic enforcement, especially on the Turnpike. After several discussions of the matter, the last one ended in shouts and Noble uttering the F word. Two days later, his transfer was ordered without explanation.

Finding out from his new boss that his transfer was part of a master plan to spy on his neighbor aggravated and enraged Noble. All he wanted to do was be a cop. Now, he was involved in some kind of covert operation to catch his neighbor doing--what, exactly? Bud hadn't concealed his past when Noble asked him. He made light of it. He wasn't living a secret life and he wasn't doing anything illegal. What was this all about? He wasn't given specific orders to conduct video surveillance. He thought of that on his own. He decided that if he ever had to defend the camera, he would say he was concerned about home security and the camera somehow got jostled and pointed at the next-door neighbor's yard. He ruled out any notion of bugging the Remmicks' home or going onto their property without a warrant. He didn't have time to follow them around. This was the extent to which he would spy on them and he did so with great reluctance.

Maggie stepped out of her Subaru in the County Complex parking lot and trudged towards the double doors leading to the lobby. Once inside, she walked the twenty feet to the elevator where she spotted Marjorie Cutler already waiting.

"Good morning," Maggie said.

"Good morning, Mrs. Remmick," Cutler responded with a pleasant smile. "How are you on this miserable Monday?"

"Miserable, huh? It's only 8:30 and we're already miserable?"

"I answer to a Commission of men whose emotional ages hover around 15. A couple of them like to email me during off-hours to suggest new ways of spending taxpayer funds foolishly. One of them, who shall remain nameless, texts me from the toilet. He told me so, and proudly."

The elevator arrived and they entered, Maggie pushing her button, Cutler pushing hers.

"So, you're like--their mother?"

Cutler pondered the question, nodded once and said, "Yes." She followed this with a look of resignation. "Elected officials are a separate breed. Why on earth would anyone want to sign up for that kind of abuse, and for what they get paid?"

"They want to make a difference?"

"Sure. We'll go with that."

The elevator door opened to the second floor and Maggie stepped out. "Have a good day, Mrs. Cutler," she said.

"Call me Marjorie."

"And call me Maggie."

The elevator door closed and Maggie turned to walk towards her office. Cutler left behind a gentle scent, probably her shampoo, Maggie thought. Her hair was bound up in that severe coif again. She wore another business suit, an elegant maroon jacket and skirt with a lovely top in contrasting shades of gold and off-white, accented by a simple gold chain with a tiny dangling pendant. Maggie caught herself reviewing Cutler's appearance and wondered why the woman fascinated her so.

Her morning was filled with routine matters--approving food orders for the meals-on-wheels kitchen, reading home care reports, reviewing voicemail messages, mostly complaints from clients or their families. One message stood out due to its length, showing 3:24 in length. Maggie positioned her cursor over the item and double clicked it. Her speakers crackled to life with the voice of a woman who Maggie knew all too well.

"Well, another day, another horrible meal," shrieked the woman. "You fucking bitches, trying to poison me again with that fucking apple sauce."

Maggie listened with a smile.

"Just once I wish you'd eat this fucking shit yourselves, just once."

Angela appeared in Maggie's office. "Mrs. Harrington, I presume?" she asked.

"Yep. She's in rare form."

"You gotta give her props. Eighty-three and still embracing the F word."

"I'll call her daughter again, just to make sure there wasn't anything actually wrong." The woman's dementia made a conversation directly with her almost impossible.

The noise of Mrs. Harrington's phone call continued as background to Maggie checking her email. She was greeted by no less than forty emails each morning from staff, clients and the public. She answered them all.

After several perfunctory replies to routine messages, Angela's voice came over the intercom.

"Marjorie Cutler on one for you."

"Thanks," Maggie replied, then pushed the appropriate button. "Hello?"

"Hi again, Mrs. Remmick. Do you have a minute to visit?"

"Oh, sure. Be up in a few." She replaced the phone on its cradle and stared at it. A little alarm vibrated in her gut.

Bud found himself sitting in his office, weary from an eventful weekend and two nights of fitful sleep. He arrived this morning with a snoot-full of attitude and a caffeine buzz. He felt dangerous, for a Monday.

He had a 9:30 interview with a reporter candidate, a young woman from the Salisbury, Maryland, affiliate. It was already 9:20 and he really wasn't in the mood. He had done significant whining to Roy Strickland to shake loose money for an additional reporter. He could offer no more than $48K to start, a joke for a reporter in the sixth largest television market. He had already seen her audition video, a formulaic collection of stories that included a weepy feature on a Vietnam vet who'd adopted three disabled children, a couple of live shots from a major fire in downtown Salisbury and the obligatory hurricane live shot showing the intrepid reporter standing her ground in 100-mile an hour winds, the only idiot on the street.

Her name was Leandra Cole, an attractive African-American woman with striking eyes that were the main attraction of her sculpted face. High cheekbones and a prominent jaw gave her a vaguely masculine look. Yet when she smiled, she looked almost demure with a kind of unaffected innocence. Her resume said she had graduated from the University of Maryland just two years ago. Salisbury was already her second on-air job. Remmick also knew that her current news director, Alphonse Mauro, was a flaming asshole who had darkened Channel 7's door some years ago. He'd gotten fired over a "Channel 7 Investigation" that involved reporters buying crack on the corner of 8th and Butler and recording the sales on hidden cameras. The series attracted the attention of the police and the district attorney, neither of whom was pleased. The reporter, photographer and producer were fired along with Mauro who approved the ill-conceived project. The media coverage of the debacle reached scandalous proportions when the photographer was hospitalized after sampling the product, which turned out to be laced with strychnine. His life was saved, just barely, and Alphonse Mauro achieved the title of Local News Pariah of the Century.

In comparing Alphonse Mauro's stupidity to his own, Bud still reserved the top prize for himself, having actually killed a man with his bare hands and some heavy reading materials. *There but for the grace of God,* etc.

His cellphone vibrated in his shirt pocket. He withdrew it and thumbed the green button in one motion. "Hello?"

"Hi, Bud," said Karen. "You're in, I see."

"Yep. Any news?"

"No, not about our Jersey boy."

"What about the rest of the universe? Do we have enough to make a noon newscast?"

"Yea, bunch of crap, but yea."

"OK, see you soon?"

"Yep, on the way in."

Both thumbed their red HANG UP buttons. At that precise moment, Leandra Cole appeared at Bud's office door.

"Mr. Remmick?" she asked.

"Yes, good morning, Leandra." They walked towards each other and shook hands. "How was the drive from Salisbury?"

"I drove in last night. I stayed at a hotel downtown, the Wyndham."

"Of course. I would've done the same. Gotta be fresh for a morning job interview."

She had no response and followed Bud's lead as he pointed to the brand new, upholstered chair that faced his desk. She sat down tentatively, as though she wasn't sure sitting was appropriate.

"Would you like coffee? Water? Bloody Mary?"

"No thank you," she replied with a half-smile that immediately evaporated.

"We don't really have Bloody Mary's. That's news director humor."

Leandra sat with perfect posture, her legs crossed elegantly in a charcoal gray suit enveloping a pale, pink blouse with silver earrings that matched a simple silver necklace. She was made up for TV, wearing a base, mascara and eyeshadow, all slightly overdone.

"Were you able to watch any of our broadcasts from the hotel," Bud asked.

"Oh, no. I had dinner and went right to bed."

"No worries. So, your agent tells me you're looking to move on to a larger market?"

"Yes. I'm from the Salisbury area and the people down there are great. But I'm ready to work in a real city."

"I see. Your audition video is good. You seem to be able to handle big stories. Of course, live shots are very important here. The consultants want us to be live everywhere, all the time, no matter how dumb it looks."

This remark elicited a furrowed brow. "What do you mean?"

"You know, live shots in front of dark buildings where there's no longer any activity. Or live shots from moving cars, live shots from five blocks away where you can't see what's going on, that kind of thing."

"Oh. That's bad?"

Her sincere response to his cynicism threw him off a little. Now he considered playing it straight so as not to confuse her. "No, it's not bad. It just sometimes seems a little dumb, that's all."

"Because I've done all of those kinds of live shots," she said, slightly alarmed.

"Yea. No, it's fine and we do them, too. I'm just being sarcastic."

Now she was thrown off. She looked puzzled.

Remmick got up and walked to the coffee machine in the corner of the office. "How about some coffee, Leandra? I know I need some."

"OK."

"What do you like in it?"

"Just some stevia."

He looked into the cup that contained the sweeteners--pink, blue and yellow packets.

"Sorry, no stevia."

"Oh. Well, um--" She seemed flummoxed and confused by his answer.

"Splenda, Equal or Sweet N Low."

"I guess, ah. Never mind."

Remmick made a mental note: *confused by sweetener*. He brought his own coffee back to his desk and sat down. "What are you looking for in an employer?"

The young woman was taken aback by the question and took a few moments to formulate her answer.

"Well, Mr. Mauro is very fair. I think fairness is good."

"Yes."

Her face lit up. "He gives everyone Christmas presents. I think that's a sign of a boss who really cares about his employees."

"I see."

"Do you give Christmas presents?"

"I believe we have a holiday party. Don't know about presents, I haven't been here during the Christmas season yet."

"Oh, OK."

"I'm sure your agent told you what this job pays."

"Yes, 48-thousand. More than I'm making in Salisbury."

Pathetic, he thought to himself. "Yep, and there are increases along the way, based on performance."

"I understand."

"When could you start?"

"Mr. Mauro knows I'm looking and he's told me I can go whenever. I just need to give them a couple weeks' notice."

"Fair enough. I'm interviewing a couple more candidates but I'll let you know soon." He stood up and walked around to her. She also stood, and they shook hands. "Very nice to meet you," he said.

"Nice to meet you too, Mr. Remmick. I would love to work for you."

"Your agent will be in touch, Leandra. Thanks again."

She turned and walked out the door and Remmick watched her walk to the elevator. When she got on, he returned to his desk, sat down with a sigh and picked up his coffee.

"Presents," he said out loud. "I got your presents."

Maggie sat in the same chair facing Marjorie Cutler's desk as the last time she was in her office. Cutler had coffee in a Styrofoam cup, one of a stack next to the coffee machine in the outer lobby leading to her office and the offices of the Commissioners. Maggie noticed a small smudge of dark lip gloss on the cup, which then led her eyes to Cutler's lips, sculptured and curved in exactly the right places and colored in burgundy to match her suit. Maggie smelled the same, faint shampoo scent she noticed earlier at the elevator. Marjorie was typing on her laptop as Maggie studied her face.

"OK," Marjorie said finally, still staring at her screen. "Take a look here." She motioned to Maggie to join her in staring at the screen.

Maggie got up from her chair and navigated her way around Cutler's desk until she was standing next to her and looking down at the laptop screen.

"This is what's happening," Cutler said, pointing to a bar graph with the heading, BUDGET. "The Commissioners are hashing out the next fiscal year budget. Here's yours. No increase, no decrease. Same as this year."

"OK," Maggie nodded. She had bent down a bit to bring herself closer to the screen and to Marjorie. "I guess that's good, huh?"

Marjorie nodded. "Yea, better than a budget cut. The Commissioners like what you're doing, so they preserved your current spending. Taking care of seniors, they've discovered, is good politics." Marjorie looked at Maggie, whose face was only inches from hers. Their eyes met and locked for a good two to three seconds. Maggie was the first to look away.

"That's great," she said, looking back at the screen.

"Yes," Marjorie agreed, studying Maggie's profile. It hadn't dawned on her to inspect Maggie, but close quarters offered an

120

opportunity she couldn't pass up. Maggie suddenly turned to face her and again their eyes met. This time, each noticed the other's eyes roaming, a mutual inspection of facial features to some unknown end. Neither turned away for what seemed like an eternity, but in reality, it was just seconds.

"Thank you," Maggie said, still looking directly at Marjorie.

"For what?"

Maggie snapped out of it. "For the heads up. It's reassuring to know I don't have to worry about my budget. That is, as long as I still have this job."

Marjorie continued looking at Maggie, but her gaze was suddenly business-like again. "As long as I have anything to say about it, you will have this job."

Maggie extended her hand. Marjorie took it. They shook for several seconds, sharing an undefined energy, each aware of the other's warm grip.

"Have a good day," said Maggie finally, letting go of Marjorie's hand.

"And you," Marjorie replied and watched Maggie Remmick walk away from her desk and out her office door.

Across the Delaware River in Trenton, New Jersey, John Ungar sat in a conference room with the Corrections Commissioner, Governor Francis Haley and the Governor's Chief of Staff. The three sat at a table, staring at a large flat screen TV at the end of the room. The images on the screen were those of Pennsylvania Governor Tom Franklin and his Chief of Staff. It was the regular monthly Skype call the two Governors engaged in for chit-chat, gossip and occasional business. Ungar and his boss were invited this time because prisons were on the agenda.

"That conference was an eye-opener," said Haley. "Fucking Germans are on the cutting edge, but I'm not sure I like the cutting edge."

"They have less recidivism and actual rehabilitation seems to take place," replied Ungar.

"Rehabilitation is a joke," said Franklin, his chief of staff nodding next to him. "Keeping them locked up and closely supervised while on parole is the way to go."

"And that's worked so well, hasn't it?" said Ungar. "We have more people in prison than any other country and it's costing us a fortune. The rate of parolees returning to jail is huge."

"And you care about this why?"

Ungar was taken aback by the question. "Um, well, I've spent my career working in and running prisons, sir, and at the end of the day, you're still talking about people. All have done criminal acts but not all should spend years in jail, not to mention those who are mentally ill. And the cost is tremendous."

The room went silent for a few moments as Ungar's words settled in. Finally, Franklin spoke. "I admire your passion, John. I don't know what it's going to get us, but it's food for thought."

Ungar sat with his hands folded on the table. His boss, the Commissioner never said a word.

"How's your budget process going, Tom?" asked Governor Haley. "We're almost done here in the land of high taxes."

"It's like rooting around in a dumpster, looking for the last edible chunks of food," said Franklin. "There's nothing left to cut."

"And your personnel issues?"

"Oh, I'm making changes, for sure. Fucking Democrats want to eliminate even more of my jobs but they don't understand--they are MY fucking jobs and I'll fill them with whoever I want."

"Spoken like a true tyrant," said Haley with a chuckle. "I admire your balls."

"John, I got my eye on the wife of one of your Kings Pointe alumni. That Remmick idiot is out enjoying his life after killing an innocent man and his wife is sucking on the taxpayer tit, for Christ sake."

"Oh?" asked Ungar.

"Her ass is mine. That job is going to someone who deserves it."

"What job is that?"

"Executive Director of a County Division of Aging out in the boonies. If I had known they were even talking to her about that job, I would have quashed it. Why should the wife of a convicted killer get a government job, I ask you? But I've got eyes on her, don't worry."

"With all due respect, Governor, what does she have to do with his past crimes?" asked Ungar.

"That piece of shit killed an innocent man, an excellent Republican. He took justice into his own hands. You really believe his bleeding-heart wife wasn't behind him?"

Before Ungar could answer, Haley jumped in. "This is all fascinating, Tom, but I have other fish to fry. Are we finished here?"

"Yes, Francis, I guess so. Talk to you next month."

"OK, Tom, till next time." Haley pushed one button to make the image and the audio go away.

Later, Ungar found himself in the capitol cafeteria, sipping pea soup out of a Styrofoam cup with a plastic spoon and eyeing up his BLT. He usually ate alone, sometimes with a newspaper. Today, he was joined by his boss, Corrections Commissioner James Portnoy, a career bureaucrat who did little or no work and smiled a lot for $160,000 a year.

"What do you think of Governor Franklin?" he asked Ungar.

Ungar pondered the question as he picked up his sandwich to take a bite. Any answer he would give might be wrong. "Is it just you and me talking here?"

"Of course."

"I think he's an ignorant hack."

"But aside from that."

"A solid citizen."

Portnoy chuckled as Ungar munched his sandwich. "Yea, I don't care for him much, either. Not sure how he and Haley got to be such buds."

"Being a governor with this president is no box of chocolates. Maybe you need all the friends you can get."

"Might just be that simple. He certainly has a bug up his ass about that one County employee. Seems like a lot of effort to take care of your cronies."

"Effort is a relative term."

"I suppose," concluded Portnoy. He wiped his mouth, tossed the napkin on his tray and rose from his chair. "I'll see you later, John."

"Later, Commissioner," replied Ungar. His sense of fair play had been aroused while listening to Governor Franklin rant about his intentions for Maggie Remmick. Would Ungar have cared if it were anyone else? Probably not. He had always liked Maggie, felt sorry for her and admired her, though he wasn't sure why. All he knew for sure was, he wanted to help her.

The single car parked in the Seahorse Inn parking lot stuck out like a sore thumb. In the dead of winter, not many motel rooms were rented in Beach City. The motel owner, an elderly man rousted from sleep when the bell rang at 10:45 in the morning, was annoyed that he had a customer in February, but less annoyed when he paid for three nights in advance. He didn't care much who the man was, why he paid from a wad of large bills or why his car seemed to be packed with plastic trash bags. He took Bill Klemmer's money, handed him the keys to room 207, then went back to bed.

Inside the stuffy motel room, Klemmer stripped down to his Hanes briefs and rooted through one of the trash bags containing clothing. He had thrown the lock box on the bed. The door had a double lock and a peep hole and a few scratches from years of use. The room most probably had not been occupied since last summer, he figured. The Seahorse Inn, on Bay Avenue at the far southern tip of the island, was about as generic a motel as there was, thought Klemmer, a perfect place to hunker down for a while. He was heartened by his encounter with the cop who let him go on 73 and thought maybe, just maybe, he was in the clear.

He found what he thought was a clean shirt and jeans in the trash bag. He gave each a sniff, seemed satisfied, then laid them on the chair that sat at the small desk in the room. He now rooted through a second trash bag and dug out a bag of Doritos and a 2-liter bottle of diet root beer. So equipped, he settled onto the bed, picked up the remote and turned on the television. It was still too early for the news, so he watched *The Price Is Right*. He crunched the chips loudly while watching Drew Carey's antics and swigged soda right out of the bottle. With his free right hand, he grabbed the lock box and opened it with the key. He withdrew the pistol, inspected it, aimed it, pointed it, then released the magazine and pulled back the slide to release the round in the chamber. Now safely unloaded, the gun was his toy to play with while watching TV and eating junk food. It was as happy as Klemmer could remember being in recent memory.

Chapter 18 - Discovery

"I have a brilliant idea," said Remmick to Karen, both of whom stood against the wall behind the assignment desk, surveying the newsroom as it prepared for the noon newscast.

"Can't wait," Karen replied.

"Why don't we just call Klemmer?"

Karen turned to look at him as though he had three heads. "Call him?"

"Yea. Like, we need him to do a job or something."

"And then?"

"And then, what?"

"Ask him if he's a psychotic, murdering whack job?"

"No, play dumb, like we don't know anything, like we just need him to work."

"Bad idea. The cops could say you're interfering with their investigation."

"But aside from your boyfriend Rosenstein, the cops don't know we know about Klemmer, right?"

"Don't do it. If he's on the run, it'll spook him. If he's not on the run, it'll still spook him."

Remmick stopped talking and looked away from Karen, turning his gaze back to the pre-show din in the newsroom.

"Fine," he said and walked away.

Karen watched him walk towards the hallway that led to the steps that led to the vending machines downstairs. She knew Bud was getting antsy. So was she. She wished the cops would scoop up Klemmer already. The sooner the truth came out, the sooner they'd be able to handle the fallout, whatever that might be.

It occurred to Karen that Klemmer probably wasn't particularly bright, having left multiple clues behind at several of the crime scenes. Her deepest fear was the unknown--what else was he capable of if he did set fires and commit murder to capture his work on video? This would be the work of a psychopath, no? *That* would be a hell of a story.

Karen found herself in a funk and made her way to her cubicle, sitting down heavily in front of her computer. She stared at nothing in particular, then sat straight up, placed her hands on the keyboard and began typing.

After visiting the vending machine to buy a Twix, Bud walked another thirty feet down the basement hallway to the ENG shop. He hadn't set foot in there since arriving at Channel 7, so he opened the door and stuck his head in. The ENG shop was an oversized garage with room to accommodate one live van and lots of shelves holding electronic equipment and the tools to fix it. Bud's eyes scanned the room, hoping to find a certain individual. Back in the far corner, inspecting a disassembled camera, was Gordon Richardson. Remmick walked slowly into the room, easing the door closed behind him and making his way around a pile of electronic gear to where Gordon was working.

"Hey, Gordon," he said as he approached.

"Hi, Bud. What's going on?"

"Nothing. Just wandering around. Haven't been to this part of the building yet."

Gordon returned his attention to the camera he was working on.

"How are things going?"

"I'm slapping together these old cameras with spit and glue."

"That bad?"

"This one is six years old. This digital technology is outdated. These built-in hard drives are for the birds. The new cameras are smaller, lighter, cheaper, 4K-capable and have high-speed memory cards."

"Uh huh. Tell it to the news director."

Gordon continued probing the camera's guts.

"On an unrelated note, do you by any chance have a number for Bill Klemmer?"

"Sure do," Gordon replied. He dropped the electronic probe he was using and put down the sick camera. He withdrew his phone from his pants pocket, gazed at it and poked at a couple buttons. "Ready?"

Remmick got out his phone, pressed NEW CONTACT and prepared to type with two fingers. "Go ahead."

Gordon read out the number from his phone display and Remmick typed it into his phone, one digit at a time.

"Great, thanks," he said.

"Sure. What are you calling him about?"

"I just wanted to introduce myself."

"He's a weird guy. Talks on the phone like a six-year old."

"OK, thanks."

At her desk, Karen typed the words "William Klemmer Philadelphia" into the Google search window. The results yielded several sites that announced things like, *Information about William Klemmer HERE starting at $9.99* or *Know Your Neighbor: Search Records Now*, etc. She thought about asking Rosenstein to run Klemmer's background but then reconsidered. Instead, she withdrew her Visa card from her bag, chose a website and proceeded to fill out the online form that would, hopefully, dredge up some of Klemmer's past for $39.95.

Tyler Rosenstein considered himself a simple man of simple needs. While it would have been more economical and healthier to bring a prepared lunch each day--a tidy tuna sandwich on wheat with some Baked Lays and a diet soda like his ex used to make for him-- he opted instead for the McDonald's down the street from the Roundhouse because he wanted the fries.

Rosenstein was married once to another cop, a mistake he swore he'd never make again. He had little patience for any human who wasn't white, male and, preferably, Jewish. His ex, on the other hand, was a Shiksa of Catholic roots who wasn't religious but had more of a world view (her words). As he got older and his cop-crust (his words) got more pronounced, he grew less patient with people in general, women and minorities in specific. She got sick of his rants, became embarrassed by his behaviors and many arguments ensued. After just three years, the marriage ended. She moved to Biloxi and became a cop there. He got promoted and became a significant force at Philly homicide.

Big Macs and fries had taken their toll on Rosenstein's body. While not morbidly obese, he was certainly not the trim man who joined the police department almost thirty years ago. But he didn't care. His womanizing days were long gone. He had enough hair to comb. He was happy to have a job, a pension, a decent place to live and a cat who mostly ignored him.

His friendship with Karen went back through her 20 years in the local news business. More than a news source, he was an actual companion for dinner and drinks from time to time after she and her husband split up. Their friendship was jocular, relaxed and had no strings of any kind. The one time it crossed into uncharted waters was the year she accompanied him to the FOP convention in Atlantic City where she learned the hard way that drinking large amounts of alcohol was a prerequisite for being part of the posse. Driving back to Philly after the last night of the convention, he was drunk behind the wheel and she was half asleep in the passenger seat. After two close calls during which he crossed over onto the shoulder half asleep, they decided to stop at the Winslow Motel off 73 which, at the time, promoted themed rooms and adult movies. They got a room, one thing led to another and they both awoke the next morning in various states of undress. Neither seemed to remember much, only that there was very little conversation and some significant effort on Rosenstein's part to perform. Still, both held on to that night as a source of vague affection, a personal connection that was better than nothing.

"I hate being at the mercy of another jurisdiction," he moaned to his boss, homicide Captain Gene Dillon, who sat behind a heavy steel desk in his office at Homicide. "Those Jersey guys trip over their own dicks."

"Patience, my son," said Dillon in a calming voice that irritated Rosenstein. "I know you want to cross the river and jack them up, but you can't. Let them do their job."

"Fuck them. They let him slip through their fingers once already."

"It would be nice to speak with this Klemmer guy and give him a chance to explain what his car was doing there that night. All we have is video of his car. We don't even know if he was driving. I know we went to his home. Have we tried getting a phone number?"

"No home phone and the cell phone companies want a warrant."

"Someone must have a number for him, Lieutenant. Friends? Co-workers? Those Channel 7 people must know how to get a hold of him."

"I'm on it," responded Rosenstein, rising from his chair and leaving the Captain's office.

"Well, whoop-dee fuckin' doo," muttered Dillon under his breath.

Rosenstein was already half way back to his office. Captain Dillon scratched his head and stared at the spot where his lieutenant was just sitting and asked, in all sincerity, "Shall I wipe your ass for you, too?"

Sitting in the Lumina in the Channel 7 parking lot, Remmick pondered his conversation with Karen. He knew she was right. Or was she? Wouldn't calling Klemmer on the phone be a logical thing for a new News Director to do, just to introduce himself and offer words of encouragement? He hadn't convinced himself since he thought he needed to hide in his car while making the call. He wondered whether the police had already tracked down his cell number. Did Klemmer have it disconnected? Would he answer if it weren't? Remmick grabbed his phone out of one pocket, fished the slip of paper with Klemmer's number out of another and proceeded to punch in the numbers. He felt his heart rate increase and he held his breath while he dialed. He then pushed the icon for CALL RECORDER, a free app he had downloaded. He waited several more pregnant seconds, staring at the green CALL icon, looking through his windshield to see if anyone else was around. Finally, he pressed it.

Karen's online search came up with a number of hits for "William Klemmer", but none with a Brill Street address. She had no other information to enter into the blank fields. She had guessed Klemmer's age to be somewhere in the mid 20's to early 30's and tried a couple of birth years, but again there were no results. It then occurred to her that the father might have had the same first name, so she did a new search and entered a range of birth years that would cover a man who might be in his 60's or 70's by now. This yielded one result, a William B. Klemmer who resided on Godfrey Avenue in Philadelphia. She clicked on the hyperlink connected to this name and a list of documents appeared. A Google map also appeared with an arrow pointing to the address. She zoomed in and to her surprise found that Godfrey Avenue was the next street over from Brill Street.

"Yes," she hissed at her computer screen. "Young William stayed close to home."

Karen proceeded to click on document after document, printing several as she read them, learning about Mr. William B. Klemmer, Senior.

Remmick held his phone to his ear and heard the sound of a phone ringing on the other end. It did so four times, then stopped. He heard a faint rustling that lasted only a second or two, then nothing.

"Hello?" he said. No sound on the other end. "Mr. Klemmer?" Still, nothing. "This is Bordon Remmick, the new News Director at Channel 7. I just wanted to introduce myself and thank you for your work. Are you there?"

Remmick heard more rustling then, "Hello?"

"Oh, hi. Mr. Klemmer?"

"Yea?"

"Hello there. Um, well, I've been seeing your work on our air with some regularity and I gotta say, you're doing a great job for us."

"Thank you."

"Yea, no problem. That crime scene stuff of the homeless guy in South Philly the other night was really awesome."

"Uh huh. My dad told me where to go."

"Oh, so your dad is still working with you?"

"Of course, just like I told Nancy the other day."

"Well, I only ask because--" Remmick stopped cold, quickly weighing whether he should continue.

"Because what?"

"Because, well, my co-worker, Gordon Richardson, says he remembers your dad from working on the street and he says your dad died a few years ago."

Remmick strained to listen. He thought he heard a faint chuckle, but he couldn't be sure.

"You are mistaken," Klemmer replied in a soft, slow voice, followed by a definite, low volume chuckle.

"He said he remembers the newspaper story, the funeral--"

"You are mistaken."

"You certainly have a knack for being in the right place at the right time. I'm just wondering, how you are finding out--"

"YOU ARE MISTAKEN," boomed an adult voice through the phone. "YOU ARE MISTAKEN! I'M RIGHT HERE, MOTHER FUCKER! RIGHT HERE! FAT BOY HERE IS AN IMBECILE! I AM THE BRAINS BEHIND THIS OPERATION, ASSHOLE. NOW FUCK OFF!"

Remmick heard a beep and the phone went dead. He looked up at his windshield again to see if anyone was around. He had to go to the bathroom in the worst way.

"You had to do it," Karen spat. "You had to fucking do it."

"I know, I know, but listen," Remmick said, fumbling with his phone, sitting in Karen's cubicle. He found the CALL RECORDER icon and pushed it, then selected his last conversation from the drop-down and touched it with his finger. The phone call began to play. Karen's anger faded at the sounds of Klemmer's voice and the change that suddenly came over it.

"Who is that?" she asked.

"You tell me."

"Was someone there with him?"

Remmick looked at her, unblinking. She returned the stare icily, then her mouth opened wider and her eyes narrowed. "No way."

Remmick nodded.

"Same guy? Those two voices were the same person?"

"Unless he's working with someone else. We know the father's dead."

"Oh, he's dead alright. He belongs dead."

Remmick was taken aback by the remark.

"Look at this, " she said while producing a stack of printouts from the internet. "William B. Klemmer of Godfrey Avenue, Lawncrest, next street over from Brill."

Remmick looked at a legal document titled, *City of Philadelphia vs. William B. Klemmer.*

"It's a criminal complaint. I'll save you the time. Klemmer Senior was a wife abuser, child abuser and generally, a sociopath."

Remmick flipped through the multi-page document. "Hm. He beat the shit out of both of them. Enjoyed it."

"A third party called 911 that time, the next-door neighbor. The cops made the arrest based on the injuries, not because the wife or kid called them. The neighbor said she heard the blows and the screams right through her living room wall. And his laughter."

"Row-home living."

"And look at this," Karen said, handing him another document. "Another criminal complaint. This time, he assaulted some kid at a crime scene while he was working as a photographer."

He took the document and leafed through it, trying to read the poor rendering of Karen's low-on-toner laser printer. She summarized it for him.

"The cop who wrote the complaint said as they were bringing the body out of the building, Klemmer Senior pushed a teenager out of the way to get better camera position. When the kid gave him attitude, Senior produced one of those collapsible batons and whacked him across the face. The kid went down, unconscious. Ended up with a concussion and seven stitches above his left eye."

"Assault and battery. He admitted it, called the kid a 'parasite'."

"He pleaded guilty to that one. Did three years at CFCF, then paroled."

"CFCF?"

"Curran-Fromhold Correctional Facility."

"Oh, right. Anything else?"

"Yea, check this out," Karen replied and handed him a document. He took it and started reading. After a few seconds, he sat down.

"Jee-zuz," Remmick said, his eyes riveted on the document.

"Uh huh," said Karen. She watched Bud's eyes as they consumed sentences, moving left to right, then repeating.

"Arson, risking a catastrophe," Bud said out loud. "Endangering a minor."

"Father and son, photographing a fire. A fire that, according to the district attorney, the father set."

"Oh, man."

"There was a trial," said Karen, producing a photo copy of a newspaper article. "Found not guilty. Insufficient evidence, according to the jury foreman. No eyewitnesses. Weak forensics."

Bud looked up into Karen's eyes. "Christ, what a pair."

"And finally, this," she said, handing him another newspaper article. It was William B. Klemmer's obituary from the Inquirer. "Died of sudden cardiac arrest while sitting on the toilet."

"It happens. Pushing out a shit puts strain on an already weak heart. I've been on a call like that. Woman was dead on the toilet, underwear around her ankles. The rigor mortis froze her body in the sitting position."

"Thank you for that lovely image."

"Actually, it was kind of--" he began with a wistful look.

Horror was evident on Karen's face.

"Never mind."

"So, let's review," said Lt. Rosenstein, sitting at a ratty picnic table in Fairmount Park, with Karen and Bud on the opposite bench under an overcast sky, in the cold. "We have an illegal recording of a phone call and a bunch of public documents obtained from the internet for forty bucks, all of which, you claim, paints a picture of father-and-son psychos, one of whom has now assumed both personalities. Does that about sum it up?"

Karen and Bud looked at each other, then back at Rosenstein and simultaneously nodded.

"That is some fucked up shit," said Rosenstein. "And I'm supposed to do, what?"

As if choreographed, both shrugged their shoulders.

Rosenstein looked incredulous and said, "I ought to lock you both up right now."

"Oh, Tyler, cut the shit," said Karen. "The only thing that is maybe slightly illegal--"

"Recording a phone conversation without permission is more than slightly illegal, for fuck sake. This is Pennsylvania, kids, two-party consent, remember? You are supposedly in the news business."

"Fine. So, you'd like us to erase the phone conversation, then?"

Rosenstein held up his hand. "No, no. Not just yet."

"Right."

"It can't be used as evidence. In fact, no one on *earth* can know it even exists."

"Fine, fine."

"Just say the word and I'll delete it," added Bud with a sarcastic edge.

Silence fell over the picnic table as a chilly wind kicked up a food wrapper that was on the ground. The high was supposed to be in the mid 30's. It felt much colder at that moment.

"I'll use it as reference material," said Tyler. "No one will ever know that recording exists."

"You're welcome," said Remmick.

Rosenstein glared at Remmick, then turned to Karen and said, "I don't like him."

"Screw you, Lieutenant Drebin," Remmick shot back. "I don't see you and Police Squad doing anything groundbreaking. Have another Twinkie while we continue doing your job for you."

Rosenstein shot up from his seat and lunged across the picnic table to grab Remmick who jumped away just in the nick of time.

"Boys, boys," scolded Karen. "Please put your dicks back in your pants. I am duly impressed, of course, but knock it off."

Both men froze and relaxed. Bud put his hands in his pockets and walked away. Rosenstein continued glaring at him, standing his ground.

"As I mentioned before," Rosenstein said, "I don't like him."

"I get that. He's trying to help. He's finding his way."

"Whatever that means."

"Will you let me know if Mr. Klemmer turns up?"

"Yes."

"Thank you, Tyler," she said and turned to walk back to her Audi. Rosenstein also returned to his vehicle, one of the few Crown Vics left in the PPD fleet.

As she arrived at her car, Bud met her at the driver's side door.

"I'm sorry about that," he said contritely. "I know better. Therapy and all."

"Those homicide guys might not be as fast as we'd like them to be, but they do know what they're doing. Cut Tyler some slack, OK?"

"Yes, yes. I guess I just want something to happen now. I'm really dreading where this is going."

"I know. Have you thought about how this will play in public if it turns out to be true?"

"Not really. I'm saving that for my next sleepless night."

Karen unlocked the car and got into the driver's seat. Bud walked around to the passenger side and got in. The Audi backed out of its space and drove out the park exit onto Belmont Avenue for the quick trip back to Channel 7.

Rosenstein sat in his car in the adjacent lot and watched the Audi pull out and drive away. He decided he needed to know more about Bud Remmick.

Chapter 19 - That's My Boy!

Maggie couldn't sleep. Part of the problem was going to bed at 9 o'clock, early for her and, in her mind, for anyone who wasn't in their 80's. She had experienced some diverse emotions during her work day--stress, anxiety, unexpected sexual tension. So, she was exhausted. She'd left Bud sitting on the couch glaring at Beulah with the television tuned to a cooking show. She raised her head from her pillow and shot a glance at the digital clock on her night table--3:12 AM.

Now that she was awake, she was ruminating over her encounters with Marjorie Cutler. There was undeniable energy that both women felt, she thought, and it was, what, frightening? Annoying? Surprising? All of the above?

Bud had come to bed at some point and he lay on his side with his back to her. The good news was, he never snored. The bad news was, he farted mercilessly in bed. It was a feature she definitely did not miss while he was in prison.

In her current semi-fugue state, she wondered if sleeping with a lesbian would be different, the actual sleeping part, that is. Lesbians fart too, right? Would a woman be territorial about bed space, that imaginary line down the middle of the mattress? And anyway, what about sex? Never having had sex with another woman, Maggie wondered about the rituals, foreplay, who does what to whom and for how long?

She was nudged out of her fantasy by a rustling sound that came from outside. Probably a raccoon, she thought, but maybe not. She got out of bed and looked out the bedroom window, saw nothing, then padded down the carpeted steps into the living room. Beulah lay on the couch, breathing loudly, completely useless as a watch dog.

She continued into the kitchen, approached the door stealthily and peeked out through a space between the closed curtains. Squinting through the glare caused by the outside light, she saw the next-door neighbor, Les, rooting around in the honeysuckle bush that separated their properties, a curious activity at three in the morning. She saw only his head peeking over the bush, then disappearing behind it. He seemed to be reaching into it, looking for something. She watched patiently, keeping still behind the curtained door. As she strained to see what he might be reaching for, she caught a glint of light, like a reflection, coming from inside the honeysuckle. It came and went, obscured by the leaves and the sheer volume of the bush. Les stopped fiddling around in there, and finally went inside his apartment.

Maggie wasn't overly curious at that moment. She was tired, but not tired enough to go back upstairs. She made her way into the living room and plopped down next to Beulah who didn't budge. She picked up the remote, which turned the television on to Channel 7 and a rerun of last night's news. She stared, but didn't listen, hoping to become tired again.

Bud was vaguely aware of movement in the bed next to him. He felt alone, and not just because Maggie had left the room. Lately, he had been thinking about his parents, who disowned him after he went away. There was a tentative, almost grudging relationship between them and Maggie. They helped her financially during those years, allowing her to keep the house and pay the biggest bills. But there had been no contact with him while he was in jail or afterwards. His mom and dad were avowed patriots who believed law and order were paramount, bragged incessantly about being Americans and had no patience for even minor infractions of the law by human beings. Bud thought his father must have gotten nose bleeds sitting on that high horse, making pronouncements about life from his Archie Bunker chair while guzzling shots and beers and falling asleep drunk. So when Bud admitted killing a man, there was no forgiveness. The old man dug in. His mom was a reluctant participant. Her tearful goodbye the day he reported to prison was punctuated by the words, "I hope you learn your lesson in there." Those words remained tattooed onto Bud's brain during his four years of incarceration and even now, lying in bed alone.

He still had Maggie and Karen, and Tiffany, all strong women who accepted his past, seeing a good person buried somewhere in that mush of pissed-off persona. Aside from them, there was no one else left. Grappling with his sublimated anger was harder than he thought it would be. Accepting it was the first step, much like admitting he was an alcoholic. Now came the hardest part: Living life on Life's terms.

He glanced at the clock on his night table--5:04 AM. He sat up on the edge of the mattress and looked around the room as he did every morning, still grateful it was his bedroom and not his prison cell. He threw on a t-shirt and trudged towards the steps, making his way down to the living room. There lay Maggie on the couch in a fetal position, Beulah curled up in the pocket created by her bent legs. The television was tuned to the Channel 7 morning news. He moseyed over and gently moved the hair out of Maggie's face, bent down and gave her a peck on the forehead. A smile appeared. Beulah raised her head in alarm

"Ungrateful cur," he said without emotion. The dog regarded Bud with suspicion, as always, but dropped her head back into the comfort of Maggie's pocket. Maggie stirred and offered a yawn.

"Hey," she said. "What time is it?"

"Little after five. I'm making coffee."

"It's Tuesday, right?"

"Yes."

"I hate Tuesday."

"Yea, me too. Tuesday has no feel."

Maggie opened her eyes and raised her head. "Seinfeld?"

"Newman," he corrected. "He was absolutely correct."

There was no further conversation as Bud staggered around the small kitchen, filling the coffee pot with water, measuring out Folger's then dumping it into the filter and pushing the brew button. Maggie dragged herself off the couch, much to Beulah's chagrin, gave her a quick pat on the head and made her way back upstairs to take a shower.

Two-hundred miles to the east, a meaty, smelly hand reached into a motel shower and turned on the hot water, felt the temperature for a few seconds, then turned on the cold and gauged the temperature of the mixture. The heaving, naked body of Bill Klemmer was bent over at about 90-degrees as he fiddled with the water knobs, then pulled back the off-white, vinyl shower curtain and eased into the stall. The hot water felt good on his ample mass, though he had to constantly shift position so the stream would hit all parts of his body. He usually avoided getting his hair wet so as not to disturb the delicate balance of chemicals and scalp gunk that facilitated the shaping of his coif. But in this case, he felt the need for a complete cleanse. The sound of the water beating down on him, the steam and the sensation of the slick, porcelain surface against the bottoms of his feet transported him to a faraway place where he had no name and no agenda. The Dorito crumbs washed away. He turned his back to the shower and parted his cheeks to allow the water to get into his crack, though he was unable to reach all the way around with the washcloth to get any soap up there.

Approximately fifty yards away, a Beach City Police car was parked on a small street that ran perpendicular to Bay Avenue, affording an unobstructed view of the Seahorse Inn and the single car parked in the lot. The officer who sat at the wheel held a small pair of binoculars to his eyes and held his breath as he studied the car. He set down the glasses, withdrew a pen from his breast pocket and wrote down the license number. He woke up his dash-mounted computer and typed in the license number and hit ENTER.

Klemmer swayed as he stood in the shower, conscious but dreamy as the water pummeled him. He had a vague memory of a phone call last night but couldn't remember who it was or what it was about. No matter, he mused, I'm all set. He thought of exploring this end of the island, finding a store to pick up more food and sodas, then figure out where he would go next.

The Beach City police officer read the information on his screen and his eyes widened.

"Whoa," he said out loud, then picked up the microphone and clicked the push-to-talk button.

A soulless Tuesday greeted the Remmicks, who navigated their respective paths to their jobs. Bud was anxious about the search for Bill Klemmer. Maggie's anxiety about her future at the County returned. She longed for action, one way or the other, because the unknown was killing her. For so long, she had wanted a seat at the table, a role as a decision-maker to better the lives of older people. Now that she had it, she realized the cost might be too high. Politics was never part of the bargain, she thought. But it was, and it sucked.

And the hits kept on coming. She logged on to her Outlook account and got a calendar alert about a conference call with Governor Franklin in an hour. It was placed there by her boss, Marjorie. She picked up the phone and dialed.

"A conference call with the Governor?" she asked. "Really?"

"It's routine," Marjorie answered. "I thought I'd include you this time so you can hear what Satan sounds like. Keep your phone on mute and just listen."

"Why?"

"It's a ritual. It's his County call. He gets a Commissioner from each county on the horn every couple months and listens to them kiss his ass and offer affirmation of his inspiring leadership. It's a pointless exercise that accomplishes nothing except it keeps the wheels of government slathered in bullshit, which seems to be necessary in Pennsylvania."

"Jeez."

"Yea, just go with it. You might enjoy it."

"I will not."

In the other part of Pennsylvania where the other Remmick worked, there was a flurry of newsroom activity revolving around a multiple shooting in Kensington, a neighborhood rife with drug dealing and almost daily opioid overdoses.

"Things sure have changed there," said Bud to Nancy. "That used to be a nice, working class neighborhood."

"Yea? What century was that?"

"Not so long ago. Maybe ten years? You were, what, 12 at the time?"

"Fifteen. You, being as old as you are, would remember."

Resisting the urge to load a pithy comeback, Bud jammed his hands into his pockets and walked away. Nancy returned her attention to the police scanner, which crackled with activity. What was it Gordon called her, a good kid?

As Bud stalked away from the assignment desk, he spied Karen waving him over to her cubicle, her phone to her ear. As he got closer, he heard her speak.

"So, where is this happening?" she asked the party on the phone. Bud stood quietly, waiting to hear the rest of her conversation. "Beach City," she said.

Bud's interest was spiked now.

"OK, call me back when you can," she said, then took the receiver away from her ear, looked at it and hung it up.

"What's up?" asked Bud.

"Tyler is on his way to Beach City, New Jersey. A local cop found Klemmer's Camry parked in a motel lot. They are deciding whether to knock on the door or wait until he comes out."

"Damn. Finally."

"They want to surprise him, minimize the risk of him trying to take off or, god knows what."

"What does that mean?"

"They assume that if he did kill someone, he might do it again. So they plan for the worst."

"And so?"

"And so, Tyler is on his way down there and he'll call us when there's something to report."

"Well, we need to go there too. Right now."

"Yea. In the old days, we'd have the chopper outside and could make it down there in twenty minutes."

"I want to go. I want to."

"*I want to*", she said, mocking him. "What are you, three?"

"I'd just be sitting around, getting pissed off at NewsCrash. Let me field-produce. Send me with a photographer and a van."

"You need to be here and be the News Director, Bud."

"I am the News Director and I am directing myself to cover the news."

Karen recognized that this had the potential to be a huge story, and having the station's News Director there to supervise coverage might not be a bad thing.

"Oh, fine."

"Sulu, you've got the con," he barked at Karen, who had no idea what that meant.

A hearty laugh came through the speaker on Maggie's office phone. After dialing in to the conference call, she placed her phone on "mute" as instructed by Marjorie and listened. Governor Franklin was in his glory, holding despotic court in a voice that filled Maggie's office through the tiny phone speaker.

"That is so very true, Malcolm," he said to the Cumberland County Commissioner. "The customer is *not* always right, eh?"

Chuckles were heard on the call. One party was engaged in a full-throated guffaw over the remark.

"Don't swallow your tongue there, Rudy," bellowed Franklin. "Jesus Christ, does anyone know CPR?"

More laughs ensued. Maggie rolled her eyes. She was staring at a spreadsheet on her screen, trying to study purchase orders and dollar amounts, keeping the conference call audio just audible.

"Hey Leonard, you still awake?" asked Franklin.

"Of course, Governor," replied Leonard Francona, the Livingston County Commissioner.

"Any progress on the personnel front?"

"Moving in the right direction, Governor. We've received your recommendations for the post in question and are setting up interviews."

"And the incumbent?"

"She is still on the payroll."

"Any opposition from the Dems?"

"We haven't actually told them yet."

"Well, this will reach a head soon. Anything else on anyone's mind?"

Sweet silence came across Maggie's speaker.

"OK, til next time," said the Governor. "Thank you all."

Each participant offered a "Have a good day" or the like, and multiple beeps were heard as the parties dropped off the call.

Maggie sat quietly, disturbed by the portion of the conversation that was about her. Several seconds later, her phone rang.

"Hello?" she answered listlessly.

"Don't worry about it," said Marjorie.

"That so-called personnel issue is me, right?"

"Yes, but don't worry about it."

"Seems like the right time to worry, don't you think?"

"Maggie. Do. Not. Worry. About. It."

Maggie sat with the phone to her ear for several seconds then said, "What magic do you command?"

"As I told you before, do your job and stay under the radar."

"Fine. Good bye."

Bud sat in the rear-most seat of the news van known as Mobile 4, surrounded by gear and strapped in by a lap belt that dug into his lower abdomen. Driving was Jonathan Carter, photographer, and Kojo, the technician, whose proper Nigerian name was impossible for anyone other than him to pronounce. They were doing 65 on the Atlantic City Expressway, which would take them to the Garden State Parkway, then to Route 9 and, eventually, the south end of Beach City. It was almost a two-hour drive.

"Are we gonna have time for lunch?" asked Carter.

"I don't know, Jonathan," answered Bud.

"Will there be overtime?"

"I don't know, Jonathan."

"Will there be hazardous duty pay?"

"Probably not, Jonathan."

"Because I don't have to perform no hazardous duty."

"Hey Jonathan?"

"Yea?"

"As far as I'm concerned, you don't have to perform any duty at all. In fact, when we get back, I'll arrange with Gordon for you to have a regular, nine-to-five shift in the ENG shop. That way, you'll get lunch every day at noon, no overtime, no hazardous duty, no photography, no glory. Just you and a soldering iron, plenty of spare time for LOLing and complaining, a regular job that will bore the shit out of you. And, I'll make sure your union rep is aware of the conversation we're having right now. OK?"

Carter had no response, but kept his eyes on the road, glancing in the rear-view mirror where he spied Remmick staring at him.

"I didn't hear you, Jonathan, is that OK?"

"I get it."

There was no further conversation during the remaining ninety minutes of the drive.

Lt. Rosenstein had already gotten off the Atlantic City Expressway and was now on the southbound Parkway doing close to 90. The old Crown Vic's V-8 was still a monster, accelerating at the mere touch of the gas pedal. He had just gotten off the phone with the Ocean County SWAT commander who had been called in by the locals, a bit of overkill, he thought, but better to be safe than sorry. They were gathering to assume a position outside a motel called the Seahorse Inn on Bay Avenue. At this point, no one had even spoken with the subject Klemmer. They only assumed he was the driver of the killer Camry and was present in the motel. Rosenstein had obtained his cell phone number from Channel 7, but the phone went unanswered, not even triggering voicemail.

The SWAT commander had arrived on scene a while ago. Rosenstein found himself hoping that this Klemmer character would open the door, raise his hands and walk freely out of the room into the waiting arms of the police. The photo he had showed a large man who might be formidable if he decided to resist. These and other random thoughts raced through his mind as he sped towards Beach City and whatever awaited him there.

Inside room 207, Klemmer sat on his bed wearing only a bath towel, watching *Star Trek II: The Wrath of Khan* on HBO and guzzling diet Dr. Pepper. He had disabled voicemail and removed the battery from his phone, remembering seeing that on *The Wire* and thinking it would prevent him from being tracked. He looked at his disassembled phone and his pistol on the bed next to him and smiled the self-assured smile of someone who had prepared for all contingencies, a mastermind adept at thinking on his feet, requiring no prompting from... anyone. He was as relaxed as he'd ever been, feeling his eyelids getting heavy and start closing.

"I am, and always shall be, your friend," Klemmer heard a dying Spock say to Kirk, words he imagined were meant for him. Tears welled up in his eyes as he watched Spock perish in the radiation-filled chamber, having just saved the Enterprise and all on board.

Klemmer was snapped back to full consciousness by a sharp knock on his door.

Maggie's world had become more claustrophobic and more uncertain, if that were even possible. Her reassurances from Marjorie were not reassuring. Hearing the Governor of Pennsylvania plotting about her on an open phone call greatly disturbed her, not only because she was the subject of the conversation but because the Governor had no qualms about discussing it with a bunch of supplicants. To them, she was just a body, a placeholder in a job that was coveted by political whores. It was all disgusting, but not surprising.

"Mrs. Remmick, line 2," came Angela's voice through the intercom. "Someone named John."

Maggie thought about all the Johns it could be and only one came to mind.

"Thanks," she said and punched line 2 on her phone. "Hello?"

"Hi, Mrs. Remmick, it's John," said John Ungar.

"Hello. What's going--"

"Please," he interrupted. "What's your cell number?"

She provided it.

"Wait five minutes, then step outside so I can call you."

"Uh, OK."

"Everything OK?" called Angela through the open office door. What does she care, Maggie wondered?

"Yea, fine. An old pal."

Maggie busied herself by signing purchase orders for a couple minutes, then rose from her desk, slipped on her coat and walked out past Angela. "I'm going out for some air," she said. Angela glanced at her as she passed, then turned her attention back to whatever she was working on.

Maggie took the elevator down to ground level and walked outside towards the parking lot. She stopped at one of the concrete benches that lined the oval in front of the main entrance and sat down, pulling out her phone. Fortunately, it was above freezing. As if on cue, her phone rang. The caller ID showed a number with a 732 area code.

"Hello?"

"Hi, Mrs. Remmick," replied Ungar. "Best we communicate via cell phone for now."

"OK. What's going on?"

"I've become aware that someone is spying on you."

"Spying?"

"I was a party to a conversation involving Governor Franklin."

"Oh? A conversation?"

"A Skype call about prisons. It's not important. But Franklin made it very clear he's got one or more people checking on you in some way. I only know that you were mentioned specifically and that he, in his words, has eyes on you."

Maggie's blood ran cold. Her chest tightened and anger started welling up. "That motherfucker."

"Sorry to upset you, but I thought you should know."

"This just gets better and better. I heard him on a conference call earlier today talking about me, indirectly, about his flunkies interviewing candidates for my job."

"Sorry, wish I knew more. I would advise you to think about who might be gathering information on you. Maybe watch what you say? I dunno."

"I'll do that. Thank you again, John."

"OK, good luck."

She set her phone down on the bench next to her and looked off into the distance. There was no wind, which made the cold tolerable. She felt tears welling up and started sniffling. The tears came hard and fast. She felt stupid and childish, stifling a sob but unable to stop the flow. It continued for a good minute or two, after which she reached into her bag for a tissue and started coming out of it. She was grateful she was alone. She reached for her phone and pushed the MESSAGE icon to send a text. She selected the photo of Bud, then typed into the message field, "The vultures are circling." She punched the little arrow icon to send it. She took a deep breath and stared off into the distance again. She stood up, turned back towards the building, took a deep breath and walked back inside.

Bud's cellphone was deep in an inner pocket of his parka so he didn't feel it vibrate. His attention was focused instead on a scene of heavy police presence two long blocks up Bay Avenue from the Seahorse Inn. Carter had navigated the van as close as the yellow barricades allowed. They parked and got out. Carter and Kojo rooted around in the van's rear compartment for gear while Remmick scanned the distant scene for any sign of Lt. Rosenstein. He approached a uniformed officer standing at the barricade closest to them and flashed his Channel 7 ID.

"We're with Channel 7," he said with authority. "Can we get closer?"

The officer looked closely at the ID, nodded his head and smugly said, "No."

"Seriously? We just need to set up--"

"No," interrupted the officer with a grin dripping with contempt.

Remmick stared at him, pondered a nasty comeback, then turned and walked back to the van. Carter was readying his camera while Kojo began setting up the dish.

"Looks like this is as close as we get," Remmick said.

"We heard," replied Kojo.

"Local cops are all pricks," said Carter. "Fucking ticket-writers with delusions of grandeur."

The officer turned around and looked at Carter.

"Yea, I'm talking about you, Goober," Carter said. The officer smiled his snotty smile and said nothing.

"You're not helping," barked Remmick. "Please shut the fuck up."

Carter glared at him, but complied. Remmick took his phone out and began to dial Karen's number when he saw the text from Maggie.

"Christ," he said under his breath. He pressed REPLY and typed, "At shore looking for bad guy... talk soon." He pushed the SEND arrow, then pushed the CONTACTS button and found Karen's number, then pushed CALL. She answered after two rings.

"Hi," she said.

"Hey. We're here. Cops won't let us near. I see the motel but no Rosenstein. You heard from him?"

"No. I'll let you know if I hear anything."

"OK, bye."

Remmick and his crew were unable to see the scene at the front of room 207. A team of six armed officers in dark clothing and helmets, three holding MP5 submachine guns and three with shotguns, were off to the side of the door while the point officer, a sergeant wielding a shotgun, knocked.

"Good morning, this is the police. Is there a William Klemmer here?"

Klemmer picked up the remote to mute the television, then picked up the pistol in a reflex motion. He froze on his bed.

Another knock. "Police. Open the door, please."

"OK, hang on," Klemmer replied in a weak voice. "Putting on pants."

"Let's go, sir, open the door right now." The police waited. The team at the side of the door tried to peer into the window but the heavy shades blocked any view. The officer pounded on the door.

"WHY DON'T YOU PISS OFF AND LET ME DO MY WORK," came a different voice from inside. The officer was taken aback. "THIS BOY WILL DO YOU NO GOOD. HE IS WORTHLESS."

The officer conferred with his team. "I think there are two people in there. Prepare to breach."

"THIS CLUELESS YOUNGSTER CAN'T HURT YOU. HE CAN BARELY DO WHAT I TELL HIM, LET ALONE FOLLOW YOUR ORDERS."

With a loud thud, the door of the motel room swung open and the SWAT officers poured in and were greeted by the sight of a large man sitting naked on the bed with a towel over his lap holding a pistol to his head.

"Drop the weapon!" came the shouts of the officers. "Drop the weapon now!"

Klemmer had a peaceful look on his face as he held the pistol to his head with his right hand. He sat on the bed, the SWAT team less than six feet in front of him. He lowered the pistol from his head.

"Drop the gun right now!" came the frenzied shout from several of the officers.

He began turning the barrel towards the team when three loud shots rang out sending projectiles at Klemmer's hand, face and chest. Klemmer slumped. The pistol flew out of his hand, unfired, as his face hit the carpet. Two members of the team split off, heading to the bathroom, then the closet, looking for a second man.

The sergeant kicked the pistol away from Klemmer, who was face down on the floor and bleeding. "Get the medics in," he commanded.

"There's no one else here," said one of the pair who split off to secure the room. "Just him."

The sergeant looked down at Klemmer as the tactical medics knelt down and started tending to the wounded man. "Pulse and breathing, contusion under the left eye, hematoma on the sternum," said one of them.

"That'll be a nasty welt," said one of the officers. "Those bean-bag rounds hurt."

The sergeant knelt down onto the floor next to Klemmer, who had been rolled onto his back so the medics could treat him. "Are you William Klemmer?"

Klemmer opened his eyes to view the source of the voice. He gave the cop a vague smile and said in a raspy voice, "That's my boy."

Chapter 20 - Turning Points

Karen edited copy as the clock ticked relentlessly towards 5:00 PM. The kids were doing their best, cranking out copy on the new lead story, editing the video to match their scripts. While it was brilliant to have a crew, live truck and producer at the scene in Beach City, it would have been even more brilliant to have a reporter. At the time, however, Karen thought the fewer people who knew what was going on, the better in case it all turned out to be bullshit. Not only was it not bullshit, it was an exclusive that would catch the other TV stations by surprise. There was no police radio traffic on the operation, so the scanner hounds heard nothing. And by the time word got out that there had been a shooting and a police operation at the Seahorse Inn, it was too late in the afternoon for the stations to do much about it except show a map.

Karen hit ENTER for the last time, putting the last piece of copy to bed at 4:50 PM. She looked across the newsroom and saw Reg sitting at his desk, apparently relaxed and waiting for the show to start. Nancy sat with a phone to her ear, as always. Rita, producing the 5:00 PM show, was already in the control room. A production assistant gathered the last hard copies of scripts, placed them in order and ran them into the studio to the anchor.

Roy Strickland appeared at Karen's cubicle. "Mind if I join you?"

"Not at all. I'm hoping you're going to like what you see."

Strickland pulled up a chair and sat next to Karen. Both were poised in front of Karen's 20-inch monitor, which now displayed Channel 7's air. Pam Whitehead was the anchor.

"Good evening. Police at the Jersey Shore resort of Beach City have shot a man who is described by sources as a person of interest in a hit-and-run killing in South Philadelphia last week. Police say the man, whom they decline to identify, pulled a gun on police as they confronted him at this motel, the Seahorse Inn on Bay Avenue, this afternoon. No police were injured in the operation, which included Beach City Police, Ocean County SWAT and the Philadelphia Police Homicide Division."

Video of police vehicles and a black, unmarked van appeared on the screen. Numerous uniformed men and women were seen in motion. After 10-seconds, the video cut to a distant shot of a large mound of a person lying on a wheeled stretcher being pushed into the back of an ambulance. It was impossible to see the person's face.

"Jeez, I guess that's him," said Strickland.

"Look," said Karen, pointing to the other monitors showing the other stations' air. "No one else has shit."

She and Strickland traded a high-five. Pam continued reading from the prompter.

"Sources tell Channel 7 News the suspect is wanted for questioning in the death of Jerome Highland, the man whose skull was crushed while he slept in a makeshift tent on Federal Street. Details of the confrontation at the motel have not yet been released. The wounded man is currently listed in stable condition at Shore Medical Center in Somers Point."

Remmick had come up for air after feeding the scene video from Mobile 4, then trying to track down Lt. Rosenstein. He thought the number of cops at this scene far exceeded the need, but what did he know? None of the uniformed cops at the perimeter knew anything. All the info Channel 7 obtained came from a brief chat Karen had with Rosenstein on the fly, who confirmed the man who was shot matched the driver's license photo they had of William Klemmer.

Remmick sat down inside the truck and punched Karen's speed-dial number on his phone.

"Hi, hotshot," she answered.

"Hello. How we doing?"

"We just kicked the competition's ass."

"Good. I don't know what more we can do here. These scene cops are useless. They're keeping us far away. It was a horror show just getting that distant shot of the stretcher."

"We're sending you some relief. Reporter Aaron James, a new photographer and a truck op. They left an hour ago, so you'll see them soon."

"Great, that'll make Jonathan Carter very happy. What a jerk-off."

"They're bringing the second satellite truck to stake out the hospital. That's where the cops will be talking later on."

"Oh, then maybe I should stay?"

"No need. Tyler is with the program, which means he'll call me."

"OK. I've had enough encounters with belligerent assholes for one day."

Karen's phone beeped the call-waiting tone. "Shit, there he is now. Later."

"Bye."

Karen pushed the green button that activated the second incoming call. "Hello?"

"What a pig-fuck down here," said Rosenstein without a greeting. "These Jersey guys are everything I hoped and dreamed for."

"I owe you big."

"Yes, you do. These cops down here *really* hate reporters."

"So, what can you tell me?"

"That Klemmer dude is whacked. His voice changes, like he's two people. I asked him if he knew where he was, what was going on. He looked at me like I was from Mars, then started babbling in this affected, raspy, deep voice, talking about his work, the boy, all kinds of bizarre shit."

"I'm surprised they didn't kill him."

"They used non-lethal, bean-bag shotgun rounds. He has a couple broken fingers, fractured sternum, fractured orbit under his left eye."

"And so, he will live to spend a long time in jail."

"Unless we get him for murder, then he will get the big squirt. As for those other jobs you told me about, I got nothing but your hunch on them."

"Not quite. There's an arson investigation underway on two of the fires, remember?"

"Oh, right."

"How quickly we forget. If they can match evidence at the fires with stuff in his house or his car, he's nailed."

"I knew that."

"Of course you did, Tyler. You are The Man."

"I have to get to the command post. The Beach City Chief is here. He's a blowhard out for his fifteen minutes. Bye."

Karen punched her HANG UP button and turned to Strickland.

"You've been a busy lady," he said to her with a satisfied grin.

"All my boys, calling in to momma," she replied. "It's what I do."

Maggie was so preoccupied she didn't even remember the drive home. She remembered getting into the Subaru in the County lot, turning on Sirius to the classical channel, then getting out of her car in the driveway. Autopilot, she thought, a scary proposition.

Beulah greeted her at the door as she did every day, and offered an animated, four-legged dance. Maggie pushed past her to enter the living room, shut the door behind her, dropped her bag and coat on the floor and headed to the far-left kitchen cabinet. She was elated to find an almost-full bottle of Absolut and a half bottle of dry vermouth. The vodka filled a rock glass about two thirds of the way. She dusted it with barely the scent of vermouth, then tossed in two ice cubes and retreated to the sofa where Beulah awaited. She sat in silence. Beulah studied her as she lifted the glass to her lips, sipped, then lowered the glass to her knee. She was depressed, bordering on despondent. How did she end up here, in the sticks, with the Governor of Pennsylvania after her job? How did she end up married to a guy who got locked up for manslaughter? Why is she a magnet for sleazy lawyers and frustrated bureaucrats of both genders?

"Why, Beulah, why?" Beulah responded by resting her head on Maggie's right thigh, an act which earned her a scratch behind the ear. She took a long hit of her beverage, then put the glass down on the coffee table, rose from the couch and went to the bedroom to grab her laptop. She sat on the bed, legs crossed, opened the laptop and clicked on the web browser icon for Indeed.com. She typed into the search window words that included *director, government, elderly*, clicked SEARCH and watched a list of results populate her screen. She rejected all the jobs at assisted living facilities and nursing homes. This left three listings--Director of Government Affairs for an eldercare non-profit, a non-paid internship at a senior center three towns away and an interim Director of Programs for the Elderly at the YMCA of Graycote County, a mere 65 miles to the west, with a salary range of $35,000 to $45,000. Maggie's head dropped in disgust. She slapped the laptop closed, frisbee'd it onto the bed and returned to the couch where she resumed drinking.

Next door, Les Noble was watching the news on Channel 7, riveted by the Beach City story. He'd never been involved in a tactical operation and was fascinated by the lingo, the video and the unfolding scenario. The video of the man on the stretcher was unrevealing but Noble caught a quick shot of a familiar face. It lasted not even a second, but he recognized the person immediately. He reached for his remote and pushed the reverse button for his DVR, taking the video back to that moment, which he paused to freeze on the screen. There he was, Bud Remmick, his neighbor, whisking past the camera for a split second.

"Huh," Nobel grunted, remembering Bud had been on a job interview. "Guess he got the job." He pushed the proper buttons on the remote to save the video for possible future use, then pushed the button to return to live TV. There was now a 50-ish man in a white shirt and burgundy striped tie speaking in front of a live camera with the words "Live: Beach City, NJ" across the bottom of the screen. The man was speaking about the events at the Seahorse Inn. The words across the bottom of the screen changed to "Live: Lt. Tyler Rosenstein, Philadelphia Police."

"The investigation is ongoing," he told a small group of gathered media. "We developed information that this individual's car was at the scene of a fatal hit and run in South Philadelphia last week. We have been looking for him to ask him what he might know about that incident. The license plate was posted on NCIC. A local police officer spotted a car matching the description at the Seahorse Inn and ran the license plate to confirm. Ocean County SWAT was called as a precaution and a tactical entrance was made to the individual's room. It was during that entry that the officers confronted the subject, who then pointed a pistol at them. They responded appropriately."

"Can you identify him?" yelled one reporter. "What's his condition?" yelled another.

"At this time, we are not identifying him," Rosenstein replied. "We are still investigating who he is and what his role was in the Philadelphia incident. We are also looking for any family members. He is listed in stable condition and he has been speaking to us."

Multiple questions were shouted, but Rosenstein raised his hands and said, "The Beach City Chief of Police has a few words, then we're done."

Noble watched with amusement as Rosenstein ceded the makeshift podium to a larger, older man in a formal police uniform, bristling with ribbons and gold-braided epaulets. The Chief made a speech dripping with platitudes and praise for all involved, turned to shake the hand of the SWAT commander, took no questions and walked away.

Noble clicked the DVR button to review his recording one more time. Bud Remmick, caught on video. What could he possibly use this for?

Later that evening, Remmick sat in the rear of Mobile 4 as he and his team drove back to Philadelphia. He nodded off a couple times. Carter drove and was silent. Kojo, riding shotgun, was also quiet. Remmick had forgotten how taxing field producing was, physically as well as mentally. He was on his feet and walking for hours, and he felt it now. He hadn't had any continuous exercise since his prison days.

"Nice work today, guys," he said to his partners. "You really hustled at every turn and I appreciate it."

"Glad it worked out," Carter replied without emotion.

Bud's eyes tried to scan the vista passing at 70 miles an hour in the darkness through the window of the van. The Garden State Parkway did not offer spectacular scenery, especially at night. He stared off into the void and enjoyed having nothing on his mind. As though the God of Pregnant Timing was watching, Bud's cellphone rang. He grudgingly reached for it, looked at the number, and pushed TALK.

"Hello," he said listlessly.

"Hi," replied Karen. "Are you ready for this?"

Bud stirred uncomfortably, his brow forming a scowl. "What?"

"He's giving it all up."

"Who? What?"

"Klemmer. He confessed to everything."

"What's everything?"

"The hit and run, the fires, more fires. Tyler was almost giddy, which is disturbing all on its own."

Bud tried to process what it all meant. He had a feeling of dread he couldn't isolate. It was poking him in the stomach.

"But he's crazy," offered Bud. "Where's his credibility?"

"He gave up specifics of each job that only the perp would know--the brand of linseed oil used, the brand of plastic tape he bound the rag boxes with. And a play by play of the murder of the homeless guy that matches the video. Says his father told him to do it. Now he's got a public defender, so the gold mine of info has been capped, but Tyler has enough to go for murder on the homeless guy and is reviewing the physical evidence in the two most recent fires."

Bud rubbed his eyes with the one hand that wasn't holding the phone. "Great. And what about us?"

"You mean, all that video that we so eagerly purchased and ran with?" asked Karen.

"Yea, all that video. I hope Strickland's getting the lawyers on the horn right now to deal with any public backlash. We need it out there ASAP that the station had *no idea* what Klemmer was doing. We need to pull all that video and *not* air it again. We can't be seen as profiting from a psychopath's work."

"You're right. I'll call Strickland at home."

"And then, you and I can figure out where our next jobs will be, maybe picking up dog shit in people's yards for $10 an hour. I've got experience."

It was cool, quiet and pleasantly foggy where Klemmer found himself, floating on a cloud of oblivion. He was on a fentanyl high, courtesy of nurse René at Shore Medical Center. Not only did he feel no pain, but he was euphoric and had no desire to think, speak or move. He was in the hands of god and his father now, with a little help from modern chemistry.

There was the lieutenant guy, Rosenberg or Rosenstein or maybe just Rosen, who spoke with his father. That was a cool conversation because dad related everything, left out no details. That would be dad all over, Klemmer thought, the king of minutia. It was satisfying to hear it all played back, nostalgic even. All that great video, the money he earned. It had been worthwhile, really, even despite today's setback. Couldn't wait to get back to it, once his visit to his private little cloud was over.

"Mr. Klemmer, can you hear me OK?" came a voice he hadn't heard before.

He snapped out of his reverie and opened his eyes.

"I'm Doctor Lorraine Cavanaugh. Can I ask you a few questions?"

"OK."

"Where does it hurt the most right now?"

"Nothing hurts right now."

"OK. Um, is anybody else here?"

"Wait, who are you again?"

"Dr. Cavanaugh."

"AND WHAT THE FUCK DO YOU WANT?" barked the second voice, raspy and deep.

"Who am I speaking with?"

"HOW ABOUT I SMACK YOUR ASS ACROSS THE ROOM, YOU IGNORANT CUNT?" Klemmer's face had taken on a blank quality, eyes focused somewhere far away, his lips tightened as he formed the words. Despite the bile, he was in no condition to act on his words.

"Why are you so angry?"

Klemmer's eyes moved over her face, his mouth remaining open. "WHY ARE YOU HERE?"

"I'm a forensic psychiatrist. I've been called in by the attending physician for a consult."

Klemmer's eyes fluttered and he took tentative breaths as he tried to speak again. "You are mistaken," he said in his original voice.

"Mistaken about what?"

"About my father," he replied in a near-whisper with his eyes closing. "He is not dead."

His head turned to the side, his eyes closed and he fell asleep. The doctor glanced at the monitor which registered a steady 58 beats per minute, BP of 110/58 and O2 saturation at 98%.

"What do we know about his father?" she asked Rosenstein.

"He died a couple years ago. He was abusive, had anger issues, did time for assault, started a fire, took the son with him at one time."

"Hm, interesting. Seems like he has assumed his father's persona."

Rosenstein looked at Klemmer as he slept and said nothing.

"And you think he committed those crimes? The tent guy, the arsons?" she asked.

"Yea, and then videotaped the crime scenes to sell to Channel 7. I'm not sure which is sicker, doing the crimes or making video of them for money."

"It's a package deal. This young man, I suspect, has nothing else in his life except what his father taught him. It has replaced any sense of right and wrong he might once have possessed. And when he is repulsed by his own actions, the father persona emerges and takes over. I'd be curious to find out who was doing the crimes, the father or the son."

"They're one and the same as far as I'm concerned. A finely tuned Crazy Machine."

"His mental state will be a major factor going forward," she said, then walked out of the room.

Rosenstein was already putting those pieces together. Whether or not William Klemmer would be found insane, Rosenstein was confident he'd never walk the streets again. Of course, this was New Jersey, and stranger things have happened.

"Christ, I think I'm gonna be sick," came the disgusted voice over Skype in Roy Strickland's office. Strickland and Karen sat on opposite sides of the desk, watching attorney Lee Cameron clutch his chest.

"This guy did crimes, then videoed them, then sold the video to your station, which you aired on multiple occasions?" Cameron asked. "Please don't tell me that."

"That's what we are telling you," said Strickland. "And today, the idiot was shot by police, but he's not dead."

"Again, you're not shitting me?"

"And, he confessed," added Karen. "In detail, in the voice of his dead father, whose personality he has taken on."

"Now you're shitting me. You're shitting me, right?"

"Lee, I wish we were," said Strickland.

There was silence in the room for many seconds. Roy and Karen watched Cameron hang his head, swing it back and forth a couple times followed by a couple of weak exhalations.

"Lee?" Roy asked.

"Quiet, I'm thinking."

Karen and Roy looked at each other across Roy's desk. Karen lifted her mug to sip the coffee that had been cooking all day in Roy's coffee pot. It was disgusting and her face showed it.

"Well," Lee said, "I see no alternative."

Roy and Karen leaned towards the computer monitor.

"It pains me to say it, even think it. It's not the way I would normally go because it's making my heart attack much more severe and, well, the drugs only do so much, you know."

Roy and Karen waited. Waited.

"We'll have to tell the truth."

Roy and Karen looked at each other. "Well, no shit, I assumed that," said Strickland.

"The truth is so fucked up," continued Cameron, "no one could possibly think we're making it up."

"Thank you, Lee, how reassuring."

"You gotta stop using his video."

"We already thought of that," said Karen.

"And I'll write you up a statement to release to the other news media and the public, something contrite and pandering and apologetic. Get your anchor to read it on the late news tonight. We gotta get out in front of this."

"Right," said Karen.

"And tomorrow, you guys are going figure out how this mental case could get away with this for, what, two years? *Two years?*"

"Yea," said Roy. "Fine."

"Good bye," said the lawyer. The screen went dark followed by a beep signaling the end of the call.

Roy and Karen stared at the dark monitor for a few seconds, then Roy said, "This could be the biggest ratings bump we've ever had."

"Or, it could be the end of all our careers."

Chapter 21 - Revelation

The headlines changed over the next 48 hours, morphing from *Murder Suspect Shot by Police* to *Channel 7 Pays Accused Killer for News*. Lee Cameron, corporate attorney for Channel 7, read the newspapers. He was earning his legal fees now, fielding subpoenas, phone calls and emails from prosecutors, police, news organizations and his clients at Channel 7. Cameron wasn't a well man-- overweight, dependent on sugar, tobacco and alcohol, gray-white hair so thin that bald would have been better and a case of A-fib and the meds to prove it. At age 69, he'd been ready to retire ages ago, but his kids' college loans stood in the way and his retirement savings were a joke. The new developments at Channel 7 gave him a stomach ache, literally.

The station had done its best to deal with the media onslaught. The statement he had crafted was read during multiple newscasts. It was emailed to every newspaper and online news agency they could think of and posted on all the station's social media channels. The statement read:

"Channel 7 has learned that an individual has been charged with committing crimes he later recorded on video and sold to our station, video which we aired from time to time over the past two years. Channel 7 had no knowledge of this alleged criminal behavior prior to two days ago when the individual was shot by police and later, police tell us, confessed to these crimes. Channel 7 has pulled all the video in question from our archives and will not use it again. We are extremely disturbed by the allegations. Channel 7 is cooperating fully with all law enforcement agencies and joins the city of Philadelphia in seeking justice for these crimes."

Cameron thought it could have been even more humble but it was fine for now. Whether it would help Channel 7 in the long run remained to be seen. However, what didn't help was that the world now became aware that the station's news director was a man who did prison time for a killing, a salacious fact that made it a much juicier story. The television column in the Inquirer was all over it and the Daily News followed suit. *Channel Seven: Killer's Heaven,* read the Daily News headline. Cameron cut that one out and taped it to his computer monitor.

"Mr. Cameron, Roy Strickland on Skype," came the voice over the intercom. "Can you join?"

"Great, thanks," he replied and stared at his computer, clicked several icons, turned up the volume and was face to face with Roy Strickland. "What?" he barked.

"Hello to you, too. How are we doing?"

"Did you see today's Daily News?"

"Yep."

"That about sums it up. Your station is a tabloid shithole."

"I don't care. We've been a shithole for years. Now, we are a highly viewed shithole."

The attorney sniffed into the phone, then popped an Altoid to open up his sinuses. "You're talking about ratings, for Christ sake?"

"Yes, of course. We haven't had a spike in viewership like this in a decade. It's an opportunity."

"God, I despise that 'opportunity' metaphor. Can't you just enjoy your bulbous, new erection without looking for new places to stick it?"

"Oh, stop being so self-righteous. You're in the same business I'm in, Lee. Have you been watching CNN?"

"No, I haven't and I won't. They have a panel for every occasion. I don't think I could stomach their so-called analysis of this story."

"Our call letters and our story are all over their screen, all day. I think the veins in Brian Stelter's head were throbbing during his Q-and-A with Bob Woodward. It's fantastic!"

Cameron squinted at Strickland and took on a look of pained horror. "Fantastic? Are you out of your mind? You and your crew are going down, man. The public thinks you're stupid. The homeless guy's family is almost certainly going to sue. And I'm not convinced the prosecutors think you and your colleagues are blameless."

Strickland appeared unfazed by Cameron's doomsday scenarios. He looked off to the side, reaching for something out of sight. He brought into the frame a banana and proceeded to peel it as Cameron watched. He glanced up at the lawyer and asked, "What do you want me to do, Lee?"

Cameron studied him for a moment, his attention on the banana-peeling process. He then offered his advice: "I want you to suspend all your newscasts until further notice."

Strickland froze in mid-peel and said, "Excuse me?"

"You heard me."

Strickland resumed peeling, then took a bite out of the banana.

"Lee," he said with a mouthful, "Good bye," and clicked out of Skype.

"Are you watching this?" Governor Franklin screeched across the room to his chief of staff. Franklin had CNN on the large TV in his office while Morris Gilder sat in the corner leather chair, trying to have his scone and coffee. "Those assholes paid a serial arsonist for video, dumb shits."

"Yea, and did you see who their boss is now?" asked Gilder. "Your very own, favorite ex-con."

"Yes, indeed. Bordon Remmick. Jesus Christ, I think I'm getting hard."

Franklin picked up his desk phone, punched several digits and said, "Get me Livingston County Commissioner Leonard Francona."

"What's on your mind?" asked Gilder, chomping on his scone.

"I'm pulling the trigger."

Two weeks into his new job, Remmick found himself nostalgic for prison. He had gotten a decent night's sleep and a day off after his Jersey shore adventure and was in a good mood during the drive to work. It was Wednesday now, almost two days after the Klemmer revelations and the media were running wild with the story. Remmick heard his name on TV and on CBS radio. He felt vulnerable and wished he were back in his prison cell, post-Levon Samuels. He kept telling himself he should call the station, but he didn't want to. He kept thinking he should reconvene with Karen, but he didn't want to. What he wanted at this moment was one of his philosophical chats with Ralphie Vignola, his prison gym pal who kept bugging him to face his demons. He wondered what ever happened to Ralphie Vig, a body builder who'd almost killed a man with his bare hands.

A pall had settled over the newsroom worse than any in recent memory, even during the darkest days of the abusive man-child

Andrew Kenner. Channel 7 was in the awkward position of having to report on itself. The scoop of the century had turned into a disaster for the ages with the revelations about Klemmer, his late father, the family psychosis and, the cherry on top, the news director's dark past.

Karen appointed herself the sole writer and editor of all copy pertaining to the story. She had been instructed by Strickland to pass all copy to Lee Cameron as a condition for keeping the newscasts on the air. The reporting would be brief, factual and to the point. There would be no extraneous chit-chat on the set, no raised eyebrows, no reactions at all. The lawyer wanted surgical cleanliness when it came to the station's handling of the story, so the less said, the better.

"I'm reading it and I still can't believe it," Karen muttered under her breath as she edited her story, then dragged it into a Dropbox cloud folder where Cameron would see it. Minutes later, she would receive a screen alert that the story was approved and she would drop it into the lineup.

She felt bad for Bud. He couldn't have known, of course, that Bill Klemmer was diseased. No one knew. Should they have known? Now, Remmick's name was associated with a scandal that threatened to sink the ship. He would have to carry that burden along with the one he came with.

Karen was thumbing through the Daily News when she discerned she had company. She looked up and saw Reg, Nancy and Rita standing in her cubicle, staring at her.

"What?" she asked.

"Are we getting fired?" asked Reg in a small voice. The others asked the same question with their eyes.

"Don't be ridiculous. You didn't do anything wrong."

"And what about our fearless leader?" asked Nancy.

"If you're referring to the News Director, he didn't do anything wrong, either. He's barely been here a week."

"He brought the evil with him," Reg said. "He told me himself, he's going to hell."

"Kids, we will survive this. No one knew Klemmer was a psychopath."

"No, just a retard," blurted out fidgety Rita.

Karen shot her a look. "That's a word we don't use in the twenty-first century, girl. Klemmer is a sick individual. Unfortunately, it took us two years to figure that out."

Rita looked down at the floor, embarrassed. The others stood quietly.

"Just do your jobs, don't talk to reporters, stay off social media and don't entertain your worst fears. I've walked through shit before and survived. So will you."

Lieutenant Rosenstein's new best friend was the shrink, Dr. Cavanaugh. The two of them dug into the task of analyzing Klemmer's cell phone, a beat-up Motorola flip phone that had to be five or six years old. With the help of a subpoena, they accessed the complete history of Klemmer's number, his voicemail messages and cloud accounts. Two things became apparent.

"He's gotten only two voicemail messages in two years, both erased," reported Rosenstein, who sat at the conference room table in Homicide. He turned his laptop so Cavanaugh could see his screen. She, accustomed to more light and less organic stench, squinted to see the small dialogue box with the Verizon logo in the center of the screen: NO MESSAGES.

"Deleted messages aren't really deleted," Rosenstein said. "They're on an archive server."

"Really?"

"One from someone speaking Spanish. Another from a Channel 7 guy named Richardson."

"What about calls?"

"There are outgoing calls to Franco's Pizza on Rising Sun Avenue. There are a couple calls received from another cell phone that belongs to that same Channel 7 guy, Richardson, and the call dumbass Remmick made to him while he was holed up at the motel. That's it."

"He told me he communicates with his father by phone, a fantasy crafted to accommodate the separation he tries to keep between the two personalities."

"Dissociative Identity Disorder, formerly called Multiple Personality Disorder."

"My, my, lieutenant, you've been reading up."

"And it mostly happens to people who were abused as children."

"Right again."

"What do we do with him?"

"*We* probably won't have to do much. If his public defender is on the ball, he will order a psych eval and steer the whole case towards insanity. Given the evidence--his present-day behavior and things he's confessed to, not to mention the evidence found in his home-- it's doubtful there will be a trial and that Mr. Klemmer will ever see freedom again."

"We can only hope."

"The sins of the father, etcetera."

"Shakespeare."

"Again, I'm impressed."

"I'm not just a pretty face."

Marjorie Cutler had an angry twist to her lips as Commissioner Francona delivered his message. He spoke for two minutes non-stop, then halted to await her response. Her eyes never unglued from his. Her hands remained folded on her lap, the soles of her feet firmly planted on the floor in front of the chair in which she sat. She barely blinked, which creeped him out.

"Tell her today," were his final words.

Cutler's demeanor now changed. She appeared relaxed, less angry. She blinked a couple times, seeming to study him closely as though looking for fleas on a dog. Then, she offered a smile and a few calmly stated words: "I will do no such thing."

"Huh?" he replied. "What do you mean?"

"Which word did you have trouble with, Leo?"

"That's Commissioner Francona to you."

"Leo, we're not firing Margaret Remmick."

"The fuck we're not!"

"We. Are. Not." Each word struck him like an angular pebble. She tugged at her suit, straightening out the collar that bunched at the base of her neck.

"Insolent *and* insubordinate, Marjorie?"

"Leo, we're not firing her because if we, or should I say *you,* fire her, a certain text message will find its way to every television station, newspaper and social media outlet in eastern Pennsylvania."

"What are you talking about?"

"Oh my, you are dumb."

"How about I kick your shapely dyke ass across the room!"

"Henceforth, I will let this do the talking." She had produced her smartphone and was manipulating it as she spoke, poking at it with her index finger as Francona fumed. Finally, one last poke. "There. That'll do it."

The Commissioner's own smartphone beeped once, signaling a new text had arrived. As he reached into his breast pocket for the phone, Cutler stood and put hers into her purse.

"I know that was meant for your fellow Commissioners when you sent it some months ago, but I was still included in the group. I'm sure you didn't mean to do that."

Francona manipulated his phone, adjusting the distance from his eyes so he could better see.

"I thought it might come in handy some day," Cutler said without emotion. She stood about twelve feet from his desk and watched as he opened the text. His mouth opened, his brow knotted into a fleshy tumor and his eyes darted up to hers, then back to the small screen. She had never seen another person's face turn ashen before her eyes. He looked at her and shook his head with his mouth hanging half-open.

Marjorie took the few short steps required to put herself right up against the front of Francona's desk, then leaned forward, putting her face level with his. "Who is that boy anyway, Leo?" Francona, frightened and angry, couldn't speak. "No matter. That little gem is safe on the cloud. It is coded to upload automatically to YouTube, Facebook, Instagram, and phillynews.com all by itself at 7AM tomorrow IF you have any notion of firing Maggie Remmick. So, you can fire her, fire me, even kill me if you want, but that video is going viral tomorrow if you do any of the above. Pretty sure that will not only end your miserable waste of a career but put you in jail as well, not to mention the excruciating, perhaps even suicidal embarrassment it'll cause the other Commissioners."

Francona had no words, only elevated respirations and guttural sounds emanating from his belly.

"Do we understand each other?"

Francona's eyes were riveted to the small screen. Margaret inched her face even closer to his and repeated, "Do we understand each other?"

He raised his eyes to meet hers and slowly nodded.

Cutler turned and walked deliberately, but not quickly, out of Francona's office, showing her shapely, dyke ass to the political hack behind the desk.

"I'm out," declared Trooper Noble. "I'm not doing this anymore."

"At ease, Trooper," commanded Major Harcourt. "I'll say when you're out."

"Sir, all I ever wanted to be was a cop. Why are you doing this to me?"

"No one is doing anything to you. It's just an assignment, like any other. All you have to do is follow simple orders."

"No, sir. I think this is all part of some bigger, darker mission to trip up Mr. Remmick."

"Not him, his wife," the Major corrected.

"Excuse me?"

The Major looked at him cautiously, silently. "Are you going to do this, or what?"

Noble rose from his chair, stood tall with his heels together and looked right through the Major.

"No, sir."

"You realize, Trooper--"

"You do what you have to do, Major. Something's not right here and I'm not going to be a part of it."

The Major regarded the Trooper with serious eyes, looking him up and down. "Consider yourself suspended. This will have to go up the food chain. Until then, get out of my sight."

Noble showed no emotion, though he felt like crying. He saluted the Major, turned and left the room.

Maggie was feeling sorry for herself by lunchtime and started ruminating over the pros and cons of eating a quick sandwich from Wawa versus not eating at all. As she had discovered time and time again, not eating at all meant a headache by 3PM and extra grumpiness by the time she got home. On the other hand, she could afford to lose about ten pounds, though it wasn't an obsession--yet.

Angela stuck her head into Maggie's office. "Got any lunch plans?"

"I'm just thinking about it. Got something in mind?"

"I'm going to run to the Wawa and get soup."

"Would you mind grabbing me one of those packaged tuna salads?"

"Sure."

"Here's money. And a diet iced tea, please."

"OK. Be right back."

Maggie was feeling restless and stood up at her desk. She wandered into the outer office where Angela sat, a sort of mini-lobby that contained a small couch, Keurig machine and a water cooler. Wall hangings included a framed photo of the County Commissioners, an ersatz impressionistic painting of a wheat field at sunset and a glossy poster explaining the details of the Equal Employment Opportunity laws. She walked through the room, cutting a roundabout path to Angela's desk, which was neat, but not too neat. Her computer screen was filled with stuff, multiple PC windows open with tabs labeled TOURISM, AMAZON.COM, BUDGET ANALYSIS, NEW DOCUMENT, and one which caught her eye, REMMICK, M.

Maggie looked around the room for something, she wasn't sure what, maybe a camera? There wasn't one that she knew of. She sat down at Angela's desk, picked up the mouse and pointed the cursor at the REMMICK, M tab. Upon double clicking, it revealed her personnel file including her state ID photo, demographics, physical description and her entire life story gleaned from her resume and job interview. Additional notes had been added by a person or persons unknown, including notations of days she arrived after 9AM and left before 5PM, dates of her meetings with Marjorie Cutler, the date of her participation in the County Call with the Governor and, curiously, the dates and times of her calls from John Ungar, whose name was noted, including the last short one during which he instructed her to go to her cell phone.

And there were quotes from their conversations.

"... your Governor has a bit of a hard-on for your husband and this has led to pointed questions about you," read one. And then, *"Hi, Mrs. Remmick, it's John. Please, what's your cell number?"*

Maggie's blood ran cold. She felt nauseous and forced herself to close her mouth. Fear was replaced by fury. She wanted to toss something across the room but she kept it together long enough to carefully minimize the window on the screen. She stood up from Angela's desk chair and sidled away from the desk and made it back into her own office just as Angela sauntered back in with a plastic bag containing their lunches.

"I'm starving," Angela announced, placing the bag down at her desk. Maggie watched Angela unpack the food, then sit down and inspect her computer screen. Maggie held her breath and watched as Angela clicked on a couple of things with her coat still on, then took her hand off the mouse and turned her attention to lunch.

Maggie walked to Angela's desk and grabbed her food. "Thanks, Ang, I really appreciate it."

"Of course," she replied with a smile as she took off her coat and hung it over the back of her desk chair. She sat down and unwrapped her sandwich.

Maggie retreated to her own desk with her salad, iced tea and a side order of revelation.

"YOU DID VERY WELL," said the voice Klemmer had become accustomed to. "YOU MET YOUR CHALLENGES AND HERE WE ARE."

Klemmer was still feeling the effects of pain killers. He was aware of the voice but was at a loss to respond.

"THERE'S JUST ONE MORE THING TO DO, A NOBLE ACT, INDEED."

Klemmer's half-conscious state prevented him from understanding. He accepted the voice as an undeniable presence, even though no one was there in the flesh.

A noise came from the front of his hospital room. The door opened and in walked a large man wearing a navy blue, hooded sweatshirt, a badge around his neck and a pistol in a belted holster. Klemmer perked up and opened his eyes all the way to take in the sight of the man walking towards his bed.

"You're awake. I'm Detective Perryman, your babysitter for the next couple hours."

Klemmer said nothing, but watched the detective through wide eyes.

"So you're the guy. I was at your house a few days ago, me and my partner."

Klemmer's eyes traveled up and down, taking in the sight of the large man, focusing on the gun at his side.

"You were quite elusive. I can't believe you weren't killed by the SWAT guys. I guess they can't shoot straight."

"HELP MY BOY SIT UP, WILL YOU?" came the raspy, guttural voice from deep inside the darkness of Klemmer's alter ego. "THE DOCTOR WANTS HIM TO MOVE AROUND."

Perryman did what he was told, moving close to the side of Klemmer's bed, helping him first sit up, then pivoting his legs off the bed so they could hang off the side. Klemmer sat on the bed's edge, breathing harder than before, chin tucked down to his chest.

"COME HERE, DETECTIVE, I HAVE TO TELL YOU SOMETHING," he said in his father's voice, gesturing with his head. Perryman looked around the room, then moved closer to Klemmer and bent down to get close to his face. "EVERYONE HERE IS MISTAKEN." Perryman's ear was just inches from Klemmer's mouth. He strained to hear the raspy voice, oblivious to Klemmer's hand inching towards his holster.

"What do you mean?"

"THEY ALL THINK I'M DEAD."

Perryman felt a tug on his belt, like he was caught on something. He turned his head to look down. Before he finished the motion, the gun came out into Klemmer's hand, up to the side of Klemmer's head and a deafening *BANG* sent a 9mm round into the left side of Klemmer's skull. It came out the right, taking with it brains and a gusher of blood that splashed against the pastel wallpaper, the monitors and onto the white sheets of the bed.

A nurse outside the room screamed and dropped a tray of instruments. Perryman twitched, dumbfounded, horrified, staggering backwards until his body collided with a rolling table that contained a meal tray. He fell backwards into it, causing a secondary explosion of noise that triggered another scream from the hallway.

The charge nurse and a doctor ran into the room and gaped at the bloody scene across the room and at the large man writhing on the floor in a puddle of beef gravy and applesauce. More people showed up at the door. A hospital security guard attempted to take charge of the commotion that lasted several minutes until Tyler Rosenstein appeared.

"Everybody move away," he said in a louder voice than he was accustomed to using. "No one goes into this room, hear me? Perryman, what the fuck?"

The detective had picked himself up and brushed as much of the food off his body as he could. "He snuck up on me. Mother fucking psycho snuck up on me, grabbed my gun and blew his brains out."

Rosenstein's look of incredulity frightened Perryman.

"I can't wait to hear the rest of *that* story," barked Rosenstein.

"It all happened so fast."

Rosenstein got right up into his face and warned, "Don't say another word."

Perryman, a hulking man with forearms the size of most peoples' legs, was on the verge of tears. He backed away, then turned to leave the room. He really had nowhere else to go, so he sat on a folding chair in the hallway next to the nurses' station and watched as uniformed colleagues and people in scrubs started milling around, wondering what just happened.

Chapter 22 - Reset

It took the rest of the week for the aftermath to settle before everyone got their stories straight and the "official" version of the Klemmer saga was written. Klemmer's final act of violence seemed to deflect some of the attention from questions about Channel 7's complicity in his malfeasance. It had become clear that he was a mentally ill individual and that not even in their infinite stupidity could the people at Channel 7 have known he was that far gone. It relieved some of the pressure on Lee Cameron, but not enough to ease his angina.

It was Friday again and everyone at Channel 7 still had jobs. The who, what, where, when and why had been exhaustively explored by the Philly media and some national. The New York Times did one story without art, buried in its National section. NJ.com was all over it for the first couple days, then nothing.

Roy Strickland was riding a wave of blossoming ratings, inflated by scandal.

The local news stories were now paying more attention to Remmick--his past and present--with a couple incidental mentions of Maggie. Bud sat in his office, staring at phillynews.com on his computer screen and seeing his name there way too often. While that was annoying enough, seeing Maggie's name being bandied about made him get out of his chair and kick the trash can across the room. He slammed his door shut and sat stewing at his desk. He wallowed in, almost welcomed, the old darkness. He'd been at his job a little more than a week and already, he felt a familiar tightness in the back of his throat, the restlessness he felt after Hilde Schimmel died and he wandered down to the Kaleidescope library to escape, only to find himself in the same room as that evil bastard Morone. The hell that ensued made him shudder, and he cleared his brain of the images. There was no one to blame for anything now except dead men--Ronald Morone, Bill Klemmer, Bill Klemmer, Senior.

A knock on his office door roused him from his funk. "Come on in."

"Hi," said Nancy, peeking her head."

"Hi."

"Karen wanted me to ask you about the Governor on Monday."

"What about him?"

"He's coming to Philly for a joint news conference with SEPTA about the new subway. Are we covering?"

"Sure. Why wouldn't we?"

"And there's a luncheon afterwards. The press is invited. They want RSVPs."

"We don't want their free food. They'll probably poison us. Yes to the newser, no to lunch."

"OK."

"Anything else?"

"Um, I just wanted to say, I'm sorry this is happening to us. To you."

"Yea, me too."

"Hell of a way to start a new gig, huh?"

"Yea, well, it's all about how we respond to things out of our control, isn't it?"

Nancy nodded with a faint smile and said, "I guess." She left, closing the door behind her.

Rosenstein did paperwork for almost two days straight following the Beach City events. His Captain wanted a detailed timeline of all events up to and including Klemmer's suicide, complete with chapter and verse on Klemmer's family history, any and all jobs he did for Channel 7 and all contacts the station had with him in the past two years. He recruited Detective Perryman as his assistant for collecting facts, dates, vouchers, any and all evidence of the life and times of William Klemmer. Perryman started after his one-day suspension for being careless with his firearm. He was glad it wasn't worse.

There were no questions about how Channel 7 knew where and when to be in Beach City. His superiors either didn't care or hadn't had time to ask. The fact was, the station's presence didn't interfere with the operation and changed nothing.

Rosenstein was intrigued by the Bordon Remmick side show. He had begun digging into his past just before the shit hit the fan at the shore. He read all about Remmick's crime, his guilty plea, obtained his prison record and saw the video of both of his parole board hearings. While he wouldn't have admitted it to anyone, Rosenstein had a perverse admiration for Remmick's refusal to feign remorse for killing Mr. Morone. He thought standing up for a victim by killing her tormentor was a singular remedy that the legal system recognized, but could not condone. The judge must have thought so, agreeing to only four-to-six years in jail. Now he was out after the minimum sentence and, theoretically, a better man. One could argue that everyone got what they deserved.

In sifting through the records of all the jobs Klemmer did for Channel 7 during those two years, evidence that he started additional fires was inconclusive. He had confessed to the two most recent ones of course, and provided corroboration to the physical evidence found at the scenes and at his home. But now that he was gone, there was no one left to interview about the thirty other fires. Of the several that had been declared arsons, other arrests had been made. It appeared the question of Klemmer's involvement in any others would remain unanswered. And whatever was in his brain at the time he was interviewed was splattered on the hospital walls.

A detailed search of Klemmer's home on Brill Street revealed a dark and insular universe centered in his stinking bedroom. Detectives found SD memory cards scattered around various surfaces. Virtually no natural light entered the room. The single light source was the 40-watt lamp on his night table. X-Box game controllers were piled at the base of the TV. Laundry piles lay everywhere. The smell of humanity was overwhelming, a cross between a locker room and a geriatric care facility. The bedsheets were colors other than the original with significant food stains everywhere. In one bureau drawer were several rolls of plastic packing tape that matched that found at the two arson scenes. In his kitchen under the sink was a half-gallon can of linseed oil. The detectives were not wanting for clues to the arsons. Rosenstein regretted only that they hadn't found them sooner.

Of the two surveillance cameras they found, only the one at the front door worked. In examining Klemmer's phone and the cloud account associated with the camera, there was nothing revealing, only multiple shots of the friendly mail carrier. Klemmer had no visitors, ever.

"This was a damaged person," Dr. Cavanaugh later remarked over coffee with Rosenstein. "He suffered a toxic mix of PTSD and a dissociative disorder with no supports at all. I mean, none. This couldn't have ended any other way. He didn't appear to have anyone, anywhere, once his father died. He had no alternatives to examine, no remedies for a life of exclusion."

"A life of exclusion," repeated Rosenstein.

"It's how I describe people who, because of their illnesses, are excluded from, well, everything normal people value. Happiness, mostly."

They sat at the Dunkin' Donuts across the street from the McDonald's down the street from the Roundhouse. Rosenstein swirled his coffee around inside the cardboard cup and looked Cavanaugh straight in the eye.

"Do you like Chinese?" he asked.

"Yea."

"The Imperial Inn is a couple blocks away, the best Hot and Sour soup in town. Any interest?"

Cavanaugh examined Rosenstein's eyes for clues to motive. Hunger? Friendship? Sex?

"Another time."

"Where do you live?"

"Marlton."

"Damn, too far."

"Too far for what?" she asked with a crooked smile.

"Nothing, It's just--far."

They got up from the small table and walked out onto 8th Street. Rosenstein turned towards the Roundhouse while Cavanaugh stopped. "My car's in the garage the other way. Keep in touch, OK?" she said, extending her hand to Rosenstein.

"Sure thing. Bye."

They parted ways, Rosenstein figured, for the last time.

Maggie Remmick was driving the last leg of the trip home, a two-lane cow path called Anthill Drive, when she saw flashing red and blue lights in her rear-view mirror. She looked down at her speedometer. The needle hovered just over 60. The speed limit on the road was 50.

"Damn," she said as the lights got closer, then right on top of her. She pulled off the road onto the shoulder and put the car into PARK.

The police vehicle followed her to the shoulder, parked a discrete distance behind her and kept its overheads on as an officer emerged from the car. Maggie reached into the glove compartment to grab her registration. As she turned to her open window, she recognized a familiar face.

"Oh, hi," she said to Trooper Les Noble.

"Hi. I don't need that stuff."

"OK. I know I was speeding. I figured you were--"

"It's alright. Can you come to my car for a minute?"

Alarms sounded in Maggie's head. A bolt of fear shot through her, almost making her gasp. "OK."

Noble backed away, allowing her to exit the car. He led the way back to his cruiser and opened the passenger door, beckoning her to climb in. He held the door open as she slid into the seat, then closed the door, walked around to the driver's side and got in. The two sat in his car. His overhead lights still flashed. An occasional car zoomed by, probably doing exactly 50 miles an hour.

"I didn't mean to scare you. I just saw your car and I needed to talk to you alone, not at your house. I don't think your husband trusts me."

Maggie stared at Noble, completely clueless as to what this conversation could be about. "Well, here we are," she said.

"I'm leaving town, leaving the State Police. I got a job back in Bucks County with a local department closer to home."

"Really? What happened?"

"Maggie, I don't know how to say this. Guess I'll just say it."

She looked at him, waiting.

"Someone way above me wanted me to gather dirt on you and your husband. It's the whole reason they helped me move to Armitage, to move next door to you guys so I could, um, spy on you."

Maggie's eyes widened. "Why?"

"I swear to god, I have no idea. At first, I thought they wanted me to catch Bud doing something illegal because of his past, to use against him in some way. But this week, they told me it was about you."

Maggie dropped her eyes and looked away. "I see."

"I was ordered to do it. Yesterday, I told my boss I wouldn't do it anymore."

"Anymore?"

"Oh, I put a little wireless camera in that bush between our two properties, hoping to see something. All I ever got was your dog pooping. I tossed it, ripped it outta there. That was after I got suspended for refusing orders. So, I quit. This is my last shift."

Maggie crossed her arms and held herself. She looked out the windshield at her Subaru, sitting empty on the shoulder. "Wow," she said in a whisper. "He wasn't kidding."

"Sorry?"

She searched his face, his eyes. She saw pain. "I learned recently that Governor Franklin is after my job. He thinks the wife of a felon shouldn't have a government job that he could fill with a patronage hack. I was told by someone on the inside, a friend, that he's got people watching me. I guess you're Exhibit A."

Noble was speechless.

"I also discovered earlier today that my administrative assistant is probably Exhibit B."

"Jesus."

Maggie wiped away tears and fought the urge to sob. "All I ever wanted was a decent job helping old people."

"All I ever wanted was to be a cop. I'm so sorry."

Maggie wiped away more tears and tried to pull herself together. "I appreciate your honesty, Les. I really do," she said, placing her hand on his right arm. "I'm sorry you got screwed by your own integrity."

Maggie got out of the cruiser and walked towards the Subaru. She got in and watched Noble drive away, turning off his overhead lights. She figured she'd never see him again.

"With all due respect, Governor, don't you have more important things to worry about?"

The question came from Morris Gilder, Franklin's chief of staff, as the two sat at a corner table at Harold's, an old-world restaurant a block from the Capitol. They snacked on chips and salsa and nursed high-octane cocktails.

"Yes, I do," Franklin conceded, taking a healthy swig of his Manhattan.

"Then, what's the obsession with these patronage jobs?"

"It's not an obsession, Morris. I like taking care of my people."

"Are you aware that this woman in Livingston County, the Remmick woman, has completely turned her agency around? They have saved a shitload of money and serve more elderly people since she took over."

Franklin had no reaction, greeting his T-bone as if it were his last meal, diving in with his steak knife, washing down a large mouthful with a healthy swig of his drink. He smacked down his glass and looked Gilder in the eye. "That agency practically runs itself. My girl Angela has it under control."

"But don't you think--"

"Stop," Franklin barked, holding up his hand. "I want the Remmick woman gone. If that pussy Francona can't get it done, then I guess you'll have to."

Gilder stopped chewing momentarily, then looked down at the table, digesting the unequivocal message. "What am I supposed to do?"

"Use your imagination, Morris, for Christ sake. You have a county official married to an ex-con, an admitted killer, who's running a TV news department that used a psychopath to cover stories. You mean to tell me you can't do something with that? Take them both down for all I care."

"It's guilt by association. She's not responsible for her husband's actions."

"She had the poor judgement to marry the fuck," said Franklin in an uncomfortably loud voice. "Figure it out."

Gilder went speechless for the rest of the meal, watching his boss ripping meat off the bone with his pearly white teeth, pink juice dribbling down his chin and porcine grunts emanating from deep within.

Chapter 23 - Monday, Monday, Can't Trust That Day

Colin Clark: Joining us on CBS Morning Roundtable now is Bordon Remmick, the News Director of Channel 7 in Philadelphia, a station that's been making news rather than just reporting it of late. He joins us from the Channel 7 studios. Thanks for being with us, Mr. Remmick.

Bordon Remmick: Sure.

Clark: It's been quite a week for your news department but especially for you personally, hasn't it?

Remmick: It's not what I expected when I returned to the business, that's for sure.

Clark: What did you expect?

Remmick: To report the news, not make it.

Clark: Many questions have been raised since the story broke about the freelance photographer who is now alleged to have committed crimes, then videotaped them for your station. Mainly, what did you know, and when, about what he was doing?

Remmick: I started working at Channel 7 less than two weeks ago. I found out what maybe three days after arriving.

Clark: So, you had no prior knowledge of this individual's activities?

Remmick: None.

Clark: I'm sure you realize that your own past history has led many to come to conclude that--

Remmick: As I just said, I didn't know a thing about it.

Clark: Over the weekend, Governor Thomas Franklin posted a Tweet saying that your lack of awareness and leadership in this saga has cast a shadow over journalists across Pennsylvania.

Remmick: He's entitled to his opinion.

Clark: He also released information about your wife, Margaret, who runs a County office up in the Poconos.

Remmick: I know what he Tweeted.

Clark: Let me put that one up on the screen--"Having the wife of an admitted killer running a government office in my state is a disgrace." He also Tweeted that she filed for personal bankruptcy while you were incarcerated, quoting the Tweet, "showing irresponsible financial behavior." How do you respond to that?

Remmick: Governor Franklin is a political hack who has decided to target my wife whose only sin has been to make her County agency more efficient and serve more senior citizens at less cost to taxpayers. He wants his own people in that and other jobs and will obviously stoop to any depths to accomplish that. My wife has absolutely nothing to do with my past actions. She applied for that position months ago, was interviewed for it and got the job based on her merits and experience. Being married to me was never an issue until, mysteriously, about two weeks ago when I showed up at Channel 7.

Clark: Do you believe the Governor is--

Remmick: The Governor is a pig.

Clark: Why do you say that?

Remmick: Where you listening ten seconds ago?

Clark: Yes, obviously.

Remmick: He is an ignorant pig who wouldn't recognize ethics if they bit him in the ass. Oops, can I say that on morning television?

Clark: So, do you believe--

Remmick: Sorry, I shouldn't have called him a pig. That demeans all pigs.

Clark: Do you believe--

Remmick: I defy you, Governor Franklin, to even attempt to fire Margaret Remmick from her well-deserved post as Executive Director of Senior Services for Livingston County, Pennsylvania. I *dare* you to fire her and I urge all seniors in Livingston County and anywhere else to look up her record, look up her accomplishments and make up your own mind whether she should be replaced by some random patronage ape who doesn't know or care about you.

Clark: Do you believe this is a partisan move by the Governor? Isn't it true you and your wife are Democrats?

Remmick: We are. As to whether it's partisan, that's a question for the Governor, a question I doubt he has the cojones to answer honestly.

Clark: And what do you intend to do today?

Remmick: Today? I'm here, at my station, doing my job.

Clark: Mr. Remmick, thanks for being with us.

Remmick walked down the steps from the studio and into the newsroom to a standing ovation. Karen led the throng but they were all there--Reg, Nancy, Rita, Gordon and two interns. Pam Whitehead whistled and waved from a desk across the room.

"Jesus," he said. "Don't you people have anything better to do?"

"He *is* a fucking pig," said Karen loudly. "You nailed it, man."

He waved off the lingering hand-claps and trod towards his office. Karen followed closely behind and managed to say, "I thought for a minute you were gonna use the F word."

"I came close."

They marched into the office and Remmick closed the door.

"I want to go to that SEPTA thing," he said. "I want to get in that fucker's face."

"Wait, the news conference this morning?"

"Yes."

"Whoa, maybe not such a good idea."

"Maybe not, but I don't care."

Karen put her hand on his arm and looked at him plaintively. "Don't do it. Please."

He caught the fear in her voice. He closed his eyes, inhaled and exhaled loudly. "What do you think I'm going to do?"

"I don't know. But you have that look."

Remmick knew exactly what she meant. A familiar feeling was back, the anger aura.

"There are always going to be assholes you can't control. Right?"

Remmick's eyes narrowed. Maggie said almost the same thing at dinner the other night.

"It's different now, Karen."

She removed her hand from his arm. He sat down at his desk, her cue to leave him alone.

Maggie dropped her coat and bag on her desk and placed her coffee down carefully. She felt apprehension merely by walking into her building. Monday mornings were bad enough. She sat in her chair and picked up the coffee, taking a sip and looking around her office as though she hadn't been there in a month. It was quiet. She felt alone.

She logged in to her computer and went to her email inbox. One item stood out, a note from Marjorie Cutler marked PRIORITY. The subject line read !!!!!!!!!. She clicked to open it and it said only, "Amazing!" Clueless to the meaning, she busied herself opening other emails, all of them routine.

After several minutes of email retrieval, she heard someone padding across the carpeting in the ante room and looked up to find Marjorie Cutler walking her way. She came into Maggie's office and closed the door behind her. She stood at the closed door for a moment, looked straight at Maggie and said, "Well, that was something."

"Huh?"

"Your husband. Quite the set of balls."

Maggie cocked her head and raised her hands. "What are you talking about?"

"Seriously? You didn't see your husband on TV this morning?"

"No. When?"

"Half an hour ago on CBS."

"I was in the car, driving here."

"Guess he wanted it to be a surprise."

"I knew he went to work early. But he didn't say anything--"

"You must see it. He was brilliant!"

"There's a TV in the main lobby downstairs."

"Let's go," said Marjorie. "I'm sure they're playing highlights by now."

Another TV, 125 miles away in the state Capitol, was still hot with Remmick's fighting words. It sat in Morris Gilder's office just down the hall from the Governor's office. Gilder, curled in a fetal position in his large leather couch, was just waiting for his phone to ring. He was biting his thumbnail, eyes darting around the room. The Governor was on his way to Philadelphia for the SEPTA news conference and may, or may not have seen Remmick's on-air tirade. Gilder was uncertain how Franklin might react, but experience taught him that the Governor wasn't one for nuanced behavior.

Back in Livingston County, after a quick trip down the elevator, Marjorie and Maggie stepped into the lobby of their building and made their way to the TV mounted over the information desk. There was a small group of County employees there, staring up at the screen. Several caught sight of Maggie approaching and pointed at her. "That's her," she heard one say. Another addressed Maggie directly. "You married an attack dog!"

Maggie's ears finally picked up the sound from the TV just in time for a soundbite of her husband saying, *I defy you, Governor Franklin, to even attempt to fire Margaret Remmick.* Her eyes widened to capacity. Her mouth opened and the words "Oh my god" escaped. She was transfixed and stood perfectly still as more soundbites were replayed in rapid succession. She looked at Marjorie, whose gaze was fixed on her. Marjorie's hand found its way to Maggie's shoulder as the two returned their eyes to the TV. They were now surrounded by a dozen other bystanders who stood silently watching.

"Maggie," said Marjorie.

"I'm going to kill him."

At least she's not sobbing, thought Marjorie.

"Why didn't he tell me he was going to do this?"

"Sometimes, boys have to show their big ones."

Maggie shot a look at Marjorie and emitted a sound that was half giggle, half moan, finished with a sigh.

The CBS program went to commercial and the crowd slowly dispersed. Two women approached Maggie. One shook her hand. The other praised her for marrying a "tough guy." In short order, Maggie and Marjorie stood alone at the information desk.

"I gotta start looking for a new job," said Maggie.

"Don't you dare," shot back Marjorie. "Don't you dare."

In the back seat of a jet-black Denali, hiding behind dark tinted windows, sat Thomas H. Franklin, Governor of Pennsylvania, Chairman of the State Republican Committee and mentor to men and women who bought deeply into the political shell game he presided over. A large man with a broad face whose over-the-top whiteness made even other white people squirm, Franklin upheld all the time-honored standards of race-baiting, xenophobia and homophobia that are woven into the fabric of America. He was elected on a platform of fiscal responsibility, advocating tax cuts across the board and cuts to government agencies. It was only after he was in office his first year did it become apparent that the voters of Pennsylvania elected a shameless gangster who prided himself on media attention, bullying, fear and intimidation. He had few friends but many supplicants, all of whom curried favor for their own purposes. As a ten-year veteran of the state Assembly, he had forged political ties that ran deep. He did favors, and accepted favors. He was also careful.

In the front seat sat two plainclothes State Troopers, one his regular driver, the other his main bodyguard. Neither was in the prime of youth or in any kind of shape to manhandle an attacker. Their chief assets were sheer size--both were well over six-feet tall and in the 300-pound range--and the Sig Sauer .45 semi-automatic each carried on his hip.

Driving ahead of the Denali was a Ford Explorer, also jet black with tinted windows, carrying two more plainclothes Troopers and the Governor's appointment secretary. Both vehicles were equipped with flashing red and blue lights and sirens, which were rarely used. The appointment secretary, a frightened young woman named Kirsten, graduated college less than a year earlier and got the job through her father, the state Controller who had worked on Franklin's campaign. She constantly tapped on an oversized smartphone and spoke only when spoken to.

After receiving a text from Morris Gilder, the Governor sat studying the CBSN app on his phone, adjusting the volume on the Remmick interview. At the words, *the Governor is a pig*, Franklin cackled almost gleefully and turned up the volume. He was riveted by the interview, which CBSN obligingly replayed for the third time. A fighter by nature, Franklin welcomed the kind of defiance that Bordon Remmick displayed. This guy's got a pair and put a saddle on them, he thought.

The drive from Harrisburg to Philadelphia was a drag, one reason he rarely came east. But he used the time to catch up on phillynews.com and the Channel 7 saga. The whole series of events, punctuated by the name Remmick, made him seethe .

"Call me a pig, will you?" he said to no one as he replayed the interview.

The setup for the SEPTA news conference was typical for that agency, whose full name was the Southeastern Pennsylvania Transportation Authority. There was a small auditorium at SEPTA headquarters downtown, already wired for sound. The stage was a makeshift platform raised about six inches off the floor with a podium on wheels set at about the center front. Rows of supremely uncomfortable folding chairs were set up in front of the platform. Reporters were typically seated in the front couple of rows. About four rows back was a raised platform for photographers.

By 9:55, the photographers were set up and standing by their tripod-mounted cameras. The front rows were populated by the men and women of the Philadelphia press corps including one Bordon Remmick who chose a seat in the front row, directly in front of the podium. Channel 7 reporter Harvey Jameson sat next to him.

Remmick attracted some attention following his morning news appearance. Several reporters chatted with him. A couple shook his hand. He sat otherwise quietly with his hands folded on his lap, awaiting the arrival of the principles. A buzz of random voices resonated through the room. Any other day, a SEPTA news conference was greeted by yawns. What was different today was the appearance by Governor Franklin, a rare event for Philadelphia in general, let alone at SEPTA's humble auditorium.

"You gonna behave now, right?" Harvey asked Remmick. Remmick gave him a sideways look and said nothing.

At 10:01, two large men walked into the room and took posts at either side of the stage, facing the audience. Several men then walked onto the stage--SEPTA Executive Director Roman Stepanick, Philadelphia Mayor Martin Wells, Governor Franklin and his bodyguard. The room quieted down immediately and Stepanick approached the podium.

"Good morning, everyone," he said into the microphone. Cameras flashed. "With me this morning are Mayor Martin Wells and Governor Tom Franklin, our partners in this ambitious project to expand subway service to many more of our citizens."

Remmick turned to look behind him at the camera platform to confirm that Channel 7's photographer was in place. She was, hunched over her viewfinder. He returned his attention to the podium where Stepanick had ceded his spot to Mayor Wells.

"The City of Philadelphia loves mass transportation," he began, "and expanding our subways is a natural evolution of our service to our citizens."

Remmick rolled his eyes, keeping his hands folded on his lap. Wells had a stock speech which he used for multiple occasions, switching-out proper nouns and verbs. By now, Remmick's eyes locked onto Franklin who stood on the stage behind the Mayor, hands at his sides. Franklin's eyes scanned the press until they landed on the man he saw on television for the first time this morning, his favorite ex-con, Bordon Remmick. If he was surprised to see Remmick at this event, he didn't show it.

As the two men eyeballed each other, Franklin suddenly heard his name spoken in an introduction. His attention snapped back to his spot on the stage and the short path he needed to navigate to the podium. He walked the seven steps to the microphone and began talking. Remmick paid little attention to the words, focusing on Franklin's face, his eyes, his tone. He was sizing up the devil.

"We understand the value of enhanced public transportation in our largest city," Franklin said. "My support of this project goes beyond state aid. It includes the political and logistical support only the Governor's office can provide."

Self-serving putz, thought Remmick.

Franklin continued speaking for another two minutes, words Remmick assessed as meaningless blather. Remmick noticed that Franklin was sweating profusely, and his eyes darted around the room as he spoke.

"He's elevated bullshit to an art form," whispered Harvey. Remmick responded with a small smile and a nod. He was noticing Franklin's continued sweating and longer pauses between phrases.

After another sentence or two, Franklin stepped back to his former spot on the stage and SEPTA Executive Director Stepanick returned. "We'll take a few questions now," he said and the reporters' hands went up. "Yes, Ms. Richards."

"Can you clarify the funding sources for the new subway?" asked Mary Richards of Channel 5.

"It will be a combination of local, state and federal funding from sources that will include bond sales, grants and investment by local businesses. We are still lining up support from the business community."

"A follow up, please," Richards said. "What's the timetable?"

"We hope to break ground this fall with completion in less than three years."

"Question for the Governor," shouted Remmick.

Stepanick looked back at the Governor and gestured for him to come to the podium. Franklin walked tentatively the few feet to that spot. Remmick thought he didn't look good.

"Governor, Bordon Remmick, Channel 7. I'm wondering if you still plan to continue harassing County governments into firing perfectly competent workers so you can stick your political friends into those positions?"

The Governor grimaced and wiped his brow with his open hand. "Mr. Remmick, this is neither the time nor the place to have this discussion. If you want--"

"I think it's the perfect time, Governor. It's a simple question. Do you?"

"Mr. Remmick," jumped in Stepanick, "We're here to talk about--"

"It's alright, Roman," interrupted Franklin. "I'll deal with this idiot."

"Yea, deal with me, you fucking *prick*," shouted Remmick, now on his feet. "You and your asshole buddies harassing my wife, harassing me--I did my time, as the whole world knows by now. She had nothing to do with *anything* I did!"

The two large men at either side of the stage began moving towards Remmick. The Governor's bodyguard moved closer to Franklin, who was now loosening his tie with his right hand while leaning against the podium with his left arm.

"What happened at Channel 7 was no one's fault, you imbecile," shouted Remmick. "You and your Tweets can go straight--"

Franklin suddenly collapsed to the floor, his massive head smacking the platform with a loud crack. His bodyguard jumped back in shock. The assembled media jumped to their feet, cameras kept rolling, flashes fired relentlessly. The plainclothes troopers ran to the Governor and stood over him, staring like children. He lay motionless on his side.

Remmick stood frozen, the words "straight to hell" were lodged in his throat. He watched as the large men around the Governor stood, also frozen, looking at each other. Someone shouted, "Call 911". Someone else shouted, "What do we do?"

Remmick snapped out of his anger-zone and ran to the stage and got down onto the floor next to the Governor. "Do any of you guys know CPR?" he asked, looking up at the entourage.

"Yea," said one Trooper.

"Help me roll him onto his back." They did so and Remmick felt for a carotid pulse at Franklin's thick, sweaty throat. No pulse. He proceeded to tear off Franklin's shirt to expose his t-shirted chest and started chest compressions. "You, get some scissors or a knife to cut off his shirt and jacket," he barked at one Trooper, then turned to another. "You, get down here and get ready to breathe for him."

"You mean, mouth to mouth?"

"Yes, when I say. Is there an AED in this building anywhere?"

"Yes, down in the lobby," said Stepanick. "I'll get it."

"Fifteen, sixteen, seventeen," counted Remmick as he performed chest compressions on his knees. "Someone should meet EMS in the lobby and bring them here."

"I will," responded Kristen the scheduler and ran out of the auditorium.

"What do you want *me* to do?" asked a Trooper without an assignment.

"You're gonna stand there for a minute. Twenty-eight, twenty-nine, thirty. Breathe for him," Remmick commanded the Trooper at the Governor's head. He did so but no air went in. "Head tilt, chin lift, remember? Hold his nose, breathe enough to make his chest rise."

"Oh, right," said the Trooper. He followed each direction and blew into his mouth once, making the Governor's chest move.

"Again," said Remmick. He did it again. Remmick resumed compressions. The Trooper at the head looked shell-shocked. The second one stood looking down at the scene. The bodyguard was on his cellphone. Suddenly, Stepanick ran into the room holding a red bag with the letters AED emblazoned in white.

"I got it," he shouted as he ran over to Remmick.

"Any training?" asked Remmick while counting under his breath.

"Give it here," said the second Trooper who'd been standing and watching. He stepped over Franklin's unresponsive body and approached Stepanick, reaching for the AED.

"Come down here with me," said Remmick, slightly breathless. "Push the big green ON button and follow the voice commands." The trooper fumbled with the package, hands trembling, as he knelt on the floor on the other side of Franklin. He unsnapped the case and found the ON button. A shaky index finger finally pushed it.

"*Connect pads*," said the automated voice of the AED. The Trooper removed the two pads, each labeled with a sketch showing where on the body to place them.

"Peel off the backing," Remmick said. The Trooper found the loose corner of the backing and peeled it off both pads quickly. He referenced the sketches on the pads and placed them against Franklin's body in the correct positions. "Make sure they're on there good."

"He's sweaty."

"Yea, press them on hard and listen to the voice," replied Remmick who continued compressions until thirty, then instructed the other Trooper to breathe again. After two breaths, Remmick resumed compressions.

"*Stop CPR. Analyzing,*" said the automated voice.

"OK, back off," Remmick said, his voice calmer now. "Get ready to shock when the voice tells you to."

The Trooper at the AED nodded in acknowledgement.

"*Shock advised. Clear the patient,*" said the voice.

"Clear, everyone clear," shouted Remmick. He and the Troopers backed away from Franklin.

"*Shock the patient,*" said the voice as the AED sounded an urgent beep and flashed a red light.

The trooper pushed the red button. The shock fired. Franklin's body twitched.

During the few seconds it took the AED to analyze Franklin's heart rhythm and the trooper to deliver the shock, Remmick raised his head and looked around. Every photographer in the room was on top of him, jockeying for a spot to capture the action. No one said a word.

"*Shock delivered. Resume CPR,*" said the voice of the AED.

Remmick resumed compressions. He turned to the Trooper at Franklin's head doing the breathing. "After this cycle of thirty, you and I will switch, OK?"

"OK," answered the Trooper, who was looking more at ease.

Remmick turned to the Trooper with the AED. "And you're just going to stand by with the AED and wait two minutes until it analyzes again, then do what it says, OK?"

"Got it."

Several police officers now rushed in to the room, trailed by PFD EMS.

"Thank Christ," said Remmick, reaching the last of thirty compressions. He was joined on the floor by a paramedic.

"How long's he been down?" asked the medic.

Remmick presented. "About five minutes. Witnessed arrest. CPR started almost immediately. One shock delivered."

"OK," said the medic. "Can you continue compressions for one more cycle?"

"Uh, sure."

"You appear to have a clue," said the medic who began applying leads to Franklin's chest and belly while his partner prepared a laryngoscope to intubate. "Huge help."

"Sure, no problem," said Remmick as he continued compressions. "I'm way past thirty compressions now."

"OK," said the paramedic calmly. His partner produced a bag-valve-mask and held it onto the Governor's mouth and nose. The partner squeezed the bag a couple times, then turned to the trooper who had been breathing for the Governor and said, "You, continue bagging, OK?" He demonstrated how hard to squeeze and how often. Once the trooper got into a rhythm, the medic got into position at Franklin's head to start tubing him.

"You've done this before?" the medic asked Remmick.

"I'm an EMT. Had a cardiac arrest just a couple weeks ago."

Remmick heard a rustle of voices coming from the photographers and reporters gathered around them. "He's an EMT," he heard someone say. "Unbelievable," said someone else.

Police now moved the reporters and photographers back off the platform. More firefighters appeared and took over for Remmick and the troopers who had been kneeling on the floor. Remmick stood back with his two impromptu partners and watched as the medics delivered a second shock. He tried to get a glance at the EKG monitor, but he was out of position.

"Let's get ready to move him," said the lead medic. The second medic had placed the tube into Franklin's throat and took over bagging him. A firefighter's hand was on Franklin's wrist. "Strong radial pulse," he announced. After another couple minutes of moving things around, a total of six people lifted the Governor off the floor and onto a wheeled stretcher. The medics were looking relaxed. One remained at the Governor's head, helping him breathe.

"Rosk, my friend," said the lead medic to Remmick. "Nicely done."

The team of medics and firefighters quickly rolled the Governor away on the stretcher. The police moved away from the reporters and photographers and let everyone mingle again.

"Rosk?" a photographer asked Remmick. "What's that mean?"

"R-O-S-C, return of spontaneous circulation," he replied. "His heart is beating on its own."

"So, he'll make it?" asked another reporter.

"It's a good sign."

"That was the most amazing thing I ever saw," said another photographer. "Who are you again?"

Several hours later, after the noon show came and went, after multiple phone calls, claps on the back, handshakes and a million questions from coworkers and strangers, Bud sat in his office with the door closed. The TVs were off. He had a Coltrane album, *Crescent*, playing on his computer. He sat in the new upholstered chair in front of his desk, staring at the wall. He listened with his eyes closed and suddenly felt emotion creeping up from his stomach into his throat, eyes and nose. He opened his eyes and was crying, the same tears that came that time in prison when Maggie looked into his soul in search of the man she married. At this moment, he had no idea who he was, who that person kneeling on the floor was, who the person who went to jail was. He sensed different people using his skin to navigate the world. Anger shared room-air with compassion and he had no idea which would emerge. For a minute, he was convinced he had multiple personalities like Bill Klemmer. Then, more tears, and a simple feeling of hopeless loneliness took over.

He didn't hear his door open behind him as Karen stuck her head in. She examined the seated figure before her, head down and shaking, sniffling, crying. She stepped in and closed the door with just enough noise to announce her arrival. Bud turned his head and looked up at her. His eyes were red and glassy. He stood as she approached him and threw his arms around her. He sobbed as they hugged for a long, long time.

Bud had no memory of the drive home. He was emotionally exhausted as he pulled the Lumina into his driveway behind Maggie's Subaru. He shut off the engine and sat there for a good two minutes, staring at his little rented house out here in Middle-Of-Nowhere, PA. He finally summoned the energy to get out of the car and trudge towards his front door. As he approached, the door opened and Maggie stood there wearing sweats and an inviting smile. She threw the door open wide and stepped aside to let him walk in. He closed the door behind him, dropped his coat to the floor and Maggie launched a hug that rivaled the Karen hug.

"I love you," she said in a voice muffled by her mouth against his chest.

"Thanks. I needed that. I love you too."

The hug lasted another few seconds until they separated and looked into each other's eyes. When in jail, Bud could read volumes in Maggie's eyes. Today, he saw his best friend.

"You're my hero," she said.

"You're my life," he replied. They kissed a hard, electric kiss. He broke if off and said, "I don't know what I'd do without you."

She reached up to his face and placed her hand on his cheek, gazing into his weary eyes. "Why don't you sit, put your feet up on our deluxe coffee table and let me get you a diet Pepsi."

He navigated around his parka, which was piled on the floor, and plopped down onto the couch. He sat and stared at the dark television, then watched Maggie return with a rock glass in one hand and a diet Pepsi in the other.

"Quite a day," he said. He turned to see her reaction. She had none. She took her place next to him and stared at the same dark TV screen.

Chapter 24 - Coping Mechanisms

In yet another display of stark survival, Governor Franklin made it through his first night at Hahnemann Medical Center with the help of two stents and meds that included painkillers for a rib broken during CPR. When he regained consciousness, it was late Monday night. His eyes flickered under the ceiling light. He moved them around, looking for anything familiar. They landed on a dark skinned, dark haired woman wearing an aqua tunic who stood to his right, staring at him.

"Hello," she said. "Can you hear me?"

His brain tried to analyze what his eyes were sending him, but there was a fog he couldn't break through. He blinked his eyes and moved them around the room again. He sensed movement coming from the other side of the room. His eyes moved in that direction and saw a dark-skinned man, youngish and handsome, in a white jacket with a name tag sewn onto the breast pocket. He was slowly realizing that this might be a hospital and these might be medical people.

"Where am--" His words hit a phlegmy obstacle in his throat and were stopped cold. He cleared his throat and cried out in pain. "Ouch, what the--" Again, the words were unable to make the full trip and he felt a stabbing pain in his side. He attempted to raise his arms to get momentum to sit up. It didn't work.

"Easy, Governor," said the handsome young man. "You're all hooked up here."

The Governor's face was wrenched in pain and he tried to grab his right side.

"You're feeling some discomfort. That's from your broken rib."

Franklin's head and eyes cleared even more and he was able to speak.

"I'm in a hospital?"

"Hahnemann Medical Center. I'm Doctor Jamdar. This is Shreya, your nurse. You're in the ICU."

"ICU? Why?"

"You had a heart attack. You're doing much better now."

"Fuck," Franklin said as he exhaled, then tried to inhale. "Ouch!"

"Your rib was broken during CPR."

"Jesus. I remember the news conference, feeling sick. Now, I'm here."

"You've had quite a ride. Ventricular fibrillation followed by full arrest, then resuscitation in the field. You arrived with a heartbeat thanks to the team who worked on you in that office building."

"I don't remember jack-shit. Got anything for this fucking pain in my side?"

"You've received fentanyl in your IV. I can set you up with a demand system that will allow you to push a button whenever you have pain. It gives a small dose in twenty-minute increments."

"Great. The sooner the better." He was now aware of the rhythmic beeps of the monitoring equipment in the room, the IV attached to his left arm and the stickers on his chest and stomach. "So, how am I now?"

"I placed two stents in your arteries which opened up the flow of blood to your heart. You are on blood thinners to help prevent clots. Since CPR was begun almost immediately, your brain was oxygenated the whole time, which means no loss of cognition or motor skills. In short, you should be able to go home in just a couple days."

"Couple of days? That's bullshit, man. I need to get back to work *now*."

The doctor moved closer to the side rail of the bed and looked Franklin in the eye. "Governor, you are lucky to be alive. You're not going anywhere until we monitor your heart and make sure there's nothing else that contributed to your condition. Otherwise, you could be right back here again."

Franklin listened intently, looking the doctor in the eye. "What are you, nineteen? Twenty? I want a real doctor, not some fucking illegal practicing his bedside manner on the Great White."

The doctor and nurse glanced at each other. The nurse busied herself preparing a syringe. The doctor walked out of the room.

"Doctor Jamdar happens to be the premier cardiac surgeon at this hospital," said the nurse. "Insulting him changes nothing. You've got the best, whether you like it or not." She injected the contents of her syringe into Franklin's IV. "This is something to help you sleep and to stop your mouth from functioning."

By the time Tuesday rolled around, the *Channel-Seven-Killer's-Heaven-Remmick-Resuscitation* story went viral across social media, cable news, online and printed venues. Karen had never seen anything like it. You couldn't glance at your phone without seeing shared posts, Tweets and Retweets showing the soundbite of Bud Remmick calling the Governor a pig, intercut with video of Remmick performing CPR on him an hour later. Accolades, analysis, opinions and speculation littered cable news to the point of absurdity. Karen couldn't watch anymore.

Bud had the day off. He went to a shooting range, rented a shotgun, bought two boxes of shells and went to town on several paper targets. They were shreds by the time his hour was up. He left the range and went to a Dairy Queen he'd passed on the way and had a large strawberry Blizzard, which he consumed in the car parked in the DQ lot. He stowed the empty cup in the space between the console and the passenger seat and headed to Big Pocono, a state park with large expanses atop Camelback Mountain. Big Pocono would be nearly deserted in the dead of winter, which was just what he was hoping for. He parked in an empty public lot, turned his phone off and stuffed it into the glove compartment before leaving the warmth of the Lumina and embarking on a hiking path that led to a scenic overlook of the valley below. There was a bench there. He sat and stared at the vista in the February cold. He lost track of time.

Maggie, on the other hand, was keenly aware of the time--10:50, to be exact--since she was late for a 10:30 budget meeting. She had forgotten about it and quickly grabbed her budget binder and jogged down the hall to the elevator, took it up one floor and walked into the conference room. Seated around a rectangular table were all three Commissioners, Marjorie Cutler and a woman she later was told was the County Comptroller.

"I'm so sorry," Maggie said as she stumbled into the room and found an empty chair. "I got caught up in something."

"Gee, thanks for joining us," cracked Commissioner Francona.

"It's OK, you haven't missed much," added Marjorie, glaring at Francona. "We're just now talking about your budget."

"I don't think there's much to discuss as far as your agency is concerned," said Commissioner Lawrence, the chair. "Your budget is basically unchanged. No cuts. Your agency is doing well and I hope it stays that way."

"Thank you, Commissioner," said Maggie.

"I watched your husband's performance on TV," Lawrence continued. "I'd call him a hero if he didn't have such a foul mouth."

"Yea, name calling," chimed in Francona. "Very professional."

"I'll be sure to pass your remarks on to him," Maggie replied. "Do you require anything else from me?"

Francona's eyes bore a hole through her as she sat and waited for a response. "No," he said with a condescending sneer.

She got up and left the room. She made her way back to her office, closing the door behind her, then taking her seat behind the desk. She sat back and looked at the ceiling, staring at the sprinkler head and wondering if she would be able to trigger it by holding a match to it. Her mind was idle, tired. She really wanted to go back home. She noticed Angela wasn't at her desk, unusual for 11 o'clock in the morning. She thought again about bailing for the day. The last few had been full of stress, disturbing discoveries and uncertainty. She longed for the simpler days of meals-on-wheels, keeping seniors fed and getting an occasional "thank you."

There was a knock on her door, which then opened. Marjorie's head appeared. "Can I come in?"

"Sure, what the hell. I'm just ruminating, obsessing, worrying. You know, the usual." She didn't move out of her chair. Marjorie took tentative steps into the office, closing the door behind her.

"What's Francona's problem?" asked Maggie.

"He's a child. Don't worry about him. At all."

"Isn't he the one who's supposed to fire me? I mean, it was him on that conference call, right?"

"I believe that threat has gone away."

"And where's Angela, my assistant?"

"Re-assigned. She's civil service, so she can't be fired short of committing a crime. She now works for County Wildlife."

"She was spying on me."

"I know. I logged in to her computer."

"You can do that?"

"A simple, 60-dollar program, installed one evening after she left work. I knew she was a sneaky little bitch who belonged to Franklin. I did what was necessary to stay ahead of the curve."

"So, I'm not a target anymore?"

"No. At least not at the hands of anyone in the County. As for the Governor himself, we'll see how that goes, but I'm hoping that since your husband helped save his life, he will now turn his attention elsewhere. Or maybe, we'll luck out and he'll die in the hospital."

Maggie rose from her chair and walked around to the front of her desk, sitting on the edge, face to face with Marjorie.

"I don't know how you do what you do around here, and I don't know why you've been such a supporter of mine. But I thank you." She said it with sincerity that leaped from her eyes into Marjorie's. Marjorie took a step towards Maggie, never breaking the connection. Maggie was aware the space between them was closing. She didn't move a muscle, never averted her eyes. Marjorie took one more step forward and was now eye to eye with Maggie, searching her face for clues to, anything.

"Well, you're obviously worth the trouble," said Marjorie. Again, looking for a sign of revulsion or fear, she moved in a swift but gentle motion and pressed her lips against Maggie's. The two women stood still, barely breathing, eyes closed, lips joined, hands at their sides. Seconds ticked by with no change until Marjorie gently backed away, opened her eyes and looked into Maggie's. She saw peace, perhaps acceptance. Marjorie turned and walked towards the closed office door. Maggie didn't move from her spot on the edge of her desk. She watched Marjorie open the door and leave without a word.

Bud's next stop was an attractive, semi-modern church, Mt. Pocono Presbyterian. It was a little past two o'clock. He had passed it on the way up to Big Pocono and decided to stop on an impulse. There were a few cars in the small parking lot. He pulled in and made his way to the front door. It was unlocked, so he walked in with no idea who or what to expect. He smelled fresh wood and carpeting, a combination that reminded him of the lodge he and Maggie once vacationed at in nearby Tannersville. He walked into the empty sanctuary where soft music was playing through speakers mounted over the dais. Perhaps he was coming in at the tail end of an event, or the very beginning? No one else was around. He walked forward to about the fourth row, then sidled into a pew and sat, looking straight ahead at the crucifix that hung high and basked in the soft glow emanating from the stained-glass windows to his right. He slipped off his parka, laying it next to him. He folded his hands on his lap and sat still, looking up at the high ceiling and scanning the beautiful windows. He tried to look into himself, but he wasn't sure how. He questioned how anger could co-exist with the instinct to save a life. He tried to confront his hate of the Governor, of Ronald Morone and the anger that was unleashed against both those men. He had the power to kill.

He heard footsteps. He looked around and spotted a man emerging from a back room and walking slowly towards him, fortyish, dressed in business casual, medium length brown hair, a generic white man. He had a pleasant smile and looked at Bud as he approached. Bud was apprehensive, but stayed put. The man finally arrived at the pew and stood in the aisle to address his visitor.

"Hi. I'm Pastor Greg. Are you OK?"

Bud smiled and replied, "Yes, thanks. I'm just--I don't know, exactly."

"May I sit? What's your name?"

"Bud, and sure, it's your place. Is it OK that I'm here?"

"Yes, of course." The Pastor sidled into the pew and sat a comfortable distance from Bud. "Our door is always open. At least from ten to six." The Pastor had made eye contact but after another minute, his look changed. "Oh my god, it's you."

Bud's eyes sank and his head nodded wearily. "Yea."

Pastor Greg sensed Bud's ambivalence. "I see now. Looking for some sanctuary in our sanctuary. I'll leave you be."

"Don't go. Can you sit for a few minutes?"

"Does the Pope shit in the woods?"

Bud turned his head to look at him with wide eyes, then chuckled. "Maybe." Both indulged in a little school-boy laugh. It passed and silence descended on them.

"When I was in prison, I once told a priest to get out of my sight and take god with him. Now, I'm thinking that might have been a little harsh."

"Really? What changed your mind?"

Bud turned away from the Pastor and gazed at the light streaming through the window to his right. "God is me. Right?"

The Pastor looked at him with a knowing smile. "I'd like to think God resides in each of us, and each of us sees him, or her, differently."

"Yea, like in AA. Higher Power. I just discovered that recently. It helps."

"Helps what?"

"Makes me feel less alone. Being alone in a prison cell is easy. Alone out here in the world, even in bed next to my wife, that's a different kind of alone." He looked for something in the Pastor's eyes. "My Higher Power fills the space."

"By the way, anytime you feel like calling your Higher Power God, it's OK. I won't tell."

"It would be easier to get the hang of that if God didn't have such a bad reputation. Look at all the shit in the world attributed to God's will, all the assholes who claim to be doing God's work, vile, evil fucks." Bud made eye contact with the Pastor and said, "Sorry, man."

Pastor Greg smiled. "Don't apologize, I get it. But don't you think good eventually wins?"

"Not as a rule, no."

"It's certainly true in the case of Governor Franklin. And only because of the good in you. It probably annoys you to be reminded that you saved his life. But you can live with that, can't you?"

"It wasn't the Governor Pennsylvania I was helping. It was a patient."

"Right. I think we're saying the same thing."

"Hey, don't confuse me with your healing words and thoughtful insights."

Pastor Greg smiled. "I don't have to tell *you* there is good and bad in all of us. Admitting it is half the battle. The other half--mediating the struggle between them--takes the rest of our lives."

Bud was watching Greg's face as he spoke. Every muscle looked relaxed. "As pep talks go, that one rates about a five, but I'll take it. I appreciate you listening." He extended his hand and the Pastor accepted it and shook.

"You've certainly made a difference in at least one life, and I suspect others, too."

Bud grabbed his parka and stood, sidled out of the pew and walked towards the door. He pulled on his parka and turned to see Greg watching him. They each gave a quick wave and Bud was gone.

"That was some epic shit, felon," said Paramedic Shaw, speaking with her mouth full, sitting at the Armitage Rescue Squad's folding card table covered in plastic.

"Coming from you, that is high praise," Remmick replied while eating from the same plate of microwaved nachos. "I wasn't even thinking about it, you know? It's like I was on autopilot."

"Yes, yes, that's the way it goes. You guys certainly did everything right. The Governor lives to annoy another day."

Remmick's last stop of the day was the nesting place of his EMS family, the Armitage Rescue Squad. The unremarkable building had an old wooden sign above the door that read *Armitage Rescue Squa* (the "d" was missing for months), a parking lot for a dozen vehicles and two ambulance bays but just the one ambulance. Inside was a small living room with several generations of overused furniture, a galley kitchen and a single bathroom containing a shower stall loaded with cleaning supplies and backboards. The rooms were separated by well-worn sheet-rock walls with missing sections of molding. The structural integrity of the folding table where Bud and Tiffany sat was dependent on whether or not they rested their elbows on it. Several more EMTs entered the building and shouted good-natured insults at the pair, then clapped Bud on the shoulder and shook his hand.

"Your chest compressions were off-center," offered Skip Milgram, the squad's resident know-it-all. "I could see in the video you were under stress and maybe weren't fully on your game."

Tiffany rolled her eyes. "And when was the last time you participated in saving a life, Skippy? The only time you've been on your knees in recent years has been--." She stopped. "Never mind."

"Don't call me Skippy," he whined. Chuckles erupted from the others in the room as Milgram busied himself at the computer.

"I just wanted to stop by and say hi," said Bud. "I'm on again this Saturday overnight. I'm not sure how long I can sustain that, though. I'm beat by the weekends anymore."

"I'm proud of you, Bud," said Tiffany. "Standing up for your wife, facing off with the Devil, then saving his ass. You might be going to heaven after all."

"Don't say that," he responded. "I have a legacy to uphold."

If felt good to bring the day to an end on his couch with Maggie and Beulah. The TV was off and the Alexa speaker was playing "Relaxing Piano". There wasn't much physical movement among them. By ten o'clock, they had downloaded every detail of their respective days to each other, though Maggie omitted the part about kissing Marjorie Cutler.

"Thanks for giving me some space," Bud said. "It was good to unplug for a whole day."

"Of course. I pretty much phoned it in myself today. I was extremely unproductive."

"And, you believe you are no longer in the line of fire?"

"So it appears, for now. The Governor could always rear his ugly head again, but maybe he won't since, you know, he owes you."

"I don't think he'll see it that way. But I don't really care. He'll do what he does, and we'll deal with it." He went quiet and Maggie had no response. They stared at nothing. Beulah grunted and shifted her ample body.

"That feeling crept up on me again," he said, "that feeling in the back of my throat, my aura."

Maggie turned her head to look at him as he spoke.

"I wanted to kill him." It took courage to say it. "I really did. Instead, I went on TV and called him a pig. That's progress, right?"

"Um, sure, progress," she agreed reluctantly. Then, she gathered her own courage to say what she'd been meaning to say for days. "I know you don't want to hear this." She grabbed his hand and held it tightly. "You can't do it again. Right? You just can't."

He had no response.

"They'll put you away for life, or worse. And me, I don't think I could live through that again. Please promise me, right now."

He couldn't control the aura, but he couldn't tell Maggie that. It just happened. When he felt it coming on, he worked to put on the brakes. How? By closing his eyes, controlling his breathing and thinking about his love for her. It was the reason he was sitting here today.

"I promise," he said as he opened his eyes and looked at the ceiling. Then he turned to her and repeated, "I promise". He bent towards her and kissed her. She threw her arms around his neck and kissed him back.

Beulah raised her head to watch for a moment, then released an audible fart.

Chapter 25 - Epilogue

Dear Mom and Dad,

I'm sure you've seen the news the past month. I wanted to write to you and explain some things. I know you haven't been happy with me, but I've missed you and hope you'll read this entire letter before tossing it in the trash.

When I got out of prison, I vowed to keep my head down, shut up and be a better person. I took a volunteer job as an EMT in this little town where we live. Getting the job at Channel 7 came out of the blue. I was invited back by my old friend Karen Sikorsky (remember her?) and the management decided to take a chance on a convicted felon. I am very grateful for this. It was hard at first. All the employees were suspicious, even frightened of me. And the nonsense with that psychotic photographer was a total shock that complicated my return to the working world. But it was good for me to manage that mess.

When I found out that politicians were out to get Maggie, I started to revert to some old ways that I'm not proud of. My anger seethed and I had thoughts that took me back to the dark time. As I'm sure you know by now, I ended up helping to save the life of the man who was threatening Maggie's job. Isn't it strange how fate plays with you? I went to that news conference to confront him and I ended up on the floor doing CPR on him. A recent conversation I had with a minister suggested it was God that guided my actions. I don't know about that, but I guess I can't deny what I did that day. If it were any other patient, I'd be happy for him. But as long as he is in power, I will always consider him a threat and it will be my burden to manage my anger towards him.

I would like to see you guys sometime. My phone number is below. Call me if you'd like to talk or visit.

Love,
Your son Bud

###

Your honest review of "Killer Competition" on Amazon would be greatly appreciated.

Other books by Tom Kranz:

LIVESHOT: Journalistic Heroism in Philadelphia
(Non fiction)

Bullets flying. Choking teargas. Angry crowds chanting for justice. Eleven dead people, five of them children. This is the epic true story of the intrepid journalists of a Philadelphia television news department whose creativity and dedication brought the 1985 MOVE disaster to a live television audience despite daunting logistics.

BUDLAND
(Fiction)

Jail didn't sound so bad to Bud Remmick, a small price to pay for erasing an abusive, blackmailing sociopath from the face of the earth. But the plan to ride out a lenient sentence starts to fall apart when prison life turns on him. Then his lawyer turns on him. Then, his wife. With nothing left but his own anger, Bud Remmick faces a reckoning with a lifelong dysfunction that plays out behind bars with a couple of unlikely co-dependents.

More information can be found at kranznotee.com